"Max, this house is huge."

He grinned and led Trenace to the back door. Standing on the porch, he gestured toward a sagging barn. "It needs work, of course, but can you imagine what sort of play area that barn would make?"

"Max, why did we come here?"

"Because I bought this place, Trena. The house, the barn and twenty acres. I want you to move here and bring the children and turn this house into a foster home."

"That's absolutely crazy, Max."

"Crazy? Look at this place, Trena. You'll have room to take in even more children than you have now. And I'll be here, too, if you'll have me...if you'll marry me. Trena, will you marry me?"

For one wild moment she was tempted to say yes. She wanted to more than she'd ever wanted anything. Then she burst into tears.

ABOUT THE AUTHOR

Since her first Superromance novel, published in 1983, Sally Garrett's tender stories of love, family and commitment have attracted a wide following of loyal fans. Sally herself has had a lot of love in her life. She raised four children and lives in Montana with her biggest fan— her husband, Monty.

Books by Sally Garrett

HARLEQUIN SUPERROMANCE
139–MOUNTAIN SKIES
173–NORTHERN FIRES
201–TWIN BRIDGES
225–UNTIL NOW
243–WEAVER OF DREAMS
275–VISIONS
309–PROMISES TO KEEP
344–DESERT STAR

Don't miss any of our special offers. Write to us at the following address for information on our newest releases.

Harlequin Reader Service
P.O. Box 1397, Buffalo, NY 14240
Canadian address: P.O. Box 603,
Fort Erie, Ont. L2A 5X3

Children of the Heart

SALLY GARRETT

Harlequin Books

TORONTO • NEW YORK • LONDON
AMSTERDAM • PARIS • SYDNEY • HAMBURG
STOCKHOLM • ATHENS • TOKYO • MILAN

Published August 1991

ISBN 0-373-70464-X

CHILDREN OF THE HEART

DEDICATION

To my younger brother,
Daniel Taylor Garrett
of Tyrone, Georgia,
and his daughter,
Suzanne Glenda Garrett,
with love and affection

ACKNOWLEDGMENTS

When I was a junior at Arizona State University, I typed a thesis for my roommate, Caroline Mitchell, who was working toward her master's degree in social services. I've long since lost track of my roommate, but the essence of the children described in the case studies of that thesis stayed with me over the years. During those decades, I've known several sets of foster parents and found them to be special people. Books by Eldon Chapman, Svea J. Gold, Albert T. Murphy and others gave me added insight into the subjects of foster care and children with special needs.

The primary care-giver in a foster home is usually a woman. Trenace McKay is representative of these women who have the gift of loving each child regardless of its circumstances.

Max Tulley sprang to life in my computer, fell in love with the heroine and refused to give up in spite of the obstacles I placed in front of him. God bless him and all the other fine men who have become foster fathers.

CHAPTER ONE

TRENACE MCKAY JERKED the plug of the electric mixer from its wall outlet and stared across the bowl of yellow cake batter at the eleven-year-old girl. "What did you say, Mickie?"

Mickie watched as Trenace filled two round pans with the thick batter. "I just said I wonder when Uncle Owen will come back. Mrs. Sewell asked me if he'd come back. You know, when she came to check on me last week?" Mickie beamed a smile across the pans. "Can I lick the beaters?"

Trenace handed the girl one of the beaters. "If she wanted to know about my personal affairs, she should have asked me."

Mickie took a taste of the cake batter and sighed. "I love raw cake batter... and I didn't say anything to Mrs. Sewell, but I wonder sometimes, too."

Trenace's frown deepened as she hurried to the oven and slid the pans inside. She knew how Mrs. Sewell felt about foster home care. Each one should set an example of stable family life, and to Mrs. Sewell that meant husband and wife in traditional family roles. If the caseworker discovered the truth about Trenace's marital situation, Trenace's license might be taken away, and the children would be scattered across the county. But the children *had* become a family while in her care. Owen had played no part in establishing the atmosphere in the McKay home.

And if her license were revoked what would happen to her? Trenace would be without a job, without a source of income—just a displaced homemaker in search of her own welfare benefits.

She swallowed her concerns and closed the oven door. When she returned to the table, Mickie had finished cleaning the beaters and scraped the bowl clean with a spoon.

"I'm ready to get back in my chair now," Mickie said, wiping the last taste of batter from her lips with a paper napkin.

Trenace slid an arm beneath the girl's legs, and in seconds Mickie was off the high stool, safely in her wheelchair and rolling across the tiled floor.

"Mickie, wait," Trenace called.

The wheelchair stopped and the girl whirled it around. Trenace knelt before her and grabbed her hands. "What did she ask you, Mickie? Exactly, if you can remember."

Mickie's thin shoulders stiffened beneath the maroon cotton knit of her T-shirt. Her black hair swirled around her pinched features. "I didn't tell her, Aunt Trenace. I promised you I wouldn't...and I didn't." Her gaze dropped, but Trenace saw the swell of tears that turned the child's eyes to shimmering sun-made tea.

"It's been a long, long time," Mickie murmured, glancing up at Trenace again. "Is he ever coming back?"

Trenace squeezed Mickie's hands gently, kissed her cheek and got to her feet again. "No, he's not coming back."

She recalled the letter she'd received from the family lawyer in January. Since then the months had slipped by, and she'd been busy taking care of the children, covering the truth and pretending to the outside world that all was well within the home that had been officially approved as a foster care residence for fifteen years.

"Is it still a secret?" Mickie asked, turning one wheel of the chair rapidly back and forth.

"Yes, it's still a secret," Trenace replied. "Mickie, you've been with me longer than any of the other children. The others don't even remember him. Mrs. Sewell can be...inflexible...when she decides to follow the rules and regulations to a T. She thinks you children should have a father image. I agree, but when Owen had a change of heart, what could I do? If she finds out he's gone, you might have to go away, all of you...and live somewhere else. Would you want that?"

Mickie's eyes widened. "I never want to live anywhere else. This is my favorite of all the foster homes I've lived in."

"Mine, too," Trenace said as she leaned to kiss the girl's cheek again. "And you're one of my favorite children. I love you as if you were my own."

Mickie frowned. "Mrs. Sewell says I won't ever be anyone's real girl. I used to hope so, but Mrs. Sewell says I'm impossible to adopt out." Her posture in the chair straightened and the tilt of her head reflected a proud heritage blended from several cultures. "I don't want to be adopted anymore. I'd rather stay here with you. Can I go outside now?"

Trenace pushed open the sliding glass door that led onto the patio and stepped aside as Mickie rolled the chair outside. The grass in the yard had been freshly mowed that morning. The giant Iceland poppies with their deep orange blossoms, the creamy tiger lilies in full bloom and the soft pink and fuchsia peonies added a rainbow of color along the weathered redwood fence that surrounded the yard. Only the lilac bush, with its winter-killed branches that she hadn't found time to remove, detracted from the yard's appearance.

In one corner a swing set stood ready for children with special needs. Owen had been good about modifying the play equipment over the years. She'd give him credit for that.

She lingered by the sliding door and watched Mickie edge the chair close to the glider and pull herself into the seat. The glider began to swing back and forth as the child clutched the hand grips and pulled steadily on the cables Owen had installed. Trenace knew the quiet times like today when the other children were at day camp were important to Mickie, for these were the times when the youngster tried to work out the reasons for what had happened to her four years earlier.

A couple of hours later the house was once again filled with the voices of children, each eager to tell Trenace about the field trip they'd taken to Spokane Riverside Park, the picnic they'd had and the games they'd played.

Trenace's attention centered on Boyd Anderson, a ten-year-old boy with burn scars down his cheek and neck, who proudly displayed his ribbons and a medal.

"I won first place," Boyd boasted. "I beat all the other guys by a mile. Coach said I have the fastest legs in Spokane. Can I have more meat loaf and potatoes? I'm starved."

"And I almost came in third," an eight-year-old red-headed boy added, pulling a rumpled yellow ribbon from his shirt pocket. "We got yellow ribbons if we finished. The kids who didn't finish got green ones for trying."

The chattering continued throughout the meal until the last spoon of ice cream and yellow cake had been consumed in recognition of Mickie's eleventh birthday.

Trenace rose from the head of the table and glanced at the wall chart. Six pairs of eyes followed her gaze.

Mickie grinned at the others. "It's Boyd and Annabelle's turn to help Aunt Trenace clean the kitchen." She turned to Trenace again. "Can we watch TV?"

Trenace brushed a strand of deep auburn hair from her forehead and looked at her watch. "Yes, but at six o'clock I want to see Channel Nine's local news. Maxwell Tulley makes his debut tonight."

"Maxwell Tulley?" Boyd asked. "Who's Maxwell Tulley?"

Trenace smiled at the two boys and four girls seated around the table. "Maxwell Tulley is a homegrown boy who made good in Los Angeles. Now he's returned to Spokane as the new anchor on Channel Nine's *Inland Empire Nine at Six News.*" Trenace smiled at the children. "I went to school with him."

"You really know a TV guy?" Boyd asked.

"Casually," Trenace replied, gathering the cake platter and dessert dishes and carrying them to the counter.

"When?" Boyd asked, pressing her with his questions.

Trenace smiled, her blue eyes sparkling as she recalled the boy from her childhood. "We went all through grade school together. My maiden name was Taylor, so we were usually near each other on the seating charts teachers used to use."

"Was he your boyfriend?" Mickie asked.

"Hardly," Trenace said, thinking back to her youth as she began to fill the sink with hot, soapy water. "We went to the same high school, but he worked on the school paper and the annual." She studied the tiny ivy-and-geranium pattern of the wallpaper above the sink. "I was earning points for my sports letter. He was in the school plays all the time, even the musicals. The girls thought he was cute.''

Boyd laughed and elbowed eight-year-old George. ''Do you want the girls to think you're cute, huh, George?''

''Shut up, Boyd. I ain't cute,'' George retorted, shoving the older boy's elbow away.

''Boys, that's enough,'' Trenace said. ''He was good-looking, tall and thin, too. Looks are important when you're on television. I'm sure he's changed over the years. I'll help Annabelle and Boyd with the chores and we'll all sit down and watch Max Tulley's debut. I think I can find my old high school annual.'' She shooed the other children out of the kitchen. ''Let's get this work done so we can see for ourselves this boy from my childhood.''

When the Spokane regional news began, Trenace and the children were seated on the carpet in front of the television. Six-year-old Libby Jones snuggled on Trenace's lap while Libby's sister Denise clung to Trenace's arm.

''Is that him?'' Mickie asked as the camera began to slowly close in on a distinguished-looking man.

Trenace leaned forward and grinned. ''That's Max.''

The man introduced himself and began to read the anchor's portion of the news. His eyes were the same intense blue she remembered from high school. His hair was dark brown, a gentle wave giving him a sexiness Trenace was positive would appeal to the women viewers, yet the lines that ran lightly down his cheeks to curve around his wide mouth gave him a masculine quality that would enhance his credibility with the male viewers.

''He looks old,'' George mumbled.

Mickie turned to Trenace. ''What do you think? Is he as cute as he used to be?''

''He's quite good-looking,'' Trenace replied, admiring the gray in his sideburns and the spark in his gaze. When he seemed to stare directly at her, she shifted uncomfortably.

"Can he see us?" Libby asked.

Trenace chuckled. "Of course not, sweetheart. It just seems that way, doesn't it? Is he looking at you, too?"

Libby nodded.

Trenace continued to admire the handsome man looking into the camera lens. What a delightful improvement a few decades had made in this man whom she remembered as a teenager with long, ungainly arms and legs.

"He looks like my grandpa," Annabelle said, edging away from the screen, "only Grandpa had gray hair." She looked down at her hands. "I didn't mean to hurt my grandpa."

Trenace reached out and pulled Annabelle onto her lap next to Libby, cuddling her in her arms. Denise tightened her hold on Trenace's arm, and Trenace smiled at her, then returned her attention to Annabelle. "I know you didn't, Annabelle. It was an accident."

George stared at the man on the screen but said nothing more.

Mickie grinned at Trenace. "Does he look like he used to?"

Trenace's mouth softened into a smile. "I'd say Maxwell Tulley wears his years with dignity. It's hard to be objective, though, since I knew him as a boy." The little girls scrambled from her lap, and she stood up and helped Mickie back into her wheelchair. "Maybe someday I'll call him and see if you children can tour the station. Would you like that?"

"When? When?" the children all asked.

"Soon," Trenace promised. "First we should give him a chance to settle into his new job. Maybe a letter would be better. He might not remember me if I phoned.

Wouldn't that be embarrassing if I called and said, 'This is Trenace from grade school.' He'd ask, 'Trenace, who?' And I'd be so embarrassed that I'd hang up and you children would never get a chance to see the studio. No, a letter would be better.''

"DO YOU LIKE KIDS?" Joshua Temple, the news director for KSPO-TV, asked.

Maxwell Tulley scowled at the gray-haired man. "Sure, I guess so. I have two of my own. They're good kids." He glanced at his watch as the makeup woman leaned against his shoulder and dusted his cheekbone for the fourth time. "I've got five minutes to airtime, Josh. Can you hold this until tomorrow?"

Josh Temple paced in front of Max's elevated seat. "Sure, but think about it. Kids are in the news these days."

"We did drugs last week," Max replied. "Gang wars are scheduled for July, and the series on teenage pregnancies should be ready to air in late August, in time to shake up all the parents just before school starts."

Josh shook his head. "No, no, I don't mean that stuff. I mean problem kids."

"Drugs, alcohol and teenage pregnancies don't make for problem kids?" Max asked, edging himself out of the chair.

Josh blocked Max's exit. "I mean younger kids, the cute kind, you know, precocious but still sweet on camera? The kind who bring tears to the viewers' eyes."

Max glanced at his watch again. "Two minutes, Josh. Do you want dead air?"

Josh stepped aside. "Would you stop in after the show? I want to talk about kids . . . and the ratings. Don't you want to know how you did your first month?"

Max smiled. "I'll see you as soon as I get off-camera."

Max slid into the anchor's chair with ten seconds to spare and clipped on his tiny microphone. When the TelePrompTer began to roll, he picked up the sheets of paper and arranged them, imagining a viewer staring back at him as he opened the broadcast. The papers were hardcopy backup, a necessary security blanket for any responsible reporter. Once the TelePrompTer had stopped cold and he'd found himself on-camera with only his memory of the story he'd read just before airtime to fall back on.

He wanted to be able to read hard-copy news. He enjoyed taking liberties occasionally by ad-libbing a few sentences that were appropriate to the story. That habit had driven his production manager in Los Angeles up the wall. Max had argued that it added a fresh aspect to the presentation and felt that his own sense of good taste kept the habit in line. He had no desire to mess up in front of a million or more viewers in the region.

Thirty minutes later he unclipped the microphone, signaling to the technicians his appreciation of a segment well-done. In seconds he was on his way to the makeup room to clean up.

He planned a quiet evening at his apartment. Since arriving in Spokane, he'd been invited to a string of dinners, cocktail parties and cultural affairs. Good public relations, Josh had reminded him, but Max had learned years earlier that he needed privacy, time to flush his mind of work and all its emotionally draining social issues. He needed two full days a week to disappear from public view and be Max Tulley, private citizen.

He shed his blue dress shirt and maroon tie and hung them alongside the jacket he kept in the wardrobe room with several others. In its place he pulled a pale yellow cotton knit golf shirt over his head and tucked it into the jeans he'd worn while on-camera. God help him if he ever forgot and stood up while still on the air.

In Josh's office he slid into the corner of the sofa and stretched out his long legs. "I'm bushed, Josh, so let's get this over with. I have definite plans for the weekend."

Josh arched a gray brow. "Really? To do what?"

"Nothing, absolutely nothing."

Josh chuckled. "I need you to do this little errand. It won't take but a few minutes."

Max crossed his legs at the ankle and frowned. "Don't make plans for me, Josh."

Josh's features had always been difficult to read, but Max had learned in the past month at KSPO that no one rushed Josh Temple, so he waited impatiently.

"Want to know the ratings for June?" Josh asked, chuckling when Max straightened, uncrossed his ankles and leaned forward. "We beat the competition by ten points at 6:00 p.m. and two points at ten." He arched a brow at Max. "Want to do double shift?"

Max grinned. "Wouldn't that be overexposure?"

Josh shrugged but didn't respond.

"The ratings are great news," Max said. "But maybe the newness will wear off in a few more months."

"Not if we keep producing great special features," Josh argued. "You know I respect your instinct for gauging the viewers' interests, but you let me be the idea man and you keep charming the viewers. I have an idea and you're the perfect anchor to pull it off." Josh leaned forward and stretched his arm across his desk, dangling a piece of yellow paper from his fingers. "I'd like you to visit this lady...just to break the ice. What do you know about something called *Wednesday's Child?*"

Max frowned. "It's a poem."

"No, no," Josh replied. "This has to do with hard-to-place children up for adoption."

Max's scowl deepened. "One of the other stations in Los Angeles did a series about older children available for adoption. I saw the pieces a few times. It was pretty sappy stuff."

Josh released the yellow paper, and it drifted toward the carpet, settling near Max's navy-and-white jogging shoes.

"I've committed us to a six-month series," Josh said, ignoring Max's remark. "There are a half-dozen companies doing the same thing with just enough variety to avoid infringing on one another's format. "I've watched promos on all of them, and I think *Wednesday's Child* is one of the best. It'll be a great way to grab the viewers. Usually it's done at noon, but we'll do it at six when most of the professional people are home trying to catch up with the happenings of the day."

Max shook his head. "Why would we want to feature kids from some big city who are unadoptable? Are you sure our viewers want to get involved in a long-distance social problem?"

"But it won't be kids from some faraway city," Josh said. "We'll feature kids from Spokane and our viewing area." He left his seat behind the oversize desk and came to sit beside Max. "Don't you see? It's exactly what we need to keep those ratings points, something with a personal touch. A child with a handicap or disfigurement or maybe emotional problems, one whose parents are dead or unfit, a kid who lives right here in Spokane...being interviewed by our own Maxwell Tulley, benefactor of the less fortunate."

Max stood up and reached for the ring of keys he'd dropped on Josh's desk. "I don't want to be a part of something that takes advantage of children who have enough problems to handle without our taking advantage of them in order to boost our ratings.''

Josh moved his hand slowly across the room, drawing an imaginary banner through the air. "I can see it now. Native son Max Tulley leaning against a pony, talking to a cute redheaded boy whose cheeks are splattered with freckles.''

"Sounds like something straight out of a Norman Rockwell painting," Max said, scowling at his production manager.

Josh ignored his remark. "You'd be leading the pony through a meadow and the little tyke would be grinning from ear to ear.''

"I'm allergic to horses," Max said, jiggling his keys uneasily in his hand.

Josh continued to ignore him. "How about a pretty blond girl in a swing, and you in the next swing, chatting with her. She'll be as cute as a button, absolutely adorable. Allergic to swings?''

Max dropped his keys onto the desk again. "She sounds pretty adoptable to me. Any reporter can pull off what you want.''

"But you're the one I want," Josh argued. "A Mrs. Sewell, a caseworker from the county health and family services agency, has been assigned to work with you to insure there's no exploitation of the children. We'll pay for the hot-line number for interested prospective parents to call, and then we'll step out of the picture. Social services will handle the legal work. All you have to do is chat with the kids and get them to open up.''

Max shook his head again. "No thanks. See you Monday.''

Josh leaned back against the sofa. "Lucky guy. I've got the biggest lawn this side of the Cascades. The shrubs all need trimming, too. Want to come help out?"

"Not on your life," Max replied. "I mowed lawns for fifteen years, and when Lucy died and I sold the house, I promised myself never again. Yard work is part of my past, big houses, too. Apartment living appeals to me."

Josh retrieved the piece of paper from the carpet. "I'll bet this woman and her husband have a big yard. Imagine taking care of six kids with special needs." He pretended to read the scribbling on the paper. "Says here she's been doing it for years. Her name is Trenace McKay. She wrote a letter to you about a month ago."

"I never received it," he said. "Are you censoring my mail?"

"My secretary opened it by mistake and showed it to me," Josh replied. "The woman wants to bring the kids in for a visit sometime. She insists they watch your show regularly. She says she used to know you."

"Trenace McKay?" Max shook his head. "That name rings a faint bell."

"The typed name read 'Mrs. Owen McKay,' but she signed it Trenace. Owen must be her husband."

Max frowned. "I used to know a girl named Trenace. It's an unusual name. She sat in front of me for several grades." He smiled. "She had curly red hair and pretty blue eyes. Her last name was Taylor. Maybe this is the same person." He shoved his key ring into his jeans pocket. "Write her back and give her a time to bring the kids in. I'll give them the grand tour and maybe put them on-camera for a human interest segment."

Josh hurried to the door, blocking Max's exit. "My secretary has already written to her. She told her you'd be getting in touch within the week." He held out the piece of paper. "Maybe you could stop by this weekend and see what's going on there. You know, meet the husband and wife? Size up the kids? Damn it, Max, this could be just the family we're looking for. Get on the good side of this woman and you'll be halfway home with the kids. They're just six little children who need good homes."

"You make them sound like six little puppies from an animal shelter," Max said, reluctantly accepting the piece of paper. "These are special children who have feelings and needs and . . ."

Josh grinned. "You're hooked already, aren't you? Let me know what comes of your visit. I'll hang around after Monday's broadcast to hear what happened. Have a good weekend, Max. Here's hoping Spokane is to your liking and we keep you here for a few years."

"Maybe," Max murmured under his breath.

MAX TULLEY STOOD at his bathroom mirror and began running his electric shaver down his cheek, squinting at the dark stubble and wondering if he needed to put on his reading glasses to make sure he didn't skip some whiskers. Maybe he'd better make an appointment to see about contact lenses. He was approaching middle age. Were the eyes the first to go?

He recalled how his mother had insisted his father shave and accompany the family to church every Sunday morning. The only exception had been during wheat harvesting time when the work continued nonstop from before dawn until long after dark. Memories of his family made him all too aware of how alone he was now, his daughters on their own, his wife gone, his parents and sisters living hundreds of miles away. His only brother lived halfway across the nation.

His parents had leased out the farm south of Spokane and moved to the San Juan Islands near Seattle. They now ran a gift shop that catered to tourists. His father, always a creative and imaginative person, had started taking lessons from a local artist to learn landscape painting. His two sisters lived in Portland and his brother was in broadcasting in Chicago. He had an aunt and uncle who still lived near Spangle. Maybe he'd give them a call and drive down for a Sunday afternoon visit.

Maybe this nostalgia had been brought on by the silly thing he'd done the evening before. He'd worked until midnight unpacking several boxes of books and arranging them on the shelves that covered one wall of the apartment's living room. In the bottom of the third box he'd found his four years of high school yearbooks. Taking a break and munching on a pizza he'd had delivered, he'd sprawled on the carpeting and sought out first his own photographs from the drama department's coverage, then begun to flip through the classes.

When his gaze settled on that of Trenace Taylor, he'd smiled, then lined the books up in a row. His photo had been next to hers in the freshman yearbook, separated by a student in the middle two, and side by side again in the senior yearbook. Pretty girl, he'd thought, admiring her young, innocent features. Now, as he worked the razor over his beard, he found himself unable to recall Trenace Taylor during high school. All his memories of her were from grade school when he'd sat behind her off and on for several years.

Yanking the razor from its outlet, he stepped backward. "Trenace Taylor, would you be surprised if a caller dropped in for a Sunday visit to talk about old times?" he asked his image in the mirror. Sometimes cold interviews turned out to be the best. The subject didn't have a chance to anticipate questions or build defenses. As he put the razor away in its case, he made his decision. A cold call would definitely give him the advantage.

CHAPTER TWO

As MAX PULLED his compact car to a stop against the curb, he glanced up and down the thoroughfare. The elm trees lining both sides of the street were mature, providing a shady umbrella overhead. The lawns were neatly mowed. He estimated the area homes had been built in the forties and fifties. Each house had a similar appearance, as if none wanted to stand out from its neighbor.

If Josh Temple's information was correct, this house on LaCrosse hid its uniqueness well. Max still didn't know why he had decided to pay the McKay couple a visit. Meeting the adult Trenace would be like recapturing a bit of his youth, when auditioning for the next school play or cheering on a winning football team had been the most important things in a teenager's life. No illnesses to tear a family apart, no career choices that still tugged at his ego, no relocations to a city that should have embraced him but instead, he sensed, suspected he'd come home a failure.

A pale blue station wagon, a decade old and with one dented rear fender, was parked in the driveway near a closed garage door. Probably filled with discarded items a family accumulates over the years, he decided. None of his business, he added as he took a deep breath and exhaled, and began the long stroll to the front door.

Max leaned on the bell and waited. No one responded, so he pressed the bell again, this time holding it several seconds. When the door opened, he stepped back.

The boy frowning at him appeared to be about ten years old. The skin at the corner of one eye was drawn downward by the scar tissue that covered his entire left cheek and the side of his neck. The boy wore a tank top and made no effort to hide the disfigurement.

Max cleared his throat. "I . . . I'd like to see . . . Mr. or Mrs. McKay. Are they home?"

The boy continued to stare at him.

"Are they home?" Max asked again. "If not, may I talk with whoever's in charge?"

"Aunt Trenace is in the backyard," the boy said, his hand still clutching the doorknob.

Max grinned. "I figured she was in the kitchen baking cookies."

"She's already done that," the boy volunteered, then grinned.

"And Mr. McKay . . . is he here, too?" Max asked.

"Uncle Owen isn't here much," the boy said.

Max tried another tactic. "My name is Max Tulley," he said, extending his hand to the boy. "And your name is . . . ?"

"Boyd," the boy said, sliding his thin hand into Max's. "Aunt Trenace is in the backyard. She said she's too busy to stop work. It's this way."

The boy turned away, his cutoff jeans brushing against the back of his tanned legs. His feet were bare.

Max followed the boy, trying to get an idea of the interior of the house as he crossed the living-room carpet, following the path worn into the nap through a combination dining room and kitchen and out onto a slab of concrete that someday might be covered with a roof. The house looked well lived in. He scanned the spacious yard and counted five more children.

"Where's Mrs. McKay?" he asked.

"Over there," Boyd replied, pointing at a huge lilac bush.

The thick foliage wriggled and shifted, then vibrated violently. Above the mass of leaves an unsightly dead limb shook and gave way, crashing through the lush green growth and onto the ground. Several dead limbs remained. Another began to shake and quiver. Max walked toward the bush, which stood more than a foot taller than his own six feet. He caught sight of a flash of red through the foliage, then a slender elbow.

"Darn it," a woman's voice muttered, and the limb groaned.

Max could hear the woman's distressed breathing as if she were at war with the bush.

Boyd walked around to the other side of the bush. "Aunt Trenace, there's this man—"

"Tell him to wait, Boyd," the woman replied. "There're only three branches left and I'll be done."

"But he wants—"

The bush stopped moving. "Who wants what?" The irritation in the woman's voice didn't seem to deter the boy, who was now smiling at the woman still hidden behind the lilac bush.

Her voice softened. "I'm sorry, Boyd, but this bush is about to get the best of me. Who was at the door? I hope it's not a salesman."

The boy shook his head as his mischievous grin grew into a full smile. "It's the guy from Channel Nine news."

"Who?" She pulled the pruning shears from the bush.

Before the boy could speak again Max stepped around the bush. His planned introductory speech evaporated as he took in the appearance of the woman standing a few feet away from him.

She, too, wore cutoff jeans, and the red he'd glimpsed was a tank top that hung down past her hips. Her torso was as slender and shapely as her arm and elbow. Not a pound of extra flesh could be seen, yet the curves of her body were womanly, accented by the green-and-white apron she had tied around her waist.

Her hair was deep auburn rather than the curly red he remembered. Her face was flushed from laboring in the July heat, making her eyes bluer than he'd ever seen on a woman.

"You really are Trenace Taylor," he said, groaning inwardly at his poor choice of words to introduce himself.

TRENACE CLOSED her eyes and wiped the perspiration from her forehead. Recognition of Max Tulley standing less than three feet from her had been instantaneous. He was the last person she'd ever expected to find staring at her. She was sweaty and flushed. She didn't usually look like this, wearing the oldest pair of cutoffs and rattiest shirt she owned. She'd dressed for physical labor, and now her legs and arms had scratches from the dead branches she'd been fighting. She hadn't even bothered to wear shoes.

Sweat trickled down between her breasts, and without thinking she pressed the damp tank top against her skin. When she opened her eyes again, Max was still there, looking cool and debonair in a pale blue knit shirt and white chinos made fashionable and contemporary with multiple tucks and pleats along the waistband. Her gaze shot to his face. He was even better-looking than the camera had revealed, his dark hair carefully groomed, and those famous blue eyes peering at her.

"May I help you?" he asked.

She stepped backward. "What?"

"With your work," he said, taking the long-handled pruners from her sweaty hands. In quick succession he removed the limbs and stepped back to survey the bush. "How's that?"

"Fine." She almost jerked the pruners from his hands and clutched them to her apron. "I . . . I used to be Taylor . . . now my name is McKay, but . . . all I wanted was for the children to be able to tour the studio." *I'm babbling,* she thought as she bit her lower lip and tried to regain her composure. She handed the pruners to Boyd, wiped her palms against her apron and extended her hand. "You don't need to introduce yourself. We know who you are, don't we, children?"

Six heads nodded their agreement. When his hand engulfed hers, she wished she'd been more reserved. She pulled her hand from his and shoved it into one of the pockets of her apron. "Well," she said, shifting her gaze to the curious faces of the children, then back to the man gazing at her. "I baked cookies this morning. Would you like to join us for cookies and lemonade?"

He smiled. "Why not?"

She motioned Boyd to put the pruners away in the garage, then pointed to the huge elm tree that shaded the swing set and a picnic table. "Why don't you children show Mr. Tulley to the table? I'll get the food." In minutes she returned to the table with a tray laden with plastic glasses, a pitcher of pink lemonade and a plate piled high with oatmeal cookies.

"Children, keep Mr. Tulley company while I shower, and remember your manners," she warned. Before she could think through the wisdom of her words, she whirled toward the house, commanding herself not to run or look back.

Twenty minutes later Trenace walked from the house, wearing a blue knit top and matching blue slacks and feeling more confident. Her hair, still damp from the shower, bounced against her shoulders, and she was thankful for its natural curl. She regretted not taking time to put on a dash of lipstick, but she seldom wore it at home, and the habit had now cost her a chance to make a better impression.

Why in the world has he come here? she wondered.

The two newest additions to her foster family, sisters Libby and Denise Jones from Ritzville, clung to each other in the swing a few yards away from the table. George and Boyd showed no bashfulness as they assaulted Max with questions about professional sports. Annabelle ignored the guest, choosing to lace asters into the spokes of Mickie's wheelchair. Mickie eased the chair slowly forward, finally stopping at the end of the table where she could study the man's profile.

The plate of cookies and the pitcher of lemonade were empty. Trenace's mouth went dry.

Max patted the table across from where he sat. "We saved you a glass and two cookies," he said, smiling at her.

An invisible line seemed to reel her toward the table, and she sat down, glad her trembling knees were hidden beneath her cotton slacks. Max and the boys chatted while Trenace tried to enjoy her snack.

Silence filled the yard when she put her glass down and swallowed the last crumb of cookie. "Someone from the station called last week and said you'd be in touch, but…I never expected this."

"The news director finally gave me your letter," Max replied, explaining the delay in response.

"I thought perhaps you weren't interested or didn't remember me," Trenace said.

"I remembered your name," he replied. "There aren't too many girls named Trenace running around the country." He studied his hands before looking across the table again. "For a while I wasn't interested," he admitted. "But the news hound in me took hold . . . and here I am. Perhaps we can make a deal beneficial to all of us."

Trenace looked across the table at Max, trying to assess his remark. "All we want is a tour, so the children will know what goes on behind the scenes when they watch your broadcast."

Max glanced at the children. "Could we talk privately?"

"I . . . suppose so, but why?"

He looked at the children again. "Are you familiar with the poem that goes, 'Monday's child is fair of face, Tuesday's child is full of grace'?"

She frowned. "Of course. 'Wednesday's child is full of woe, Thursday's child has far to go.' I don't remember the rest."

" 'Friday's child is loving and giving, Saturday's child must work for a living,' " Max continued.

"Now I remember." She smiled more happily. " 'The child that is born on the Sabbath day is bonny and blithe and good and gay.' I haven't thought about that poem for years."

He stared at her for a moment, then glanced at the children. "You look very comfortable surrounded by all these children."

Mickie rolled her wheelchair to his side. "Did you really know Aunt Trenace when she was a little girl?"

Max nodded.

"What was she like?" Mickie asked. "How was she in school? Did she make good grades?" She grinned up at Trenace. "I bet she *never* got into trouble."

"Everyone gets into trouble sometime," Boyd challenged.

Max winked at Mickie. "Let me think." He scratched his head and tried to look thoughtful. "She had red hair but not exactly bright carrot red."

"Freckles, too?" George asked, touching the scattering of dots across his own cheeks.

"Some," Max replied. "Of course, I sat behind her, so I know more about her backside...excuse me, the back of her hair. It was curly. She always knew the answers on tests, too."

Boyd smirked up at Max. "Did you ever look over her shoulder?"

Max laughed. "I plead the Fifth Amendment on that question, young man."

"What does that mean?" Boyd asked.

Trenace laid her hand on Boyd's shoulder. "That he probably did, but if he admitted it he'd be in deep trouble, just as you would be if you ever tried to copy someone else's work. Now why don't you children all go play for a few minutes before we go inside for quiet time?"

"Do they still take naps?" Max asked.

"No, but they go to their rooms and rest and do whatever they want as long as it's quiet." Trenace waited until the children were all out of earshot. "Why did you really come to see us?"

"Wouldn't a casual visit be enough?"

"No, Mr. Tulley, it wouldn't."

"Max. Call me Max."

She tried to look away. "Your secretary could have called us about taking a tour of the studio. This... this personal touch is thoughtful but unnecessary."

He walked over to the fence at the back of the yard, and she followed him. Leaning against the wooden panel, he studied the six children playing around the swing set. "Are you familiar with the *Wednesday's Child* program?"

She shook her head. "I thought we'd watched all the children's television available including cable reruns."

"No, you don't understand," he replied. "It's a news segment that local stations can buy into, either showing filmed segments from elsewhere or produce its own. Our news director has this bee in his cap that KSPO should get involved."

Trenace straightened. "What do they do on these segments?"

"Feature hard-to-place children who need families."

She frowned at him. "I don't think we'd be interested. These children have been hurt enough. You don't know their situations."

He lowered his voice. "That's the point. We'd tell a little about their backgrounds and try to find them permanent homes."

She shook her head. "I've picked up the pieces when the dream of adopting older children becomes reality. Thank you, but no thanks. It's a heart-breaking experience for both the child and the couple when the children come back. I try to help them feel good about themselves, but it takes time. They're innocent, but they always blame themselves." She shook her head. "We would love to tour the studio sometime, though. Thank you for coming, but the children really do take a quiet time break." She called to the children. "Time to go inside."

She gathered the empty glasses and put them back on the tray, then began to hustle the children into the house, knowing she must look like a mother hen with her brood of chicks. She didn't care. Max Tulley's charm had worn thin when she'd realized the true nature of his visit.

He took the tray from her hands and walked beside her toward the house. "Please don't be angry with me," he said as her left hand slipped from beneath his. "Could we at least visit while the children are quiet, unless you nap or read with them."

She suppressed a smile. "I have no time to nap. There's always chores to do around here, and I start preparing dinner."

"Could Mr. Tulley stay for dinner?" George asked, strutting beside Trenace and Max.

"I'm sure he has plans."

"Not a thing," Max said.

"He knows some of the players on the California Angels and the L. A. Raiders," Boyd added. "Please let him stay. George and I will do dishes, even if it's not our turn."

Trenace reached the glass door and slid it open. Max, still holding the tray of glasses, paused with one foot inside and one outside. "I promise to mind my manners," he said.

The two boys began to elbow each other excitedly.

Trenace rolled her eyes heavenward.

"So will we," Mickie chimed in, speaking for all the girls.

"Okay," Trenace conceded, "but only if you have an extra quiet, quiet time. If any one of you makes a peep, Mr. Tulley can't stay."

"Does that apply to me, too?" Max asked, his features overly serious, but the twinkle in his eyes was obvious to both her and the children.

"I guess you're exempted."

"Great," Max said. "We can catch up on old times." He grew serious. "I'd forgotten about your husband. Will Mr. McKay be joining us for dinner?"

The spark of enthusiasm left her voice. "He's out of state, so, no, he won't be with us. It's just me and the six children."

"That'll do," Max replied as he stepped into the kitchen with the tray of glasses.

WHEN TRENACE MCKAY returned from the bedrooms, she found Max comfortably settled at the harvest table in the kitchen, reading an editorial in the Spokane newspaper.

He glanced up as she passed by. "Coffee?" she asked over her shoulder.

"Sure."

As she prepared a fresh pot, she listened to the rustling of pages and glanced over her shoulder. He grinned up at her from the open high school senior yearbook she had forgotten to put away.

"The children were curious," she explained.

He strolled to the counter and turned, leaning against it as he held the book. "Hard to believe we looked like this twenty years ago, isn't it?"

She looked up at him but didn't reply, admiring the strong lines of his profile.

He chuckled. "I was six feet tall and weighed a hundred and thirty pounds." He closed the book and handed it back to her. "I remember you more from elementary school when you sat in front of me for several grades running. I used to play with your curls."

She blushed. "You couldn't have. I would have known."

"You had this habit of flipping your hair over your shoulder," he recalled. "I'd catch a curl with my pencil and touch it. It was in math class...seventh and eighth grades. I hated math. Still do."

"I loved math," she replied. "I was good at it, too."

"I know. I copied your work occasionally. They were the best scores I ever made."

She turned sideways, resting her hip against the counter. "You cheated?" She found herself caught in an aura of excitement as she met his gaze.

"I needed you in my freshman algebra class," he continued. "I had to learn to study just to get a passing grade."

"Poor boy," she teased, enjoying his company. "I took advanced algebra and got an A."

The electric coffeemaker stopped perking and the ready light came on. She reached for one of the mugs hanging on hooks beneath the cabinets. Their hands touched briefly, then his moved away to another mug.

When he put his mug on the counter, he shoved his hands into his pant pockets and turned away to stare out the window at the backyard while she concentrated on the coffee. "Sugar or cream?" she asked.

"A little sugar," he replied, his back still toward her. The muscles beneath his knit shirt flexed as he pulled his hands from his pockets and leaned his shoulder against the doorjamb.

She carried the mugs to the table and sat down. When he joined her, sitting directly across from her, he concentrated on the hot, steaming brew.

"Tell me what you've done since high school," he asked. "How did you get from senior class valedictorian to foster mother?"

"You remembered that?"

He took a sip of coffee. "That was one of your accomplishments mentioned in the senior yearbook, but I remembered it, anyway, because out of a graduating class of two hundred thirty-five, I came in about seventy from the bottom."

She tossed her head and chuckled. "Oh, Max, you couldn't have. You were in all the plays and you were on the school paper, and didn't you run for class office?"

"I tried to, but my grades disqualified me," he admitted. "I was a ham, albeit a serious one at times. My mother always said if school success had been based on drama and speech rather than math and science and history, I would have been the star of the class." He smiled. "You haven't answered my question."

She ducked her head. "I married two weeks after graduation and was pregnant by the time all my friends were heading off to college. My husband joined the army and served two years in Vietnam. I was home with our two young children."

"Boys or girls?"

"One of each," she replied, motioning to a collection of photographs on a nearby wall. "Steven is twenty. He'll be a junior at Washington State this fall, majoring in forestry. He has a summer job with the National Parks Service on Mount Rainier. Suzanne will be a sophomore and wants to be a teacher. She's a summer employee for the Parks Service, too, but in Yellowstone."

"It's expensive having two kids in college," he said.

"They're both on academic scholarships. And it's a good thing, too. I could never afford tuition for them. Do you have children?"

"I have twin daughters," he said, taking a photo from his wallet and handing it to her.

"Pretty girls," she observed, smiling. "They look identical."

"They are," he said, accepting the photo back. "But how did you get to be a foster mother?"

"While Owen was in the service, I started taking care of other women's children to help pay the bills. One thing led to another and now, here I am, foster mother to children with special needs. I suppose we've had close to two hundred children over the past fifteen years. Some of them stay only a week or two. Others like Mickie have been here for years." She glanced up at him. "I love the work, but it has its downside...like whenever the children leave. I keep reminding myself not to get emotionally involved...but I can't help it."

"I doubt you'd be a good foster mother if you didn't get involved," he said. "I think I understand."

"What about you?" she asked. "With those grades were you able to get into college?"

"My father was on the school board off and on, and he knew someone who convinced the registrar at Oregon State University to let me in on a trial basis," he said. "Maybe I matured over the summer, because I surprised everyone, especially my parents. I loved my college classes. I majored in drama and minored in journalism, learned to lower my voice and enunciate my words clearly, and presto, I got a job offer in Portland."

"In television?"

"Not quite. I was a disc jockey on an FM station from midnight to six in the morning. But it was a start. I switched to television in Sacramento as a field reporter in the legislature, later moved to Los Angeles, and now I'm back home."

"I think you've skimmed over a few details," she said.

"And you, too?"

She shoved her empty cup aside. "Tell me more about your own family. Do they enjoy living in Spokane?"

"I came here alone," he said, sliding the photo back into its place. "Lucy and I met at Oregon State and got married our junior years. Ashley and Amanda were born a year later, a little sooner than we'd planned, but they're great kids. They're both enrolled in the engineering program at the University of California at Los Angeles." He chuckled. "They certainly didn't take after their father. They're a year ahead of their class. This summer they're studying in England as part of an exchange program. They've never given me a day of grief. When I hear horror stories about raising teenagers, I wonder why our girls gave us no trouble."

"And your wife?" Trenace asked, unable to resist learning about his marriage.

A troubled expression darkened his features. "She died three years ago. That's why I'm back in Spokane."

"I'm sorry," she murmured.

"I loved her very much."

"I'm sure."

He glanced up. "I didn't mean for the conversation to turn morbid. What about you? You must miss your husband, with him gone so much of the time."

She cleared her throat. "I've learned to get along. I enjoy making my own decisions, but sometimes, when the children are having problems... Well, it's hard to hug and reassure six children at once." She smiled across the table. "My husband works in construction. It can be difficult with jobs ending and new ones opening up somewhere else. He never knows where the next job will be.''

"I assumed foster homes had two parents," he said. "Did you have trouble getting into the program with him gone so much?"

"He wasn't always away from home." Her lips narrowed. "Weren't we going to discuss this *Wednesday's Child* thing? We'd better get to it before the children get up."

"You're right," he agreed. "Here's how it works. We would select a few children and do short segments on each of them, then feature them during the six o'clock news with a hot-line number to call if a viewer wants to learn more about adoption."

She frowned. "You've oversimplified the adoption process."

"No, we haven't," he insisted. "I'll interview the children, but the social services people will handle the details. My news director wants me to get to know each child ahead of time, film them and then do a follow-up piece on the placements."

"What about the failures?"

He shifted on the bench. "We'll deal with those if they happen."

Her gaze narrowed. "You haven't thought about the failures, have you? What the rejection will do to the children? The emotional damage you're exposing the child to? You'd better go talk to your director and make him understand the possible consequences of this."

"Maybe I've presented this all wrong to you, Trenace." Suddenly he smiled, his blue eyes twinkling. "Didn't we call you Trena in Mrs. Wilson's seventh-grade class?"

Some of the steam went out of her, and she settled down on the bench again. "Yes, but that was years ago."

"At least give the program some thought," he coaxed. "Talk it over with your husband and Mrs. Sewell."

"You've talked to my caseworker?" she asked.

"She's our liaison with family services," he explained. "I haven't met her, but Josh Temple says she's all for it."

"That's because it would get the children off her welfare rolls and under the adoptive parents' financial responsibility," Trenace said bitterly. "Many of these children have extensive medical needs, and if they're placed, the county dumps the costs into the laps of the unsuspecting new parents."

"Don't they tell that to the adoptive parents up front?"

"They're supposed to, but they don't dwell on the negatives. They make sure the children are healthy-looking when they meet. Would you want to take a child who will need surgery soon? An AIDS baby? A boy like Boyd who will have years of skin grafts? Annabelle who will be in counseling for a long time? There's no end to the expenses. Sometimes the new parents ignore what lies ahead of them because they're swept up in the excitement of getting their very own little boy or girl."

"You sound bitter," he said. "I'm surprised."

"If you'd been in the program as long as I have, you'd see through the glamour and excitement to the children and their needs. We can't lose sight of the children."

"But if you exclude these children from this opportunity, you might be guilty of just that," he argued. "What if we could place some of these children in happy homes? Would you deny them that opportunity? A chance to have parents who love them?"

"I love them."

"Of course you do, but they're yours only temporarily. Please don't close the door on these boys and girls. They need a chance. Will you at least hold off on your decision until you talk it over with your husband. Will you do that? Not for me or KSPO, but for the children?"

She sat quietly for several minutes, mulling over his words. "You're a powerful persuader," she said. "I'll think it over before I make up my mind." She glanced up at the clock. "Good grief, I forgot all about supper."

Max reached across the table and patted her hand. "Let me take you all out for hamburgers."

She shook her head rapidly. "No, some of the children don't handle stress well. Libby and Denise are from an abusive home. If anyone raises a voice, they burst into tears. They've only been with me for two months... we tried it once and the outing was a total disaster." She hurried to the refrigerator and yanked the door open. "I'd planned on a pot roast, but now there's no time. Darn it. Maybe macaroni and hamburger, but all the hamburger is frozen."

"It can still be my treat," Max said, rising from the table. "Do they prefer hamburgers or fried chicken?"

Trenace stepped backward and whirled around. Her confidence was doubly shaken when she bumped against his chest.

He frowned as he grasped her shoulders. "Don't fall."

She sidled away, bracing her hands against the counter ledge behind her.

"It's my fault you didn't get dinner started on time," he said. "I enjoyed meeting the children and visiting with you."

She pursed her lips, thinking how excited the children would be. "Let me give you some money."

"All you have to do is tell me if they prefer hamburgers or chicken," he insisted.

Gradually a smile replaced her frown. "Boyd and George love chicken," she said, "but the girls like hamburgers without cheese, except Annabelle who's nuts about cheeseburgers." She reached for her purse and extracted a ten-dollar bill.

He took her hand and rolled her fingers into a fist around the bill. "I'll put it on my expense account if that makes you feel better."

She brightened. "I have ice cream for dessert."

"Great, especially if it's chocolate." He pulled a ring of keys from his pocket and dangled them in the air. "Is Division still the street with all the fast-food places?"

"Worse than ever," she replied. "Go straight down LaCrosse and you can't miss it. Be careful," she murmured, then wished she hadn't said such a foolish thing.

"I will," he said. "No one's told me that for years. Thanks, Trena." He glanced over his shoulder once and was gone.

TWO HOURS LATER the children were still gathered around the table, but they were growing restless and irritable.

The clock struck eight. "He should have come back long before this," Trenace said, knowing the children's patience was growing thin.

"Maybe he had an accident," George said.

"Nah, he's a good driver," Boyd challenged.

"Maybe he got sick," Libby said.

"Or maybe he had to go back to the television station to do the news," Annabelle offered.

"This is Sunday, silly," Mickie said. "That other man does the news on Saturday and Sunday."

"Girls, please don't bicker," Trenace said, laying a hand on each girl's shoulder. "Whatever Mr. Tulley's reasons for not coming back, they're not going to provide supper." She opened the cupboard door and scanned the contents, then removed a large jar of chunky peanut butter. "We'll have sandwiches and vegetable soup. Annabelle, can you get the bread? Libby, you and Denise get the lettuce and margarine and jelly. Boys, set the table and don't forget the napkins."

Boyd's enthusiasm for the makeshift supper matched the pout on his thin face. "What if he comes after we've eaten. Can we still have the chicken?"

Trenace took a deep breath, concerned about the disappointment reflected in the children's faces. This would be nothing compared to the sense of rejection they would feel if the program Max was promoting failed them. "If Mr. Tulley shows up later, well . . . we'll see. He's a busy man." She lowered her voice. "You can't depend on other people's promises. You must learn to take care of yourselves."

"You always say we should keep our promises," Mickie said. Her brown eyes grew moist, and she whirled her chair away from the table, turning her back on the rest of the children.

"And never fight and scream," Libby added.

"Does he really want to put us on TV?" Boyd asked.

"Who gets to go first?" George asked.

"It's too early to decide," Trenace said. "Please don't get your hopes up. We'll talk about it after I've discussed it with Mrs. Sewell."

"Maybe Mrs. Sewell is wrong," Mickie said. "Maybe someone would like to have me, after all."

As Trenace poured soup into their mugs, her thoughts centered on the missing man. Max Tulley had swept through their afternoon, filling them with hope and promise. Even though he had spoken quietly about the *Wednesday's Child* concept, some of the children had obviously overheard him.

Now he seemed to be letting them down.

CHAPTER THREE

BY THE TIME the late news came on television, Trenace had the children in bed, the living room tidied and two loads of laundry done with a third waiting for the dryer.

She folded the last pair of jeans and carried the stack into the boys' room, quietly laying them on the dresser.

When she dropped into her favorite overstuffed chair and pushed the power button on the remote to the television, all remaining energy seemed to drain from her. Automatically she selected Channel Nine, then abruptly changed her mind. She couldn't watch KSPO news, not tonight. She had memorized its format, knew just when the major story would air, how they slipped the less significant tidbits of news between regional and national news, how they teased the viewer with promos.

Would Max himself be watching? If so, was he alone? He'd been in Spokane only a month, but was his social life already full and satisfying? Perhaps he'd remembered a previous commitment for the evening. Why hadn't he had the courtesy to call? Knowing she was sulking, she settled back into the soft cushions of the chair to watch a competitor's channel. If that was the way he wanted the matter to end, so be it, she thought. They could do without him. A tiny smile tilted the corners of her mouth. *I really did enjoy his visit.*

Half dozing, she listened to the promos to the next segment of news. "KSPO's recently hired anchor was injured in an accident earlier this evening. Details after these messages.''

Trenace grabbed the remote and jumped from the chair. Max? Injured? But how? She switched to Channel Nine. His own station would have had a report. She waited several seconds, perplexed by this tiny bit of explanation. If the story had been accurate, KSPO would have featured it early in the broadcast and she had probably missed it.

She groaned and changed back to the other channel. *Why didn't I give him credit for trying to keep his promise?* she thought, and a wave of guilt swept through her. How seriously had he been hurt?

When the program resumed, a still shot of a small white car with a crumpled front end and a spiderweb mosaic of cracks across the front windshield filled the screen with an inset of Max's face for a few seconds, then the camera returned to the newsman.

''Police reported that the intersection of Division and LaCrosse streets was littered with numerous containers from fast-food establishments in the area. Officers arrested two teenagers at the scene for trying to steal a bucket of fried chicken. They have been turned over to juvenile authorities. A KSPO spokesman said Tulley sustained minor injuries but would be kept overnight at a local hospital for observation. Maxwell Tulley, a native of the area, returned to Spokane recently to assume the anchor position at KSPO.''

Without a pause the reporter switched to a regional story about the arrest of several members of a white supremacist group in the Hayden Lake area of northern Idaho.

Trenace turned off the television and stared at the blank screen, shaken by the reason for Max's failure to return. Before he'd left he'd given her his business card. She retrieved it from the kitchen counter and punched in the numbers on the phone. When a woman answered, she asked about Max's welfare.

"Good gracious, ma'am," the woman said. "You're just about the umpteenth caller. Ninety percent of them were women! He's fine, but he banged his head pretty hard, so they're keeping him overnight at the hospital."

Trenace cleared her throat. "What hospital is he in?"

"Oh, ma'am, can you imagine if I'd told all those women who called ahead of you the same thing?"

After a brief explanation of Max's visit to her foster home that same afternoon, Trenace convinced the woman to inquire further and the woman put her on hold. When she came back on the line, she said, "Mr. Temple said he could vouch for you, ma'am. Max is at Saint Vincent's over on Sprague. Tell him hi from all of us if you get through, okay?"

"Of course," Trenace said, then thanked her and hung up.

But when she tried to speak to Max, she found herself against a barricade. No phone calls to patients in the emergency room. No phone calls to any patients after ten o'clock. No information given out except to family members. "Are you family?"

She was tempted to lie but decided against it. "Could you at least tell me when he'll be discharged?"

"I'm sorry, ma'am."

"Thank you," Trenace replied.

Later, as she lay in bed in the darkness, she thought about the coming day. She'd call the station and leave a message for him. She had medical appointments for three of the children in the morning. After the appointments at the clinic, she would drive Denise, Libby and Mickie to the day-camp facility for the rest of the day, then do some shopping.

At times Trenace longed for a few hours alone, but not often. These children were her responsibility, her life, and she was thankful she had them, especially since Owen had left. Mrs. Sewell, the social worker, had been a wealth of information and advice over the years, but more recently she'd hardened, turning cold and withdrawn. Now she always ended her visits with a terse reminder that the children had been placed with foster parents on a temporary basis.

"I know it's hard, but it's for your own welfare. It's not good for the children, either, to get too attached."

WHEN MAX FINALLY convinced the staff physician at Saint Vincent's that he felt fine, the woman signed his release, admonishing him to rest for a few days. He listened but didn't say a word. He had no intentions of resting. He'd done that overnight. They had kept him in the emergency wing. None of the rooms had phones. He'd pleaded with a nurse to sneak one in or let him go out to the desk and use one, but all that had gotten him was a sedative.

He'd given Josh Temple's name and phone number when the medical staff asked for someone to notify. Josh had come to the hospital, sided with the physician about keeping him overnight and offered to assign a field reporter to fill in as anchor for a few days. When Max refused, Josh had insisted he not report to the studio until midafternoon, and that if he changed his mind to give him a call in time to draft another reporter.

He'd been too dizzy to think straight, and his head had hurt like hell. He should have asked Josh to call Trenace

McKay and explain his failure to return to her house with the food.

If he could just get to his apartment, shower and shave, and get a decent cup of coffee, he'd give her a call and apologize.

After an erratic taxi trip by a driver new to Spokane, they reached his apartment building. The manager waved to him as he walked past the office door.

"Hey, how are you?" the manager asked. "We heard about your little accident on the news last night. What happened?"

"A guy in a four-by-four truck tried to run a light and I was in his way," Max replied. "I got banged up a little bit."

"And a black eye?" the manager observed.

"Yeah, to go with the goose egg on my head," Max said. "Actually, it feels even worse than it looks." They chatted for a few more minutes, then Max excused himself. In his apartment he made a fresh pot of coffee and headed for the shower.

His car would probably be totaled, the investigating officer had hinted. Well, he'd been thinking about trading it in for something more rugged, anyway. He lingered in the shower, letting the pulsating hot water ease the soreness that was beginning to make itself known throughout his body. With a towel wrapped around his hips he sat on the edge of the bed and dialed Trenace McKay's home.

No one answered. Ten o'clock by his watch. Maybe she was out in the backyard. He tried the number again, letting it ring more than a dozen times before giving up.

Concerned, he called a taxi and dressed. Outside, when the cab arrived, he climbed in and gave the driver Trenace's address. A short time later, when they pulled to the curb, he said, "Wait until I see if she's home." No one answered when he rang the McKay doorbell.

A large desk clip had been attached to the doorjamb. It held a pad of paper with a pencil tied on a string. He took the pencil and wrote, "Sorry about last night. Will be in touch later. Max."

"Take me back to where you picked me up," Max told the driver. As they traveled the few miles to his apartment, his thoughts lingered on Trenace and her children. He'd only met them once, yet he felt a commitment. Probably the children, he decided. They were children with tragedy and sadness in their past. "Wednesday's child is full of woe," he mumbled.

"What did you say?" the taxi driver asked as he pulled up in front of the apartment building.

Max shook his head. "Nothing." He paid the driver and returned to his apartment. Inside, he gazed around the tidy set of rooms. Tastefully decorated, comfortable—everything he needed—but the rooms were sterile, devoid of human touches. No fingerprints, no dust, only his lone coffee cup in the sink. No one to fight with over the morning newspaper. The complex provided a cleaning service. A laundry service picked up his soiled clothes once a week. He had no lawn to mow, no household repairs to worry about, no one to be concerned about or be concerned about him.

"Quit feeling sorry for yourself, Tulley," he mouthed, refilling his cup just to have something to do. In the living room he dropped into the nearest chair. Not nearly as comfortable as the McKay house, he thought.

His head still throbbed, but the medication he'd been given at the hospital had made him drowsy. He couldn't afford to be dull-witted until he finished work. He considered flushing the pills down the toilet, then decided he might need them later that night.

Could needing an aspirin or two justify another call to the McKay household? He smiled. Knowing that one excuse was as good as another, he reached for the phone. A deep burst of pleasure filled him when he heard her voice.

"Hi, do you have plans for lunch?" he asked.

TRENACE MCKAY'S HEART fluttered strangely at the sound of Max Tulley's voice. Her throat went dry and she couldn't speak.

"About last night, I hope you and the kids forgive me," he said. "I tried, I really did, but—"

She interrupted his apology. "I saw the car on Channel Two last night and explained the accident to the children this morning. How are you?"

"Fine," he said. "You probably have a houseful of kids," he hinted, giving her an out if she wanted one.

"Actually I'm alone," she replied, settling on the kitchen stool near the wall phone. "The children are all at day camp. I dropped the last three off there after visits to the clinic."

"Oh, are they sick?"

"Just preschool examinations," she replied. "Dr. Brockman says they're fine."

"When do they get home?" he asked.

"About 4:00 p.m."

"Then have lunch with me."

"You mean . . . just the two of us?" She thought of all the things she'd planned to do, but now they faded in importance. "I'd like that. I have some more questions about *Wednesday's Child*. Where shall I meet you?"

"I'll get a taxi and come get you," he said. "I have a headache that won't quit," he admitted. "I'll stop at a drugstore on the way for some aspirin."

She read through his bravado. "Don't call a cab. I'll come pick you up instead."

"I accept, but only if you can bring some aspirin with you."

"Of course," she said. "Give me your address and let me do the driving." She jotted it down and promised to be there within the half hour.

"I'll be outside waiting," he promised.

Anticipation filled her with energy she hadn't felt in months as she changed into a pink-and-white striped sundress. Even though this was business, she looked forward to seeing him again. She leaned against the dresser drawers and closed her eyes. She had enjoyed his company immensely the previous afternoon. He was unmarried.

Her eyes flew open. He thought she had a husband. Maybe she should tell him the truth about Owen. But would he keep her secret? She wasn't sure. He was a person easy to trust, but perhaps that was a trait he'd developed for career purposes. *Consider him an old friend,* she told herself. Most of her friends had drifted away as her involvement in the foster children program had deepened. Knowing she was wasting time, she grabbed her purse and keys, locked the door and ran to her car, wishing she had time to clean out the interior.

As she pulled into the parking lot of the apartment building and found a parking place, he waved from the entryway. Through her rearview mirror she saw him step off the curb and break into a brief run. He stopped abruptly, and she lost sight of him in the mirror.

Twisting in her seat, she spotted him again several yards from her car. He was clutching a light pole, his eyes closed.

She leaped from the car and raced toward him. "Max, you're not well," she cried, steadying him with her hands. "Let me help you." She slid an arm around his waist as he leaned against her.

"Just don't move for a moment," he said, his voice wavering.

"I should get the car," she suggested, beginning to feel embarrassed at standing here in public at high noon, her arms around a man she barely knew.

"No, don't leave," he replied. The arm he had draped around her shoulder tightened as his hand pressed against her for balance, curling her slowly around and into his arms. His chin pressed against the top of her head, forcing her cheek to rest near his throat.

Scents of soap and after-shave surrounded her, clean, masculine scents that complemented the firmness of his torso, which she could feel beneath his cotton shirt. Her hands moved on his back, alternately patting and stroking him. "You'll be okay," she crooned. "You'll be fine."

"Just...don't move for a minute," he mumbled. "I'm dizzy."

"I'll hold you as long as you need me," she whispered. Another minute passed. He swallowed, and for an instant she wanted to kiss his throat. Knowing her own emotions were running riot, she tried to ease away, only to find herself firmly in his embrace. "Maybe I should get help," she whispered.

"I got dizzy, but it's passing," he explained. "I shouldn't have run. The doctor said to take it easy. Maybe she was right." He stepped away.

"I think I can make it to the car now," he said.

She kept her head averted. "Take my arm, just in case," she said, and when he did, they made their way to her car.

Inside the vehicle he touched her shoulder. "I'd have been flat on my face without your help."

She turned to him, noting the greenish cast to the skin around his mouth. "Maybe lunch isn't such a good idea."

"I never got to eat last night, and this morning they tried to feed me some unidentifiable coagulations they insisted were scrambled eggs," he countered. "A decent meal might settle my stomach."

"You have a black eye, your nose is swollen and that goose egg will be a challenge to the makeup people. Are you off tonight?"

"I'm checking in at three," he replied. "I have a top-notch crew of field reporters who are editing their stories as we speak. But Josh Temple has the final say on what gets aired, so I'm free until then. Let's enjoy this time alone. I'm sorry. I just meant you usually have six kids looking on and I'm often buried in story material."

She smiled and slid the key into the ignition. She nodded her understanding, wondering if he might feel the same subtle chemistry between them that she'd felt when she first found him watching her at the lilac bush. As she drove toward the restaurant he'd suggested, she recalled the poem about the children. Perhaps she and Max were Wednesday's children, too. She carried her own share of woeful secrets, and his wife had died. Moreover, something told her there was more to his wife's death than he'd revealed. But she didn't know him well enough to ask.

IN THE RESTAURANT, they ordered soup and sliced turkey sandwiches. When the food arrived, his appetite returned with a vengeance.

"This is great," he said, enjoying the taste of food for the first time in months.

As she finished her soup, Trenace laid her spoon down and opened her purse. "Here's the aspirin." She handed him the tin.

He smiled and took two, then returned them to her. "Now let me tell you more about *Wednesday's Child*."

Over their meal he described the concept again, shared a few possibilities of how he could present the children's stories and answered her questions.

"We'll feature many other children from other foster homes, as well, but Mrs. Sewell and Josh Temple feel that it will be easiest for me to begin by getting to know you and your husband and some of the children who have gone through your home over the years. We'll want to do one segment on you and . . . Owen? Mrs. Sewell thinks it might generate some interest in prospective foster parents. I'd like to spend time with both of you as soon as he returns."

He swallowed the last bite of turkey sandwich and glanced up in time to catch a flash of naked trepidation in her eyes before she began to shake her head.

"Telling the children's stories will be okay as long as you clear it with Mrs. Sewell, but I won't agree to an interview about Owen and me," she said, refusing to look at him.

"Why not?" Caught off guard by her change in attitude, he pressed her. "Would Owen disapprove?"

"He has no say in the matter."

"But he must. He's your husband and—"

"No, he's not."

Max put his salad fork down and stared at the woman sitting across from him. Maybe he'd heard her wrong. He'd found himself attracted to her. He'd known from the beginning that she was married but that hadn't stopped his interest. He'd decided early on to channel that interest into a top-notch series that would benefit both of them, and enjoy her company along the way. Couldn't a man and woman be friends without becoming involved more deeply? He didn't want a relationship, and he'd accepted the limitations of their circumstances.

Now she'd suddenly changed the ground rules. "Would you care to clarify that remark?" he asked. She met his gaze directly, but he suspected it took all her courage to avoid taking flight. "Please, Trenace, what do you mean, he's not your husband?"

"He left for good almost two years ago and moved to Nevada," she said as her mouth softened into a sad smile. "He met someone. She got pregnant and he wanted to marry her." Her eyes remained dry. "They have a son now."

"The bastard," Max said. "What about you? Surely he had to think about you." How could a man hurt a woman as sensitive and caring as Trenace McKay? Surprised at the intensity of his own reaction, he waited impatiently for her to explain.

"Owen said that since our two children were grown, we had no reason to stay together, and he wanted this new family very much." She traced the damp ring on the table left from her glass of tea. "We discussed it like two mature adults. No emotional outbursts, no accusations, no nasty words." She glanced up at Max. "I did insist that he pay off our mortgage. I knew I could manage if I didn't have that to worry about."

"You make it sound as if your marriage was a business arrangement that had gone sour," he said.

She ignored his comment. "He made the final payment on the house last December in order to have a tax deduction, and he signed the deed over to me. We live separate lives now.''

"And that's it?" he asked. "A tax deduction, a deed transfer, and a twenty-year marriage ends? Trenace, that's cold as hell. Didn't you care whether he stayed or left? Didn't you love him?"

"When I was eighteen, I thought so, but a teenager's love is based on hormones and insecurity," she said. "We aren't all able to meet and marry our true loves like you did.''

"What about passion? Surely you had an active love life," he said, knowing he was prying into her private affairs.

"I don't think that's any of your business," she replied. "We're talking about love, not passion.''

"Can you separate them?" he asked.

She stared across the room, past the other customers, and once again ignored his question. "As the years passed, I began to have my doubts, but marriage vows are forever and I intended to keep mine. We'd drifted apart, and I'd become too involved with the foster children. As the years went on, he began to resent that. When he had an offer to become a field supervisor at the construction firm where he'd been the office manager for several years, he jumped at the chance.''

"Are you legally divorced?" he asked, wanting to take her hand, to touch her and let her know he cared.

"He filed in Nevada, and it was granted the day after Christmas," she explained. "I agreed to cooperate all the way on condition we kept it a secret. If Mrs. Sewell finds out about it, I might lose the children. She carries a lot of influence within the agency, and she prefers foster homes to be headed by a male role model." She looked directly into his eyes. "But I'm doing fine without Owen. Max, the children are all I have right now. They need me, and I need them. They give me reason to keep going. Will you keep my secret?''

This time he did take her hand, squeezing it gently. She didn't pull away. ''What would you do if you didn't have the foster home?''

''I don't know.'' Her shoulders stiffened. ''You're looking at a woman who's never held a job outside the home in her life.''

''Never? Not even during high school?''

She shook her head. ''Maybe that's why I was able to get straight *A*'s in school. I had few demands on my time other than studies. I can run an efficient house and relate to troubled children, but those skills neither pay well nor warrant respect or admiration, and I've learned the hard way that it doesn't offer job security or a pension plan. Did you ever do a story on unemployment benefits for displaced homemakers, Max?''

He stood up. ''Let's get out of here,'' he said, taking the check and heading toward the cashier. Outside he walked beside her to the station wagon with the crumpled fender and around to the driver's side. Instead of opening it for her, he leaned against, it, glowering down at her.

The sun turned her auburn hair into molten flames as potent as the turmoil churning inside him. He wanted to touch it, to feel its silky strands slide through his fingers. She wasn't married. Why hadn't he picked up on the signals before? She was free, as free as he was.

A sharp pain shot through his midsection. Maybe he shouldn't have eaten. Lingering effects from the accident were bringing aches and pains to parts of his body that he hadn't realized had been injured.

''What's wrong?'' she asked.

"I don't know," he replied, waving his arms in the air. "I feel mad as hell and I don't know why." He grabbed her shoulders. "I wanted to produce an interesting series that would touch the viewers. I wanted to learn about the problems of adopting older children, and damn it, I wanted to have a hand in helping the kids find good homes."

She touched his shirtsleeve. "You will. You're doing exactly what you'd planned to do. The accident is a temporary setback. Give yourself a week and you'll be as good as new. You have no reason to be angry. Why are you so upset?"

His mouth softened. "I thought you were married and I was glad. It meant no involvement other than old friends meeting again." His brain buzzed with an ache that loosened his tongue. "Now I'm not so sure. I needed you to stay married."

"I can't change reality," she murmured.

When she looked up at him, he recognized his own vulnerability. He was standing on the brink of change, as if his life might take an unexpected turn, but the logic of his mind held no influence over the confusion of his emotions.

Her mouth invited caressing. It would be soft and warm. *She isn't married.* The buzzing in his head increased to a throb, crippling his ability to think rationally. His hands slid to her face, and as his fingers splayed across her cheeks, he tilted her head slightly.

She gasped as his mouth settled on hers, and only later did he realize her arms had moved up his shirt to encircle his neck.

CHAPTER FOUR

"WE SHOULDN'T HAVE done that," Trenace said. Her arms had turned to lead as she became aware of her willingness to explore the contours of his mouth. One brief kiss and he had ignited a passion she had forgotten she could possess.

His hands slid down her arms to clasp hers. "You're right. We shouldn't have, but we did."

She looked into his eyes. "I wanted us to be...friends."

"We will be."

"For the sake of the children."

He nodded.

"Good," she replied.

He dropped her hands and touched his right temple.

"Your headache has come back," she said.

He grinned. "Maybe another kiss will make it better."

"Not on your life," she said, glad the mood had changed. "You're a big boy."

"You noticed?"

"Little boys don't..." She recalled his reaction to holding her firmly against him. "Little boys don't have...character lines around their mouths." At the mention of his mouth her gaze lingered there for several seconds before turning to his eyes, only to find herself reaching upward to meet his mouth once more. Their surroundings were forgotten until a warm summer breeze touched her moist lips and she realized he had released her once more.

His somber expression unsettled her already-teetering composure. She fumbled inside her purse. "Here," she exclaimed, shoving the tin into his palm. "Take two every few hours, and eat something so they don't upset your stomach."

"Yes, ma'am," he murmured.

She glanced at her watch, unwilling to risk looking into his eyes again. "Goodness, it's almost three o'clock. Where did the time go? The children will be home soon, and I haven't thought about dinner."

He grinned. "We could try for chicken and hamburgers again."

She laughed. "You have a job to go to. Have you forgotten?"

"Only at moments like this," he said. Before she could think of an appropriate response he turned and walked to the passenger side of the car and slid inside. In minutes they were at the front doors of KSPO.

"Take care," he murmured. "I'll make amends to the kids. Expect the unexpected."

He squeezed her hand and left the vehicle. Sadness enveloped her as she watched him disappear through the glass double doors. Irresponsible emotional reactions on their parts would be counterproductive to their mutual objectives. The children needed him. He needed a successful series. She wanted happiness and a promising future for the children. They needed to step back, put distance between them.

But what did she want for herself? For a few moments, when they'd stood locked in each other's arms, their lips savoring the pleasures of newfound intimacies, she'd wanted much more than mere friendship.

She closed her eyes and tried to think rationally. She had no right to even think of such a thing at a time like this, especially with a man like Max Tulley. They moved in different circles. They had nothing in common. Unless...

"No," she murmured, and the sound of her own voice in the enclosed automobile startled her. *Impossible. Physical attraction. That's all it is. It's been a long time since Owen walked out.*

TRENACE HAD a large pot of spaghetti cooked and the sauce simmering when the doorbell rang. "Anyone in the living room?" The bell rang again, and she grabbed a dish towel to wipe her hands. When she opened the door, she couldn't believe her eyes.

A clown in full costume grinned at her. The clown was at least six foot six and as thin as a rail. His hair was orange on the left, bright green down the middle and flaming red on the right side. His smile could charm the worst cynic.

"Yes?" she asked.

"Ma'am?" the clown asked, taking a deep bow. "Is this the residence of six little children who had to go to bed without their supper last night?"

Trenace smiled and nodded, for only one person could be responsible for this visit. She felt a tug on her apron and glanced down to find shy Denise peeking around her hip.

Libby, more outgoing than her sister, slipped past and stared up at the strange-looking man. "Who are you?" Libby asked.

"Jocko McPocko, a direct descendant of a long line of royal clowns," the clown replied. "Do I have the right house?"

Libby looked up at Trenace, waiting for Trenace to answer the clown. Trenace smiled down at her. "Do you want to answer him?"

Libby nodded. "We live here. The balloons are very pretty."

"Would you hold them for me, please?" the clown asked, presenting her with the bouquet of two dozen colorful balloons. He scanned the area. "I have a heavy load in my car. Are there helpers among these children?"

"I can help," Boyd called.

Trenace glanced behind her to find the other children gathered.

"Me, too," exclaimed George.

"I can carry stuff on my lap," Mickie offered.

Trenace stepped outside, and Mickie followed, wheeling her chair out the entryway, down the ramp and sidewalk to a Volkswagen Beetle painted to match the clown's hair. On the side a sign read Clowns Unlimited. In tiny letters was printed the slogan, You Pay, We Play, and a phone number.

The children returned with sacks from several fast-food restaurants and a large bucket of chicken on Mickie's lap.

"My assignment isn't complete," the clown said, winking at Trenace. "May I have permission to enter your lovely home?"

"Did Max send you?" If the man was a lecherous maniac who meant them great harm, they would all meet their end with smiles on their faces, she thought.

"Max?" The clown arched his bushy brows, then wriggled them. "Who's he? The king of these United States?"

"No," the children sang.

"Prime Minister of the British Empire?"

"No," they cried.

"Is he the governor of Spokane?"

"No." The chorus grew louder.

"Is he your monkey's uncle?"

"No," they cried, bursting into giggles.

"Then who is this Max fellow?"

"He's that TV guy who came to see us," George said.

"The only guy I know from a television station is an old grouch who gets sulky from time to time," the clown insisted. "Unless the camera is on. Then he drips with confidence. Could this be the same guy?"

"Maybe," Boyd replied. "Max knows about baseball, but he sure isn't a grouch." He glanced over at Trenace and grinned. "Aunt Trenace says he's not old, either."

The clown chuckled and scratched the green stripe of his wig. "It's a big mystery to me, but I'm sure I have the right house." He reached into one of his oversize pockets and removed an accordion-pleated piece of adding machine paper, allowing it to unfold and ripple downward, its end settling on the floor at the tips of his shiny red shoes. "Let me see now. The chicken belongs to two boys." He turned to Libby and wiggled two blue eyebrows. "That must be you . . . and you!" He pointed a finger at Annabelle.

The girls giggled and pointed to Boyd and George.

The clown puffed out his chest and frowned at his note. "Are you sure?" he asked. "I'd hate to give it to the wrong kids."

"We're the only boys who live here," George insisted.

The clown winked at Annabelle, then relinquished the bucket of chicken to Boyd. Annabelle, struck with shyness, hid behind Trenace's skirt. The clown turned his full attention to the girl in the wheelchair. "You must be Mickie. I have a hamburger and fries for you. No cheese."

Mickie's eyes widened as he presented her with her meal. She looked up at Trenace and asked, "How did he know?"

Trenace shrugged.

The clown leaned toward the chair. "Clowns know a lot, almost as much as Santa Claus." He stuck out his chest. "I know that Annabelle loves cheeseburgers. What do you think of that?"

Annabelle squeezed through the milling children. "That's me," she said, politely accepting her food.

Libby had lost some of her confidence and now held her sister's hand. "What about us?" she asked.

He looked the girls up and down. "You look like hamburger girls to me, no cheese and no pickles. Am I right?"

Libby and Denise nodded and accepted theirs.

Trenace smiled at the clown. "Won't you join us? It looks as if you've brought enough for the whole neighborhood."

"Can't stand hamburgers, actually," he whispered.

"How about spaghetti?" she whispered back.

"Sounds great," he replied. As the children rushed to the kitchen, the clown turned to Trenace. "I told Max that no rational woman would let me inside, but he said you'd be a good sport about all this."

She smiled. "No one but Max could have put you up to this. Who are you really?"

"Jocko, ma'am," the clown replied. "Didn't you listen?"

She escorted him into the kitchen and motioned to the high stool near the breakfast bar, where they would be away from the excited children. He served himself a plateful of spaghetti and meat sauce, and she waited patiently while he ate. When his appetite was satisfied, she confronted him again. "Who are you really?"

He touched the corners of his painted mouth with a flourish and grinned. "My dear sweet mother named me Jacob, but I've been called Jocko for as long as I can remember. The last name is Grimes. I'm a cameraman for KSPO-TV. My wife, Becky, used to be a secretary there, but now she runs this clown service and I help out once in a while. When Max told me what happened last night, I suggested Jocko McPocko make a house call."

"That's very sweet . . . of both you and Max," Trenace said.

He held up a long finger. "There's method to our madness. He asked me to work with him on this assignment and wanted me to meet the children ahead of time so I could think about some camera approaches to handle any potential problems." He glanced at the children. "The oldest boy's face could be a challenge, depending on whether we wanted to downplay the scars or be honest and show them the way they are."

Trenace glanced at Boyd, who had taken charge of parceling out seconds on the remaining food. "He's still having reconstructive surgery and will for several years," she said. "He's a great kid, but his father couldn't see past his tendency to cry when he got hurt. Boyd's father threw gasoline on him when he was four years old. Why? Because he'd stumbled and skinned his knees." Her mouth tightened. "For acting like a typical preschooler he got doused with fuel and set on fire. It's a miracle so much missed him. The garage caught fire, then the house, and the rest of the family was burned to death. Only Boyd and his father were spared."

"Where's his dad now?"

"In prison for second-degree murder of four people. Boyd has been with me for ten months. He's a great kid, but he has his moments, especially when he thinks one of the other children might get hurt. He's a worried old man in a boy's body.''

Jocko grew solemn. "Maybe we should start with one of the girls. Are they all eligible for adoption?''

"Not Denise and Libby," Trenace replied. "Their mother has petitioned the court to get them back, but her past performance isn't very promising.''

Boyd swallowed the last bite of the fourth piece of chicken and looked up at the wall clock. "Max is coming on in five minutes,'' he announced.

The children scurried about, clearing the table and carrying their dishes and silverware to the counter.

"Can I watch, too?'' Jocko asked.

Taking his arm, Trenace escorted him into the living room, then adjusted the television set. When Max Tulley's image flashed on the screen, she was sure her heart had stopped.

"Wow, look at that bandage," Boyd said, whistling softly.

A neat white two-inch square of gauze covered the abrasion and welt on his forehead. No amount of makeup could have hidden the darkness surrounding his left eye or the swelling across the bridge of his nose. In spite of the accident he was as handsome as ever. He gave a brief opening remark about the accident. Then he added, "If the kids at the McKay house are listening, I have a message.''

"That's us!" Mickie exclaimed as the children scooted closer to the set.

"Be extra nice to Jocko and Mrs. McKay. They're special people who mean a lot to me," Max said, bestowing a smile at the camera that brought Trenace's heart to an abrupt halt. With a slight pause he launched into the lead story.

Trenace curled up into the overstuffed chair, confused yet pleased by his remarks.

Jocko chuckled. "That cost the station a commercial break."

"What do you mean?" Trenace asked, still watching the screen and Max as he read the lead-in to another story.

"Seconds count with this business, even in the news department," Jocko explained.

She turned to him. "Will he get into trouble?"

"It's doubtful," Jocko replied. "With what he must make he can buy the time himself."

"I wouldn't want him to be called on the carpet because of us . . . but the children loved it. Look at their faces."

"You should see your own face," Jocko said, grinning.

Trenace glanced away. "He did it for the children."

"You're sure?" Jocko teased. "The man is magic in the ratings. The viewers love him." He stretched his unusually long legs. "It always amazes me how a person can project an impression of openness to the public and still keep his true self hidden."

She turned to Jocko, troubled by his comment.

"He's a man nursing some deep hurts," Jocko explained, as if thinking aloud. "He pretends to the outside world he's recovered, but how could a man recover when something like that happens to him."

"Do you mean his wife?" Trenace asked.

"You know about her?"

"He told me she died a few years ago."

"And that's all?" Jocko asked, frowning at her.

"Yes . . . is there more?"

Jocko turned back to the screen. "I've said too much. You'll have to ask him." As the news program ended with a final remark from Max, Jocko stood up. "It's time to hit the road."

"What about that?" Boyd asked, pointing at the huge patchwork bag whose drawstring Jocko had looped over his fist.

"Oh," Jocko said, looking innocently into the round bag and bouncing it once against the floor. "You noticed?" He slowly pulled on the cords that held the opening of the bag and reached into it, extracting a rubber ball at least three feet in diameter. "Max said you could kick this around outside. It's supposed to be indestructible." He reached into the now-limp bag again and brought out several envelopes. "These are from KSPO management. Mrs. McKay had better take charge of them."

They followed him to the door and watched as he drove away in the colorful Volkswagen. Back inside the house Trenace peeked inside one of the envelopes, startled to see a hundred-dollar gift certificate to a nearby shopping center. The other envelopes held similar certificates. A note from the president of KSPO read, "We realize funds must be scarce, so perhaps these will help ease the burden. Enjoy them, compliments of myself and the staff here at KSPO."

A nagging thought disturbed Trenace as she began the evening bath routine. "George, you're first, then Boyd, and Boyd, leave George alone and no teasing." The girls watched a comedy show, and Trenace kept them company, clutching the six envelopes as she mulled over the significance of what she held.

She would have to notify Mrs. Sewell. This windfall could cause more problems than it solved. She hoped not. The children could use new clothes. They were active and growing rapidly. She received a clothing allowance from the county, but it was never enough. She'd dipped into her personal savings more than once, especially for the older children. Shopping at three nearby thrift stores and passing outgrown garments down helped ease the problem.

Whenever a child was removed from the McKay home, Trenace made sure he or she left with as complete a wardrobe as possible. New children seldom arrived that way.

George came skipping down the hallway, wearing baggy pajamas, his feet bare, his red hair standing up in spikes. He held a black comb in one hand and gave it to her. "I can't see in the mirror without climbing onto the sink, and you told me I shouldn't do that anymore." His blue eyes twinkled as she began to comb his hair. When she finished, she kissed his shiny, freckled cheek. He grinned at her. "Can I sit on your lap?"

"Of course," she murmured, pulling him into her arms. He settled against her, tucking his legs beneath him. A few minutes later he slid his left thumb into his mouth, unaware of the curious gazes from the girls as he fell asleep.

She carried him to his bed and covered him with a sheet and a light flannel blanket. In spite of the warm night air the children seemed to need the security of the flannel blankets.

In succession the girls took their baths and received the ritual of hair combing. After the younger ones were in bed, Trenace helped Mickie into the tub and waited within calling distance if she needed help. Mickie had been with her the longest of any of the children, and each time Mrs. Sewell called or visited, Trenace was afraid that it would be Mickie's turn to leave. But so far it hadn't happened.

Mickie and Boyd were allowed to stay up an extra hour. Soon after they went to bed, Trenace showered and changed into a lightweight gown and robe, then curled up in her favorite chair to wait for the ten o'clock news program. As the credits for the show in progress began to roll, the phone rang.

"Hello?" she said, hoping it wasn't Mrs. Sewell with a late-evening emergency placement.

"Good evening, Trena," Max Tulley said.

"Max? Oh, goodness, you didn't have to call," she said. "Are you home?"

"No, the ten o'clock anchor quit after an argument about a news story and I'm filling in," Max said, his voice low and steady.

"But you should be home resting. Gracious, I sound like a worried mother."

"I took a pain pill," he said. "If I look spaced-out or fall asleep during the broadcast, you'll know why."

"How will you get home? You don't have a car."

"I'll call a cab. Did Jocko get there?"

She laughed. "With enough food for a week. Thanks, Max. It wasn't necessary but . . ."

"I wanted to do it."

"But the gift certificates?"

"That was Joshua Temple's idea," he explained. "He thought maybe the kids could wear some new clothes for the filming, which is the main reason I called."

Disappointment edged some of the thrill of his call from her mind. "Are you starting soon?"

"On Thursday if possible," he said. "Jocko and I would like to come by after we finish the six o'clock show and film outside."

"That sounds fine," she said. "Who chooses which child?"

"I talked to Mrs. Sewell and asked about the little girl Annabelle," Max said. "She's photogenic and the audience should respond to her. Mrs. Sewell said her family had already signed papers releasing custody, although I don't understand how any family can just give up their own child.''

"Max, Annabelle is ..."

"Sorry to interrupt," Max said, "but I should be miked up by now, so I'll say goodbye. Trenace?"

"Yes, Max."

"About what happened at lunch ... don't take me wrong, but I'm glad your husband is out of the picture. What I mean is, now we don't have to wait for his approval or ... hell, forget it. See you on Thursday."

Before she could reply the dial tone hummed in her ear.

WHEN THE VAN from KSPO-TV rolled to a stop in front of the McKay home, several neighbors peeked from their windows. Max glanced at one woman who was curious enough to step outside and stare. He nodded, then motioned Jocko to follow him.

Trenace opened the door before he had a chance to press the bell. Her eyes shone brightly, accented by the navy-and-white splashy knit top she wore over navy slacks. He wanted to reach out and touch her, to convince himself she was real. She had been in his thoughts incessantly since that unplanned kiss in the restaurant parking lot.

This is business, he warned himself. *Keep it that way.* Trenace extended her hand, and he took it, trying to hide his disappointment at her formality.

"Good evening," she said, barely glancing at him but smiling at Jocko. "The children are anxious and excited." She stepped back and motioned them into the living room. "They're in the backyard, but ..." She turned to Max and touched his arm, her fingers as light as a feather.

As he gazed into her eyes, he could see sensual confusion and found himself comforted by the realization that their attraction was mutual. All that stood between them were six children and an assignment to complete. Perhaps after the taping they could find a quiet corner and talk.

"Would it be best to do the interview without the other kids?" Trenace asked.

He covered her hand with his before she could remove it. "We need to keep the background noises down, but I don't see why the others can't be there." He pressed her hand and felt her begin to withdraw. "Let's try it together, and if that doesn't work, we'll do it again with just you and Annabelle and Jocko."

"But only Annabelle in front of the camera," she insisted.

He wondered about her reluctance to appear on camera but decided not to press the issue. "If you prefer it that way."

In the backyard he found Annabelle perched on the picnic table bench, smoothing a pink dress primly over her knees. Perfect, he thought, taking in the little girl's blond pigtails with pink ribbons tied halfway down them. "If she isn't placed immediately, I'll eat Jocko's wig," he murmured, then walked to the picnic table and sat down next to Annabelle. First he planned to chat for a few minutes, then send a signal to Jocko to zoom in on the real interview. The video camera would be rolling from the beginning, and they hoped to get some good material from the informal portion as well as from the heart of the interview.

"Hello, Annabelle, do you remember me?" Max asked.

"Yes, sir, you're the man on TV," she said, her voice so soft that he wondered if a microphone would pick it up.

"May I clip on a mike?" he asked, waiting until she finally looked up at him and nodded. He fastened the tiny mike to the lacy-edged Peter Pan collar and smiled. "Do you know why we're here talking?"

"Yes, sir," she said, still solemn with no trace of a grin. "Aunt Trenace says you're gonna find me a new mother and daddy."

"That's right," Max said, relieved when he finally coaxed a smile from her. "Somewhere out there are two people who are just waiting to love you as their very own little girl."

She nodded, carefully keeping her hands folded in her lap.

The wooden slats of the bench began to turn to unforgiving steel beams. "Would you rather go to the swing and talk?"

"No, sir."

Max glanced up, spotted Trenace standing next to Jocko and arched an eyebrow. She gave him an encouraging smile, and he turned his attention back to the uncommunicative little girl. His mind went blank for several seconds, and the silence on the film lengthened. They could edit it out, but what if he couldn't think of a way to draw her out? "What kind of a mom and dad would you like to have?" he asked, hoping he could use her answer to liven up the tape.

"I want a mom and daddy who won't get mad at me."

He frowned. "Did your mom and dad get mad at you?"

She took a deep breath, and Max waited expectantly.

"My daddy keeps a gun..." She looked up at Max, a bewildered expression in her blue eyes. "My daddy always told me never to touch his gun."

"Your daddy is right. Guns can be very dangerous," Max agreed.

"My momma said he should get rid of it, but my daddy said he needed it in case burglars got in our house," Annabelle explained, her voice still timid. "They used to fight about it."

Something rang a bell in Max's mind, but he couldn't get a grasp on it. "How old are you?"

"Eight years old," she replied, "but I was only six when my grandpa came to visit us. I never meant to hurt him."

"Of course you didn't," Max said, patting Annabelle's hand.

"I told my momma I didn't mean to hurt my grandpa, but she said I was lying. She said it was my fault, and then she said it was my daddy's fault. That's why they got a divorce and my daddy went away." She looked up at Max again, her blue eyes shiny with tears. "My momma hates me because she says I did it on purpose. That's why she gave me away to Aunt Trenace."

"No matter what you did, I'm sure your mother didn't just give you away," Max said, putting his arm lightly around her shoulders.

"I got the gun out and showed it to my grandpa, and it went off, and my grandpa got blood all over his shirt, and he died . . . but I didn't mean to hurt him."

Max's ears rang with her words. "You killed your grandpa?" He didn't recognize his own voice.

"But I didn't mean to hurt him," Annabelle cried, her chin quivering as tears streamed down her flushed cheeks.

Trenace swooped the hysterical little girl up in her arms and ran into the house, leaving an ashen-faced Max and a stunned Jocko alone in the yard with the other five children.

CHAPTER FIVE

TRENACE COMFORTED the distraught child, who fell quickly asleep, exhausted from reliving her traumatic experience. As she rocked the little girl, Trenace felt furious with Max, but when she returned to the backyard and saw him with his face buried in his hands, her feelings of outrage where shattered. She sat down beside him on the picnic bench and touched his shoulder. "Annabelle's asleep."

He leaned back against the table. "I handled that like a rank amateur. I asked all the wrong questions and made a little girl hysterical. I'm the world's biggest heel."

She shook her head. "I should have told you about her background. How could I have been so stupid?"

Max ran his hand over his face. "I think I read a piece in Los Angeles on the case. It made the national news, didn't it?"

Trenace's mouth tightened. "I'm afraid so, and the intrusion of the media helped to break up what was left of the family." She turned toward the other children and gathered them around her. "Annabelle will be all right. She's never talked much about her grandfather before. Sometimes it's very painful to face the truth, and today she did."

Mickie rocked her wheelchair close to Trenace's knees. "She was crying."

"Yes, dear, because she loved her grandpa and didn't mean to hurt him, but he died and no amount of wishing can bring him back." Trenace gazed at the worried young faces of the children crowding around her and Max. "If I had the power, I'd give you all two loving parents and promise you happiness." She blinked her tears away and smiled at the children. "But then I'd never have had you come live with me, would I? Maybe with Max to help us we can work some miracles in the next few months. Now why don't you all go inside? It'll be getting dark soon. We'll have a snack and say goodbye to Mr. Tulley and Mr. Grimes."

Jocko packed his camera away and shifted from one long foot to the other. Max stood motionless, his notepad dangling from his left hand. She waited until the children were inside before speaking to the two men. "Either Mrs. Sewell or I will tell you about each child's background before you start the interview from now on. When do you want to come back?"

Max stared at her. "You still want to continue... after what happened?"

She swallowed. "Yes. Today was a breakthrough for Annabelle. She's been in counseling for over a year, but the psychologist says she refuses to talk about her grandpa except to say she didn't mean to hurt him. Max, don't you see? Today she talked to you. Come inside and I'll tell you more about her."

"I don't think so," Max said, shoving his notepad into his pant pocket. "I've got to go talk to Josh Temple about this whole damn program. It's not working."

"MAX, I'VE WORKED with you on a lot of stories since you got here," Jocko said as they rolled into the television station parking lot, "but I've never seen you like this. I agree it was upsetting, but I think you're ready to kill the whole project."

Max opened his door. "Not a good choice of words." Without a backward glance he went into the building and directly to Josh's office. It was empty. In his own office he dropped into his chair and tipped it back, closing his eyes. If only he could erase the little girl's image from his mind, if only he could have chosen a different child, one without problems or disfigurements or emotional scars.

The casters on his chair thudded against the mat as he leaned forward and stared at his cluttered desktop. *But that's why they're with Trenace McKay, because they are scarred.* He turned the swivel chair around and stared out his window, trying to think clearly.

His own two daughters had grown into young women with hardly a day of turmoil. Even as teenagers they'd been honor roll students and never broke curfew. *Model children?* As a father, had he been insulated from the real world of parenting? But what was real?

A picture perfect little girl who shot and killed her own grandfather? A boy like Boyd whose father doused him with gasoline and set him on fire? The sisters Libby and Denise had been victims of child abuse, but what kind? Mickie seemed spunky in spite of her confinement in the wheelchair. Was there more to her situation? And little George, cute as a button? He should have been adopted as a young child. Did each of these children hide a secret so terrible that society had rejected them?

Trenace McKay must be a martyr to work with these children. She'd said hundreds of children had passed through her home. Maybe Owen McKay had run away from his wife's emotionally draining occupation. Could any man live with a martyr for long? A flash of her face materialized in his mind's eye, almost as clear as if she'd entered the room—beautiful, caring, understanding, always there when the children needed her. Had she been there when Owen needed her?

What were her own children like? Angelic saints like his own? For the first time in his life Max felt as if he should apologize for his daughters' good behavior.

For the next two hours he studied the copy for the ten o'clock broadcast, making notes along the margins, asking a reporter to verify two points in a specific segment. When he headed to the makeup room to change into a dress shirt and jacket, his head was throbbing, but he decided against a pain pill. Buttoning a gray dress jacket over his pale blue shirt, he adjusted a burgundy tie. In the studio he clipped on the mike, and for two full minutes he sat in the anchor's chair, trying not to think about Trenace McKay and Annabelle and all the little children of the world who needed someone's loving arms to protect them from harm.

"Max, come alive!" the camera operator called.

Max looked up in time to catch the countdown from the technician behind the glass panel. For an instant he wondered if he'd fallen asleep, but as he read the introduction to the major story, a little girl's tear-filled eyes and a beautiful woman's compassionate face haunted him.

TRENACE WATCHED Max work his way through the half-hour news program. His dignity and professional manner was the same, but the spark in his eyes seemed hooded tonight. Glad the children were asleep, she sat down cross-legged on the carpet and gazed at the screen.

A movement of his hands, a glance down at his notes, an informal remark to his sports reporter—she scrutinized each small nuance carefully, wanting to understand the man behind the facade. Earlier in the evening she'd sensed he had faced his own vulnerability. But to what? Jocko had hinted he was still recovering from his wife's death. Could that have been worse than having one's husband skip out for another woman?

She reached out and touched his face on the screen. A spark shot from the screen to her fingers, and she jerked back. Staring at his solemn features, she edged away, but when he smiled and said good-night to the audience, she murmured, "Good night, Max." Her heart skipped a beat when she glanced back at the screen to find him leaning back in his anchor's chair, staring at the camera. The screen went blank for a few seconds before swinging into a commercial.

The expression on his face continued to haunt her, and she knew she would only toss and turn if she went to bed. Flipping channels, she watched a few minutes of a mindless talk show, then a movie old enough to have Roy Rogers as a supporting actor, on to a hospital drama in syndication featuring two diseases she'd never heard of before. The station signed off and she turned to another. She'd pay for this restlessness the following day.

Going to the kitchen, she warmed a mug of chicken noodle soup in the microwave. As the display bleeped at her, the doorbell rang. She flinched. Surely Mrs. Sewell wouldn't bring a new child this late at night without a warning phone call. Cautiously she walked to the front door. Peeking out from behind the curtain, she saw a vehicle drive away in the darkness. The doorbell rang again. Clutching the doorknob, she checked the dead bolt. "Who's there?"

"Max."

Fumbling with the security devices, she unlocked the door and jerked it open. In the darkness of a moonless night his silhouette filled her door. He seemed taller tonight, but thinner, and when he didn't move, she reached out to touch him.

He took her hand, and the warmth of his skin filled her with a need to be close to him. She stepped outside. As his arms encircled her, she clung to him, pressing herself against his body and forgetting her own scanty gown and robe. Her cheek rested against his chest, and through his shirt she heard the thudding of his heart, deep and powerful.

His hands splayed across her back, stroking her, comforting her, yet as she savored his caresses, she remembered that she should be the one comforting him. She eased away, but her hands sought his face, not content until her fingers traced the worry creases down his cheeks to circle the grim line of his mouth.

"Why are you here?" she whispered.

"I . . . I needed you," he confessed.

She frowned. "I was worried about you."

"I've been a basket case all evening."

"I could tell . . . but I don't think anyone else could."

"You know me so well?" he asked, his hand moving to her neck.

"Maybe."

His fingers began to stroke the softness of her earlobe, and she found herself breathless.

"Trenace, I need you," he murmured. When he sought her mouth, she lifted her face willingly.

His mouth molded itself to hers, changing the warmth within her to hot passion. His arms tightened around her, drawing her upward, almost lifting her feet from the porch floor. The strength in his arms made waves of longing wash over her. She wanted to know him more intimately.

A warning flashed through her muddled thoughts. They had no right to be standing on her porch in the darkness, like two teenagers, pawing each other with lustful desire. If he continued to touch her in this incredible way, she didn't know what she might do next.

They'd agreed to be friends, and friends didn't— She refused to speculate on what friends might or might not do. Regret hung heavily in the dark shadows of the porch as she stepped away. "I was having a mug of soup. Care to join me?"

"Sure." His hand settled comfortably on her shoulder as they walked through the dark house to the well-lit kitchen.

She filled another mug, set the controls of the microwave and turned to him. His gaze drifted down her robe, and a wave of embarrassment swept through her. She fumbled with the buttons, managing to confirm they were all safely fastened. "I don't normally entertain handsome men after midnight in nightclothes."

"You look lovely," he said, stepping closer to brush a strand of auburn hair from her cheek.

She had a crazy desire to turn her cheek and kiss his hand, to keep his fingertips on her face. The buzz of the microwave sounded, and feeling relieved at the distraction, she opened the door.

Handing him one of the mugs and a spoon, she motioned him to follow her to the living room. Before he sat down he pulled a vial from his trouser pocket and removed a small white pill. "My head is splitting again," he said. "The doctor said I might have headaches for weeks. I try not to take these unless it gets really bad but . . . tonight it's worse than usual."

"Sit down," she suggested after he'd taken the pill with a sip of broth. They enjoyed the soup, the silence between them comfortable. "Are you feeling better?"

"Yes, but the pills make me drowsy," he replied.

"Stretch out on the sofa. I'll sit on the hassock." She smiled. "We'll talk and you can relax."

"I should call a cab and head for my apartment."

"Is there someone there to talk to?"

"Four walls and an empty bed," he said, his gaze lingering on her. He frowned. "I'm sorry. I shouldn't say that."

She pulled her legs up and tugged the robe and gown over them, forming a tent of protection. "That's okay. It's late and you're tired. You've had a trying day. Please lie down and rest a few minutes. I couldn't sleep, anyway."

He removed his jacket and tie and unbuttoned the top two buttons of his shirt. Then he stretched out on the sofa, his head resting on a tufted blue pillow she'd made years earlier. Slipping one hand behind his head, he turned to her. "How are the children?"

"They're survivors," she said, her gaze drifting down the row of buttons on his shirt. When they disappeared beneath the small brass buckle of his belt, her attention jerked back to his face. He'd been watching her. His gaze held hers captive.

With his free hand he reached out to touch the arch of her foot, which was sticking out beneath her robe. "You have incredibly soft skin wherever I touch you." His voice sounded soft and intimate. "Your eyes hold me. I don't know why, but they do. Why didn't I notice you in high school?"

She smiled and eased his hand from her foot. "Because I was trying to be a female jock and you were bent on being America's next greatest actor."

He smiled. "You? A jock?"

"I finally earned my sports letter my senior year," she said. "It was a heck of a lot harder than making good grades. I'm surprised you didn't become a movie star."

"I've seen what can happen to actors when a career turns sour. I'd rather report on depravity than be part of it."

She gazed down at him. "You insulate yourself, don't you?"

"Insulate myself? I don't understand." He closed his eyes and folded his hand across his flat stomach.

"You report the news but aren't part of it." She gave in to the urge to caress the back of his hand as it lay across his middle.

"Tell me about Annabelle," he murmured. "I want to come back and film her, maybe this weekend, but I need to know what happened, so I can avoid another experience like today."

Trenace straightened her legs to restore the circulation.

"Put them here," he said, patting the sofa cushion near his hips. When she did, he closed his eyes again and smiled, but when his hand found her leg and settled on the back of her calf, she suspected she'd made the wrong move.

"More soft skin," he murmured.

"Please, Max, don't do that," she said, easing his hand from her leg. "Behave yourself, or I'll call that cab myself. We've agreed to be friends, for the children's sake. Remember?"

His head turned toward her, his eyes stormy and dark. "It was easier when I thought you were married."

"Then pretend I still am."

"Didn't you say once that we should deal with the real world?"

"Yes, but I was talking about the children, not us."

"Are you telling me that for us it can be a world of fantasy?" he asked, watching her every fidgeting move.

She grinned. "I won't dignify that question with an answer."

"Afraid to delve into the possibilities?"

"I thought you came here to talk about Annabelle," she reminded him. When he didn't reply, her thoughts began to undermine her determination to keep him at arm's length. "Friends don't touch each other at every excuse. Friends don't kiss each other the way we have."

"You're irresistible," he said. "But you're right. I came here to talk about Annabelle. Would it be too much to ask of a friend to hold my hand while she tells me about Annabelle?"

"You drive a hard bargain."

He closed his eyes again. "Jocko and I will come back Sunday afternoon, if that's okay with you, and I'll keep the interview on what she wants in her new parents, what she likes, her favorite things. I'll do the introduction and narration at the studio." He held out his hand.

She nested his hand in both hers and held it in her lap, then tucked her toes between his hip and the sofa cushion. "It was the mother's father who died. The media hounded them, camped at their front and back doors. Whenever the father would come out to go to work, he found a camera rolling and a microphone stuck in his face. He and his wife began to fight, and Annabelle got forgotten in the trauma.

"A coroner's inquest concluded that it was an accidental death, but then one of the national affiliates did a special on handgun carelessness in homes. They focused on poor little Annabelle's family. Max, it was terrible what the reporters did to her and her parents. Her father filed for divorce, relinquished custody of Annabelle and disappeared. Her mother's grief turned to anger, and Annabelle became her target.

"A teacher called the authorities when Annabelle came to school with bruises. There was an investigation, during which her mother said she couldn't bear the sight of her own child. She signed papers to put Annabelle up for adoption, but two placements were unsuccessful. The shooting and her parents' divorce, her mother giving her up, two failed adoption efforts, and three foster homes all in a little more than two years have taken their toll."

"Poor kid," Max said, squeezing her hand. "You're good for her. You're good with all the children. How do you do it?"

"I love them."

He smiled and closed his eyes again. "And I'm sure they love you. It would be hard not to love you, Trena."

Her gaze shot to his face, but his eyes were still closed, his features unreadable.

"You give out hugs and kisses and bake sweet cookies and provide warm meals at all hours. You're a remarkable woman. Do you know that?"

She looked down at his hand, so large and masculine as it lay unmoving on her robe. With her finger she traced the large veins just below the skin that snaked toward his wrist. "Max?"

He didn't respond.

"Max, are you asleep?"

His fingers curled and relaxed and his hand grew heavy. She lifted his hand to her lips and kissed it, then laid it gently back onto his stomach. "Max, you're pretty remarkable yourself," she said. She considered calling a taxi for him, then decided against it. Why disturb him when at last he was getting some rest? She hadn't broken through the wall of invisible protection he surrounded himself with, but she had seen a few cracks in the mortar tonight. He was a caring, loving man. She was sure of that. What had happened to him to make him build this wall?

She covered him with a crocheted afghan and went to her own room. Crawling between the sheets, she thought about the man asleep on her sofa. She had literally fallen into his arms the moment she'd seen him. Other than Owen, she'd never found herself attracted to a man enough to respond to him with sexual interest.

Is that what I feel? she wondered. Sexual interest? Lust? If he had been more aggressive, would she have invited him into her bed and comforted him in a different way? She'd never had to deal with a situation such as this before. Max had been single for... how long? Three years? Surely he didn't live a celibate life. But if there was a woman in his life, why had he come to her door after midnight?

While he'd been kissing her, she hadn't wanted to stop there. If she'd let the kissing continue, would they have stopped there? Would he be alongside her now, satiated with lovemaking instead of chicken soup?

She smiled into the darkness. What would he think if he could read her thoughts? An image of Max making love to her flashed through her mind, and she savored the fantasy for several minutes.

She tensed when she heard footsteps in the hallway as one of the children made a trip to the bathroom. How could she be having these thoughts when six children were asleep only a few yards away? And what would the children think when they woke up to find Max, the TV man, asleep on the sofa?

THE SUN STREAMING through Trenace's window jerked her awake, and a glance at her clock swept the cobwebs away. She never slept past eight o'clock. She dressed and ran to the kitchen to find six children sitting around the table eating cold cereal and toast.

"I fixed the toast," Boyd said. "When I got up, the coffeepot was perking. Did you go back to sleep?" He grinned at the other children. "I told 'em to hurry 'cuz the van will be here in ten minutes for day camp. This is our last day. You promised to go with us and see the program we've been working on."

She frowned at the children, then glanced at the red glowing light on the coffee maker. "Just a moment." In the living room she found the afghan neatly folded on the hassock. All sign of Max's visit had been erased from the house, but when she returned to the kitchen and spotted the two mugs in the sink, she knew she hadn't dreamed his visit.

She smiled at the children. "I'll be there for sure, but I'll drive the station wagon. On the way home let's stop for hamburgers. It's time I got you all out and about more often. Libby? Denise? Would you like to try McDonald's again?"

The sisters leaned against each other. "We'll be good."

"You two are always good," Trenace replied. "Then we'll come home to see our friend, Max, the TV man."

SHE WATCHED Max on the screen twice daily, but he didn't call or stop by. The darkness around his eyes changed shades and gradually disappeared as did the bruise on his forehead. A visit from Mrs. Sewell distracted her, but a sense of loneliness disturbed her ability to concentrate during the visit.

"Mr. Tulley called me this morning," Mrs. Sewell said as Trenace poured her a cup of coffee. "He said he's coming to film Sunday afternoon and asked me to be present. I'm pleased that little Annabelle will be the first child filmed. Will Mr. McKay be home this weekend?"

"He's in New Mexico, and we really can't afford airfare," Trenace replied. She recalled the gift certificates given to the children by KSPO and told Mrs. Sewell about them.

"Oh, my goodness, that does complicate matters," Mrs. Sewell said, smoothing her gray hair. "We could overlook clothing and toys but a gift of money? I'll have to put in an order to adjust their checks accordingly."

Trenace frowned. "You mean the agency will deduct six hundred dollars from what I get to run the household just because of KSPO's generosity?" She mentally calculated her monthly grocery bill and the summer utilities. "All at once?"

"You know the rules and regulations, my dear," Mrs. Sewell replied, tidying the contents of her briefcase.

"But the money was meant for clothing and some little extras," Trenace argued. "The children are always outgrowing their clothes and school is coming soon. There's never enough money, and they all need new winter coats and gloves. I need to replace some of our books, too. I can't always get to the library. I never imagined you'd be cutting grocery money." Angry at this upsetting news, she rose from her chair. "Do I ask the children to stop eating for a week or two? Do you know how much I spend on groceries? Do you realize how inflation has boosted the cost of a box of dry cereal alone? Can't you at least spread it over a few months? These children are being punished enough without this."

Mrs. Sewell smiled. "I'm sure Mr. McKay earns enough money for you to make ends met. After all, I warned you that being a foster parent isn't a profit-making venture. It's a labor of love, my dear. You seem a little upset today. Is there something I can do? Perhaps six children are too many for a woman who must play both mother and father. I do wish Mr. McKay would get a job in this area so that he could be here to help you. You know we prefer couples in our program. The regulations have loosened, but most of us who have been in this service for a long time disagree with the concept of just one adult. And with one like Mickie in a wheelchair... Would you feel better if I began to look around for a new home for her?"

"Of course not," Trenace exclaimed. "Mickie loves it here. It would be very upsetting for her to be moved. Please, Mrs. Sewell, don't disturb what I've worked so hard to achieve here. Mickie is happy. Boyd is blooming. Annabelle is finally beginning to heal. Even George is coming out of his shell."

"The little sisters from Ritzville will probably be going back to their mother soon," Mrs. Sewell warned. "The mother is in counseling and her boyfriend is out of the picture."

"They're very fragile little girls," Trenace said. "Are you sure returning them to their mother is the wisest thing to do?"

"Our primary goal is to keep the natural family together," Mrs. Sewell said, as if reciting a department policy.

"But at what price?" Trenace asked.

"We try to anticipate the best, not the worst," Mrs. Sewell said. "A birth mother's love is always better than a foster parent's affection. I've told you that before. You foster parents always wonder why I repeat this at every visit, but if you'd seen how many still get emotionally involved, you'd understand the burden I carry in my profession. Well," she said, standing up and smoothing the wrinkles from her gray cotton jacket, "I have two more calls to make, so I must be on my way. Please get the Ritzville sisters ready to go home."

THE NEWS DIRECTOR'S secretary had called late Friday to notify Trenace when the filming crew would arrive. Still, she grew progressively more nervous as the day and hour approached.

She smiled at Annabelle. "Are you ready?"

Annabelle tugged at her newly purchased blue knit top and matching shorts. Perhaps she had overdressed the child the last time. Today everyone would be more relaxed, more at ease. Annabelle had responded to two recent therapy sessions, and now Trenace assured her that Max knew all about her grandfather and that they would be talking about happier things.

"But I won't ever forget my grandpa," Annabelle said.

"Of course you won't." Trenace gave her a squeeze.

Annabelle threw her arms around Trenace's neck. "I love you, Aunt Trenace."

"And I love you, too, sweetheart," she replied. "Now let's go out back and wait for Mr. Tulley and Jocko."

As the children waited, they talked about what they would say to Mr. Tulley when their turns came. Thirty minutes later the crew arrived. Trenace felt her heart thud against her ribs when Max smiled at her. They hadn't exchanged a word since their midnight visit. She knew it was probably for the best. They'd hinted at subjects she didn't think she could deal with.

"Good morning, Mrs. McKay," Max said, extending his hand.

"It's afternoon," Jocko whispered loudly.

Max cleared his throat and held her hand for several seconds before letting go. "How are you and the children?"

"We're fine and Annabelle is ready," Trenace said motioning them to follow her through the house.

The afternoon flew by as they filmed Annabelle and Max on the swing set and then sitting on the grass. He seemed to ask all the right questions, and Annabelle charmed him with her answers.

Annabelle smiled at Max. "Are we finished now?"

Max nodded. "You were great."

"Can I hug you now?"

"I'd like that," Max replied, accepting the little girl's gesture of confidence. Jocko kept the video camera rolling.

"We're ahead of schedule," Max said. "Boyd, would you like to have your turn?"

After a quick change of shirts and a combing of Boyd's unruly brown hair, they were able to film a second session. The scars on his face and neck were touched on briefly as he leaned over the huge colorful medicine ball.

"I gotta have skin grafts, but they don't amount to much," Boyd said in his serious "little old man" voice near the end of the interview. "I've had dozens of 'em already, so I know all about what the doctors do."

"You're a brave young man, Boyd," Max said, giving the boy a warm hug as the session ended. He glanced up, searching the crowd for Trenace.

She knew the expression in his eyes would stay with her forever, for another piece of mortar had fallen. She blinked away her tears and smiled encouragingly at him. Jocko began to pack away his equipment, chatting with the technician who had come with them.

Mrs. Sewell went to Max. "Mr. Tulley, this has been most enlightening to see your work. I know we'll get calls right away once you begin airing the segments. Thank you for a superb job." She bid everyone goodbye and left.

"You're all welcome to stay for dinner," Trenace said.

The men exchanged glances and Max shook his head. "We have another story to film across town, but we'll be in touch."

As the crew left, Jocko leaned toward Trenace's ear. "Make that 'he'll be in touch,'" he whispered, giving her a lecherous grin before he ambled from the yard.

CHAPTER SIX

A WEEK LATER when the doorbell rang Trenace whispered a prayer that Max Tulley had returned. He'd called once to apologize for not stopping by but he and Jocko had been busy filming children at other foster homes. He'd mentioned in passing that he'd complete the assignment Sunday afternoon and then would be free for several mornings.

"Could you get away for breakfast?" he'd asked.

"Oh, Max, I'm afraid not," she'd replied. "Day camp is finished and the children are home until school begins."

"How about getting someone to stay with them for a few hours?"

"Sitters are very hard to find. Most of them don't have the patience. I'm so sorry."

"Then I'll come to you," he'd said before hanging up.

But now, when Trenace opened the door, a grim-faced Mrs. Sewell greeted her. "May I come in?" Inside, the woman looked around the living room. "Where are the children?"

"In the backyard," Trenace said, tensing with uncertainty.

"I have good news about Annabelle," Mrs. Sewell said. "You know how important this program will be for us if it proves successful. Three couples called about Annabelle, and we're screening them now, but one couple looks extremely promising. They've been on our list of prospective applicants for over a year, so they've already been checked out. They'd originally requested a newborn. Now they want to meet Annabelle and take her home for the weekend. Isn't that exciting?''

"Annabelle? Leaving us so soon?" Trenace's heart tightened. She looked out the window at the children playing. "Of course, that's wonderful."

Mrs. Sewell handed her a photograph. "Good. I know you get attached to the children, but we can't let that happen, can we?"

"Can I show this to Annabelle," Trenace asked, staring at the photograph. "Tell me a little about them, and I'll prepare Annabelle for the visit."

"Mr. and Mrs. Peterson will be here at nine o'clock to meet Annabelle and take her for the weekend," Mrs. Sewell explained breathlessly. "They'll have my number in case problems arise, but they know all about her situation. The man is a high school counselor and the wife is a former teacher. She quit teaching last year to be ready whenever a child became available. They're very excited about Annabelle."

"WORKING DOUBLE SHIFTS is getting old," Max said as Josh Temple scowled across the desk at him. "Haven't you found a replacement for the ten o'clock slot yet?"

"Strange that you should ask," Josh said. "I've hired a young woman from Butte, Montana. She'll be here the first of August. And here, take these." He handed Max a fistful of ivory envelopes. "The sales manager has been soliciting some sponsors for a dinner to keep the *Wednesday's Child* program rolling along in financial health. We're having a dinner August eleventh, and you're one of the guests of honor. I thought you might want to invite a few close friends."

"Why am I a guest of honor?" Max asked.

"Because this is making you famous," Josh boasted.

"Not to mention boosting the station's rating?"

Josh shrugged. "See that Mrs. McKay and her husband get one. Warn Mrs. McKay that I'll be introducing her and she'll be expected to say a few words to the audience. That little girl of hers has already found a new home."

"Annabelle?" Max stared at the handful of envelopes. Trenace must be heartbroken, he thought. He'd avoided calling her. She'd asked for friendship, but his body and emotions had begun to have their own ideas. He didn't want to become involved with anyone, especially not a woman who was tied to a houseful of children. He couldn't even ask her to dinner. She'd mentioned that finding someone to stay with the children had proved almost impossible.

What did other foster home couples do? he wondered. Well, of course, in other foster homes, there was a spouse to ease the burden. There was a second income to pay for a sitter. Trenace carried it all alone.

"Did you hear me, Max?"

Max looked up and guessed at the last question his production manager had asked. "I'll deliver it personally," he promised.

"What I asked was how is the filming going?"

"Oh, fine, fine," Max said. "We're doing several more this weekend." He turned to leave.

"Don't forget what I said," Josh said. "You and Mrs. McKay made the perfect combination to get this program off to a running start and you deserve to share the limelight. So be there, both of you."

After the six o'clock broadcast, Max phoned the McKay home. The sound of Trenace's voice made him vividly aware of how much he needed to see her again. "Will you be home this evening?"

She chuckled. "I'm home every evening. Can you stop by? I . . . the children have been asking about you."

"I'm on my way." *Keep the home fires burning,* he thought, acknowledging on the drive across town how much he'd missed them all. When she opened the door and smiled at him, he knew he'd been smitten by this quiet, strong woman whose beauty shone from a source far deeper than her creamy skin. He wanted to pull her close against him, but she was flanked by Boyd and George. "Hi, boys, what's happening?"

"Annabelle's got a new mom and dad," George said excitedly. "They took one look at her and said they wanted her." He tried to snap his fingers but couldn't.

Max frowned at Trenace. "So quickly?"

"It's not final," she explained, "but the first weekend went so well that they have her for two weeks now, and the paperwork is being processed." The boys raced from the room, and she filled Max in on the backgrounds of the prospective new parents. She laid her hand on his arm. "When will Boyd's piece air?"

The warmth of her touch made his blood surge, and when she smiled, he couldn't resist touching her cheek. "It'll air the middle of the month," he said, admiring the incredible softness of her skin. One of the children called from the sliding doors and she turned. His hand slid from her cheek through the curls at her temple to sink against the back of her head. Before he realized what he was doing he'd leaned down and brushed his lips against the side of her neck and felt the tremor move through her. Without a word she took his hand and led him to the back-yard.

When the children saw him, they surrounded him.

"Who's next?" Mickie asked, wheeling her chair back and forth restlessly.

"We're gonna go home," Libby said, and her sister Denise nodded.

"That's wonderful," Max said. "That leaves only Mickie and George to film. Who wants to be next?"

Mickie shook her head. "I don't want to be adopted," she said. "I wanna stay with Aunt Trenace forever."

"No one wants to adopt me," George said, walking to the swing set and sitting in one of the glider seats with his back to them.

Max glanced at Trenace, but she shook her head. "He's been dealing with some problems, and I think they all miss Annabelle," she said. "But we're getting two new children once Libby and Denise go home. Mickie may change her mind. Maybe we can film her and just pretend she's staying here."

"Good idea," Max said, and ambled over to the swing set. "Can I sit with you?" he asked George. The little boy nodded, and Max eased himself down onto the seat opposite him, hoping his weight wouldn't break the seat. "I bet I could find someone who would like a little boy like you. Can I try?"

George looked up. His cheeks were pale beneath the freckles, his blue eyes bright. "Do ya really think so? Mrs. Sewell tried once and the man said I looked like Ronald McDonald."

Max leaned forward. "Did you know that when I first met Aunt Trenace she had hair almost like yours?"

"Ah, you're kidding me," George said. "Her hair ain't red."

Max winked. "Can I tell you a secret?"

George nodded and leaned forward as Max whispered into his ear. "But keep it a secret, okay?" Max said when he finished.

"Sure," George said. Suddenly he leaped from the glider and raced to Boyd. "Guess what?" he said. "Aunt Trenace had freckles when she was in the second grade. All over her arms and her back. I know because Mr. Tulley said so." He broke into a fit of giggles. He quit laughing as quickly as he had started when he remembered Max still sitting in the glider. His thumb went into his mouth and he walked back to the glider, his head and shoulders drooping. "I'm not very good at keeping secrets."

Max grinned. "Then I'll tell you another one."

The boy's eyes widened. "You'll tell me another secret even after I told?"

Max whispered in George's ear, then leaned back in the swing and tried to look solemn. "Keep it this time."

George glanced at Trenace and back at Max. "Okay, but I'm gonna see for myself."

Max groaned at his failure to teach the boy the art of discretion. He watched as George walked over to Trenace, who was sitting in a nearby lawn chair. Casually George strolled to the back of her chair and leaned against it, peering at her skin above the scoop neck of her French-cut yellow knit shirt.

"Can I help you, George?" Trenace asked, twisting to see him.

"Just checking," George said. He strolled back to the glider and leaned close to Max. "You're right. They're all gone."

Chuckling to himself, Max came to Trenace and dropped into the empty lawn chair next to her and pulled the ivory invitation to the dinner from his shirt pocket. "This is for you," he said. "I'd like you to be my guest."

She eased the engraved invitation from the envelope. Looking over at him, she asked, "What were you and George up to?" She began to read the invitation.

"He was confirming that your freckles have disappeared," Max said, avoiding her startled gaze.

"How do you know?"

"I've been peeking myself," he admitted. "Will you go with me? If you can arrange a sitter, I'll cover the costs. Josh Temple says you have to be there and that he's holding me personally responsible if you don't show up."

She grinned. "I don't believe a word of it, but I'll go, especially if it will help the program. How dressy is it?"

He shrugged. "Dinner dress, not long. I'll wear a suit."

"I can manage that," she replied. "If it had been formal, I would have declined. Maybe Mrs. Sewell can help me find someone who's dependable."

THE NEXT WEEKEND Max and Jocko returned with their equipment and filmed a segment with George. As the interview began to wind down, George looked directly into the camera. "I want a dad who looks just like me, so he won't say I'm ugly."

His grin of confidence brought tears to everyone's eyes, including Max's. "I'm sure there are some redheaded men and women watching who will understand, but I think you're a handsome boy. And didn't you know that freckles on the neck mean money by the peck?"

George looked puzzled. "What's a peck?"

Max laughed. "An old-fashioned measurement," he explained. "It means you'll earn lots of money when you're grown up." He gave the boy a high-five hand-shake.

After some coaxing, Trenace and Max convinced Mickie to have a turn. When she finally agreed, Trenace took her inside to change her top and comb her hair.

"Why is she in a wheelchair?" Jocko asked.

Max frowned. "I'm not sure. A spinal injury, but I don't know what kind. I'll skirt around that if I can."

When they returned, Max took the handles of the chair. "Can I push it?" Mickie nodded, and they began to walk around the yard, Jocko walking backward several feet in front of them with the camera rolling. They talked about Mickie's likes and dislikes and her favorite music. Max sat on the ground at Mickie's feet, and they continued to talk. "How old are you?"

Mickie smiled. "Eleven. Aunt Trenace says I'll grow someday maybe, but my mother wasn't very big, either."

"And your father? Was he tall?"

Mickie stiffened in her chair. "He was mean. I don't want to talk about him."

"Okay," Max agreed, wanting to avoid another episode similar to Annabelle's. "Do you like to read?"

"He and my mom drank all the time," Mickie said, staring past Max's head to distant memories. "We lived on the reservation 'cuz my dad's grandmother lived there. He threw me one time."

Max frowned. "That's okay. You don't have to tell me."

She shook her head, sending her shiny black hair across one cheek. Her voice grew soft as the memories seemed to grow. "Dr. Brockman says I was born with spina bifida. That means a hole in my spine, but I was operated on to close it." Her dark gaze shifted to Max's face. "I used to know how to walk. I could use crutches that had bracelets on them and I could really walk. I practiced and practiced, and I wanted to show my daddy how I could walk, but he didn't come home for a long time, and when he did, he was drunk, and..."

Trenace came to them and knelt next to Mickie's chair. "Sweetheart, you don't have to say all this," she murmured, handing Mickie a tissue. "Max will understand."

"But I remember," Mickie insisted. "He came home and I tried to walk for him, and he kicked one of my braces away and grabbed me and threw me against the wall. I...I tried to get away, but I couldn't get up. He laughed at me. He said I was like a worm."

"Damn the man," Max said, taking Mickie's hand. "The bastard should be put away."

"They took him to jail," Mickie said. "My mom went with him, and I don't see them anymore." She held her head up proudly. "Someday I want to walk. I keep hoping, anyway."

Max squeezed Mickie's hand. "I think you're a beautiful young lady, and I know there's someone watching who will want a daughter just like you to love." He turned to Trenace. "Mrs. McKay, can you tell us something about Mickie?"

He hoped Trenace would forget about Jocko's camera.

She wiped her eyes and smiled up at Mickie. "Mickie is a very intelligent child. She's small for her age, but she's very healthy now except for a tendency to catch cold. She does well in school. She reads beyond her grade level and she's learning to cook. We...my husband built a worktable with adjustable legs. If...she finds a new home, the table will go with her."

She touched Mickie's cheek. "Mickie is very special to me. She's been with me for more than two years now. She's like my own child." Her eyes widened and she turned to Max. "I shouldn't have said that. Can you edit it out?"

"The truth will out," he murmured, getting to his feet. He turned his full attention to Mickie. "And you, young lady, were superb. Someday you may be a great actress. You keep trying, and I'll help wherever I can." He kissed her cheek and gave her small shoulders a squeeze. He helped Trenace to her feet and turned to the children. "What do you all say? If I order two pizzas, would you help me eat them?"

"You betcha," Boyd said, "but last time you didn't come back."

"We'll have them delivered," Max countered.

Boyd gave a hoot. "Aunt Trenace won't order pizzas. She says they're too expensive."

"Not today," Max said. "This is a celebration. Everyone whose eligible for adoption has been filmed and Denise and Libby are going home soon, so let's eat." He looked across the children's heads to Trenace, and she nodded her approval. His gaze lingered on her face as the children milled around them. If he didn't watch himself, he'd be putting her on a pedestal right alongside the Virgin Mary and Joan of Arc. He looked away, acknowledging that the thoughts that often troubled him were anything but saintly.

They had exchanged a few kisses and embraces, a poor record, he thought. He watched her casually, comparing their lives and finding few similarities, but that didn't stop the growing attraction he felt each time he saw her. It had been a long time since a woman had excited him in a physical way. Why did it have to be this woman, with her house so full of children that she made him think of the "Old Woman Who Lives in a Shoe"?

Except she wasn't old. Whenever he saw Trenace, he seemed to lose control of his body's reaction. She'd be appalled if she knew, for what he felt at this moment had little to do with friendship. He excused himself and went into the house to call for the pizza. He stayed there until the delivery had been made.

MRS. SEWELL ARRIVED Saturday morning to pick up Denise and Libby. Trenace hugged them both and bid them goodbye, wondering as they climbed into the case-worker's automobile if this reunion would work. Many attempts to reunite broken families failed, leaving Trenace to wonder if the system needed to change. She had been warned from the beginning that there were no easy answers to caring and placement of abandoned, orphaned and abused children. For now, all she could do was open her home and offer them a temporary sanctuary.

The hours dragged into late afternoon. Max Tulley would come for her at six sharp. He'd called twice, once to chat and once to let her know he'd finally purchased a new vehicle to replace the one that had been destroyed in the accident.

She ran her fingers through her hair. He'd been back in Spokane for two and a half months. Was he pleased with his return? KSPO's reformatted *Nine at Six* news had bumped its strongest competitor out of first place for June and July. A press release in the *Spokane Review* had attributed it to Max Tulley's professionalism and the *Wednesday's Child* segments.

The phone rang again and it was Max. "Hi, Trena, I wanted to make sure you hadn't changed your mind about tonight."

She smiled. "I keep my commitments," she replied. "Did you have to work today?"

"We finished filming the last two children at a foster home north of Spokane," he replied. "We have enough segments to run the program well into October. I'm sorry some of the children have to wait so long to have their stories told."

"Many of them have waited for years," she replied. "A few more weeks will seem like seconds in their lives."

"Boyd will be featured next Wednesday," he said. "George is scheduled the following week. I'm holding Mickie's for a while."

"Thank you, Max. I don't think I could stand to lose all my children at once."

As she hung up the receiver, Trenace thought about her reaction to the success of the program. Did other foster parents feel the same sense of loss when a child was placed? She should be thrilled when they found new parents to love them, but deep inside she missed each child who had passed through her home over the years.

She went outside to check on Boyd, Mickie and George, who were playing a card game at the picnic table. "Who's winning?"

"Boyd always wins," George complained.

"I pay attention, stupid," Boyd replied.

"But he never cheats," Mickie added. "We watch him like a hawk. He's just a good player."

Trenace smiled. "I'm taking a shower and getting dressed for the big dinner tonight," she said, and turned toward the house.

"Are you and Max going on a date?" Mickie asked.

"We have a dinner to attend, so we're going together," Trenace explained.

"I think he really likes you," Mickie said. "He looks at you all the time when he's here."

Boyd arched an eyebrow. "I'll agree to that. He looks at you kinda funny and hangs around more all the time."

Mickie giggled. "Maybe he loves you."

George moved his game piece. "I love Aunt Trenace, so why shouldn't Uncle Max?" He looked up at Trenace. "He said we could call him that instead of Mr. Tulley."

"He can't love her because Uncle Owen might come home," Boyd said. "Then there'd be a fight and she would get hurt . . . or killed."

Trenace returned to the picnic table. "Max and I are just good friends. We like each other, but as friends."

"I think he loves you," Mickie said.

"Mickie! Don't say that," Trenace exclaimed. "What would people say? Mrs. Sewell would never understand."

"She doesn't understand anything, anyway," Mickie mumbled.

"What did you say?" Trenace asked.

"Nothing, but he looks at you all drooly, and he gets this funny look in his eyes. I like to see him that way, 'cuz then he always offers to buy us food."

"Mickie's right about that," Boyd agreed. "If he didn't look at you that way, we'd never get anything good to eat."

George glanced up from his move. "I like your food."

Trenace laid her hand on the little boy's shoulder. "Thanks for the vote of confidence, George, and as for you two," she said, unable to suppress a smile, "I'm sorry you've been so deprived since you came to stay with me.''

Mickie and Boyd grinned. "We like him," Mickie said, "So it's okay how he looks at you, and we won't tell Mrs. Sewell. We'll keep it a secret, too, just like the one about Uncle Owen never coming back."

Boyd nodded his commitment to the secret.

"Why isn't Uncle Owen coming back?" George asked. "You guys never tell me nothing!"

Trenace sighed. *So much for secrets.* "I'm sure you talk among yourselves, but please don't say a word to Mrs. Sewell about either of them—Max or Owen. Mrs. Sewell has strong opinions, and she could cause trouble at the agency. Promise me you'll keep quiet? She would never understand if she thought Max and I were...involved, which we aren't, of course." She waited until each child pledged his or her silence, then hurried into the house.

In the shower her thoughts lingered on what the children had said. Did Max look at her "all drooly"? She doubted it. The children's imaginations were running wild, as occasionally did her own. If he was as interested in her as the children had suggested, he'd come by more often. The children may have thought his visits were frequent, but she had been more aware of the times between. She understood why. His career had first priority on his time. He had a life of his own beyond his work. He had relatives still in the area. His reputation had grown, and his social calendar was probably full.

He could have asked hundreds of glamorous women to be his guest, but his job was important and Josh Temple had requested that he bring her. "Seems logical to me," she whispered aloud as she rinsed the shampoo from her hair, pushing the billowing white suds down her body. As her hands brushed her breasts and down her slender waist, her unruly mind played tricks on her.

What if they were Max's hands? Would he come into the shower and pretend to help her? How long would it take for his desire to get out of control? Would he claim her in the shower or carry her to her bed? She'd never taken a shower with a man. Would Max be so daring?

Daring or not, he'll be upset if he arrives and I'm still soaking wet, with dripping hair. She grabbed the slippery bar of soap and began to wash her body, but the fantasy returned more vividly than before. She'd soap his back and her hands would play games on his skin. She'd trail her fingers down his spine to his hips, then slide her arms around his soap-slicked torso and whisper against his shoulder. He'd turn and . . .

She lost her grip on the bar of soap and it skittered past her foot. What in the world was wrong with her, letting such fantasies take control of her mind? Max wasn't drooling after her. She was a thirty-eight-year-old divorced woman with responsibilities, and that was the only reason she was going out tonight.

If she and Max let their aging hormones get out of control, what could she expect? An affair? A brief encounter that would make them both realize the attraction had been a mistake? No, she vowed. That wasn't in her future, and she thought too much of Max to allow it to happen. He was still recovering from the loss of his beloved wife. Each time he mentioned his "Lucy" a look of pain would creep into his eyes, and she could tell he hadn't forgotten the woman who had given him two perfect children and shared his life for almost fifteen years.

She would enjoy the evening, meet new people and bid him farewell. He had filmed all of her eligible children. Once the *Wednesday's Child* program ran its course, he would move on to other special features and forget he had ever met good old Trenace McKay and all her children.

As MAX KILLED the ignition of the minivan, he patted the pale blue padded dashboard, pleased with his decision to buy the van instead of a red four-wheel-drive truck that had first caught his attention in the dealership showroom. The vehicle's handling was superb and the seats comfortable. The minute he'd spotted the van, images of Trenace and the children accompanying him on trips had made him smile. If he'd jumped to an invalid conclusion, it would be an expensive one. Time would tell. For now, he'd settle for taking Trenace to dinner and having her to himself for a few hours.

Boyd answered the door and grinned up at Max. "Aunt Trenace isn't ready yet. Mickie's helping her." He peeked past Max and spotted the white van. "Wow," he said, whistling his approval. "Can I drive it sometime?"

"Show me your license," Max replied.

"I can't get it for five and a half more years," Boyd admitted.

"How about a ride sometime soon instead?"

"It's a deal, man," Boyd replied. He turned. "Here comes Aunt Trenace now. Want to see her?"

The woman coming toward him was a vision of softness. The bodice of her ivory silk dress covered her full breasts, but her shoulders were almost bare. The fabric caressed her skin, bringing out the delicate sculpture of her body.

A narrow piece of lace formed a deep V down the front, giving him hints of skin he longed to touch. He wondered if she might be braless. A fabric belt clutched her waist, allowing the skirt to flare around her hips and fall to just below her knee. Matching two-inch ivory leather heels accentuated her shapely tanned legs. He knew they were the most exquisite legs he'd ever seen.

"I have a jacket if this is too..." Her voice trailed off. "I had my hair trimmed." She laughed nervously.

Her auburn hair had been trimmed to form a cap of waves around her head, and she had brushed it away from her face. Her eyes shone.

"You're beautiful," he said, taking her hand. She smiled, and for a moment he thought he saw her eyes fill with tears. He must have imagined it, he decided.

"I told you he'd say that," Mickie called, rolling down the hallway and almost colliding with Max.

"Smart young lady," he agreed. "Is the sitter here?"

"She's with George in the kitchen," Trenace said, sliding on a jacket that matched her dress. "I'll say goodbye and we can be on our way."

Outside, Max escorted her to the minivan and helped her in. When he settled himself in the driver's seat, he noticed her hand glide over the upholstery.

"Very nice," she said. "Is this the new car you mentioned?"

He nodded. "Yep, it's all mine. I picked it up yesterday."

"I would have expected you to get something sporty."

"This caught my eye, and I've never had a vehicle I could carry things around in, so here it is, and if you and the children will accept, I'd like to take you all somewhere tomorrow. Anywhere. I need to break it in."

She glanced at the interior. "Will Mickie's wheelchair fit?"

"I asked the salesman and he insisted it would," Max replied. "The salesman showed me a catalog of lifts that can be installed."

"That would be very expensive. And this van must have been expensive, too."

He chuckled. "All new cars are expensive, but insurance paid for most of it." He glanced over at her in time to catch her staring at him.

She looked away. "My station wagon is a bucket of bolts, but as long as it runs I'm not complaining. It must be nice to be able to afford a new car."

"Then maybe I'll give you this one," he replied, as surprised by his suggestion as she was.

"Don't be silly, Max. No one gives away a vehicle like this." She stroked the cushion near her thigh. "But we'd love to go with you."

"Any suggestions on where we could go tomorrow?" he asked, concentrating on his driving.

"Along the Spokane River. The children love it down there and much of it has wheelchair access."

"Good," he said. "We can make it a picnic. I'll provide the food and transportation."

"What can I bring?"

He grinned. "The kids."

A half hour later they arrived at the hotel where the dinner was taking place. Inside, Josh Temple met them at the banquet room door. "You must be Mrs. McKay," he said, extending his hand. "Nice to meet you. You two are at the second table from the center up front."

"We have assigned seating?" Max asked, noticing the placards at each napkin.

"Yes, unless someone starts playing musical chairs," Josh replied, leading them to the front of the room. "We've mixed them up to keep cliques from forming. They need to get to know each other, don't you think? You two have to be near the front, since you're both on the program, so I put you together. Hope that's okay."

He didn't wait for a reply. "Sorry Mr. McKay couldn't make it, but I'm glad Max talked you into coming. It's good meeting you after our phone calls, Mrs. McKay." He glanced at Max. "You've been keeping secrets?"

Max opened his mouth to deny whatever Josh was getting at, but Josh had turned to greet other guests.

They found their seats and chatted with the others at the round table that accommodated ten diners. Max leaned back in his chair and scanned the room. Josh Temple had outdone himself. The room had been set up to accommodate at least five hundred people. He recognized many of the local television media people and a few reporters from the newspapers. Corporate names were displayed on tall centerpieces at each table, indicating who had underwritten the cost of the gathering.

A woman he'd dated twice since returning to Spokane stopped at their table to say hello, but he couldn't remember her full name and skipped over introductions.

Josh Temple went to the microphone at the head table and cleared his throat. "Folks, you'll find name tags and black markers at each table. Glad you could all come. Enjoy yourselves, and we thank you for your support in this worthwhile project for Spokane's special children." He left the podium and returned to mingle with the guests.

Someone started passing the name tags around the table, and they busied themselves for several minutes. Max glanced at his watch. Dinner had been scheduled for seven, but there was no sign of any waiters yet. He turned to Trenace, who finished her conversation with the man next to her, then smiled at Max. He draped his arm along the back of her chair and leaned closer. "Let's stand up and stretch. We'll be seated for hours once this begins. See anyone you know?"

Trenace scanned the milling crowd. Suddenly she clutched his arm and motioned to a couple three tables away. The man, three or four inches taller than Max, waved at Trenace and whispered to the woman with him, and the couple began to make their way through the crowd.

Trenace smiled. "Max Tulley, this is Dr. Laudon Brockman, the children's physician. He's an absolute miracle worker."

The two men shook hands.

Dr. Brockman put his hand around the shoulders of a slender woman about Trenace's height and eased her forward. "And this is my wife, Michelle. Michelle, this is Mrs. Trenace McKay, the woman I've told you so much about. She's one of my favorite foster parents, and she's a miracle worker, too. We've been at this ever since I moved to Spokane, haven't we, Trenace?"

Trenace laughed. "It's been at least eight years. How are the children?"

Michelle's gaze darted away, and she tightened her hold on her husband's arm. "The girls are fine. Excuse me, but I need to...find the ladies' room before dinner is served." She ran her fingers through her wheat-colored curly hair and hurried away.

They watched the attractive younger woman leave.

"Did I say something wrong?" Trenace asked. "I've always wanted to meet your wife. You've told me so much about her and the horses. I'm sorry if I've upset her." She turned to Max. "Michelle breeds and shows Arabian horses."

Dr. Brockman's gaze followed his wife through the crowd. "She's restricted her work to the breeding now. She...we lost a child several months ago. A little boy. He was premature and lived for two weeks. My wife has had problems adjusting to his death. Strange how easy it is to give counsel to others and so hard to find the answers when something happens in one's own family."

"I'm so sorry," Trenace said, laying her hand lightly on the physician's coat sleeve. "I have an appointment for Mickie next Tuesday. We'll see you then."

Max's gaze shifted from Trenace back to the tall man with the stooped shoulders and unusual amber eyes. "Do you take care of all of Trenace's kids?"

Dr. Brockman nodded. "And about thirty other foster kids. I volunteered because I was just getting back into medicine. Now it's a major part of my practice."

Max's reporter's instinct kicked in. "You were out of medicine for a while?"

Dr. Brockman either failed to hear his question or chose to ignore it. "You're the anchor on KSPO, aren't you?"

Max nodded. "I'd like to dig a little deeper into the foster home program. Would you give me an interview sometime?"

Dr. Brockman frowned. "If you'll keep it professional. No personal questions. My family is out of the public eye."

"He's too modest," Trenace said. "He teaches classes at Gonzaga and Spokane Falls and he's written two books."

"I'm giving up teaching for a while," Dr. Brockman said. "I want to spend more time with my family."

Max felt as if some underlying meaning had escaped him.

"Max, why don't you come with us when I take Mickie?" Trenace suggested. "Would that be okay with you, Dr. Brockman?"

Dr. Brockman nodded. "Wonderful idea, but no cameras or anything like that. Fair enough?"

"Agreed," Max said, shaking the man's hand again.

The waiters began to distribute salads at the tables.

"Excuse me. I'd better find Michelle," Dr. Brockman said, a distracted expression on his rugged features. His hair was a mixture of cinnamon brown mixed with gray, giving him an air of distinction mixed with heavy concern. At the moment Max was sure his concern was for his pretty wife.

CHAPTER SEVEN

"SOMETHING'S WRONG THERE," Max said as they returned to their seats.

"Losing a baby is a terrible thing for a woman to have to go through," Trenace replied, taking a sip of water.

"Have you? Lost a baby, I mean?" Max studied her face. He knew so little about her as a woman. The only part of her life she had let him into was the one involving foster parenting.

"Not my own children, but each time a child leaves I feel the loss," she admitted. "At first Owen said I wasn't cut out for it because I'd cry. But he was wrong." She reached for her salad fork and began to eat.

During the meal, they talked with the couple next to her. The man was a local banker and his wife was involved in volunteer service at a homeless shelter in the heart of Spokane.

"Those children are only a step away from your foster home," the woman said. "Our goal is to keep them out of the system, but it gets harder every winter."

The husband described the financial help he'd convinced his bank to underwrite. "Every year I have to make my pitch a little stronger," he said, and his wife touched his arm.

"But we don't give up," the woman said.

"Neither do I," Trenace said.

While dessert was being served, Josh Temple stepped to the podium and started speaking. The hum of conversation around them quieted. "I'd like to introduce the person whose charm with the kids has made this program a huge success, Mr. Maxwell Tulley, a native of Spokane. His moving to Los Angeles was Spokane's loss, and now KSPO takes full credit for enticing him back home."

The guests applauded as Max rose from his chair, touched Trenace briefly on her shoulder and walked to the podium. He pulled a pair of tortoiseshell half-lens reading glasses from his inside pocket and put them on. The glasses gave him an air of seriousness she found enticing. He was a blend of sexy masculinity and solemn gentleness as he began to describe his part in the program.

After several minutes, Max laid his notes aside and looked directly at Trenace. "Without the cooperation of the foster parents I've worked with for the past few months none of this would be possible. These children aren't the blond-haired, blue-eyed babies most couples want to adopt. I'm told that some of them aren't sweet and innocent, but I've yet to find those children. The children I've met are all the victims of society and often victims of their own parents. These children would fall through the cracks and be lost forever if not for these caring men and women who open their own doors and give them love and security for the time they live in their homes."

He gazed thoughtfully around the room, then back to Trenace and smiled. "I'd like to introduce a woman who has been in the foster home program of Spokane County for a decade and a half. She introduced me to the world of foster care and recently told me that more than two hundred children have stayed with her and her husband over the years. Mrs. McKay, would you come up?'' He held out his hand to her.

At the podium she looked at him, uncertain, but his encouraging smile put her at ease and she smiled back, then turned to the microphone. Ten minutes later she thanked the audience for their attention and returned to her seat amid a burst of applause.

''Great, just great,'' Max said, squeezing her hand beneath the linen tablecloth.

Trenace stared at the pink index cards still lying beside her cup of cold coffee. ''I forgot my notes,'' she whispered. ''I have no idea what I said.''

He laughed and leaned close to her ear. ''No one will ever know. You were magnificent,'' he whispered, his lips brushing her cheek as he withdrew.

Several other speakers described their involvement in the program, then Josh Temple closed the evening.

''I'm pleased to announce that KSPO will be presenting a two-hour special on December 15 to give the viewers an update on how the children have fared. We'll be filming segments starting the first of October. Many of you will be asked to participate, and I hope you'll be as cooperative then as you've been this evening. Thank you and good night.''

The diners around the table shook hands and promised to stay in touch. ''Ready?'' Max asked, and Trenace nodded.

On the way home she asked, ''Will you take part in the special?''

''I'm going to be one of the executive producers and do most of the narration,'' he said. ''Will you be a resource person?''

''Of course,'' she replied. ''I don't know quite what that involves, but I'll help wherever I can.''

When they arrived at Trenace's house, she turned to him. "Won't you come in? For coffee or a glass of wine?"

Inside, Max insisted on settling with the sitter in spite of Trenace's protestations. "Getting you to go with me was worth every cent. Thank you, Mrs. Miller." He held the front door and waited for the woman to reach her car before he closed it again.

In the kitchen Trenace turned to him. "Coffee or wine?"

"Wine sounds great," he said. "May I turn on the radio?" She nodded, and he fiddled with the dial until he found a station with soft music. "Do you dance?"

"It's been a long time," she murmured, pouring two glasses of white wine and handing him one. "These juice glasses are the closest I have to wineglasses," she apologized.

He took two sips. "Very tasty."

She glanced away, suddenly feeling awkward, being alone with him with only the romantic music surrounding them.

He set his glass down. "Dance with me."

She looked around the kitchen. "Here?"

"Let's go outside." Retrieving his glass, he pulled the sliding glass door open and bowed gallantly for her to exit. He stepped back into the kitchen and brought the radio outside, then carefully closed the door. He slid out of his jacket and helped her out of hers, then removed his tie and unbuttoned two of the buttons on his pale peach shirt.

He drank the rest of the wine, set his glass on a nearby table and held out his hand again. "Pretend I'm your Prince Charming and you're beautiful Cinderella and we're at the ball. We must dance before I turn into a frog and you prick your finger and fall asleep again."

She tossed her head and laughed. "I think you have your fairy tales mixed up."

"No cue cards to prompt me," he replied, chuckling. "We're on our own out here to do what we feel, to be natural." Shadows from the kitchen slanted across his features, accentuating the angles of his cheekbones. His eyes were darker blue than usual. "Will you dance with me, princess?"

She stepped into his arms, and they began to dance. For several minutes they were quiet, adjusting to each other's movements and letting the music envelop them as they swayed to the swell and ebb of traditional waltzes played by symphony orchestras and swing music of the thirties and forties.

A string of commercials began to play, and he hummed and sang softly near her ear. "Stay in my arms," he crooned, and they continued to dance.

"You always had a good voice," she said, leaning back to gaze at his features. "My girlfriends and I would drool over you in the musicals in high school. We'd go to every performance."

He smiled but didn't speak. His arm tightened, and she settled against his body, resting her forehead against his shoulder and enjoying the comfort his arms offered.

"Easy," he warned as he guided her off the concrete slab and onto the grass. The music resumed, and he whirled her around in ever-larger circles until they had danced across the lawn to the lilac bush.

She gazed up at him, one arm around his neck with her fingers resting against the nape of his neck. "This is where we first met," she murmured.

"You were stunning," he replied.

"I was sweaty and sunburned."

"All I saw was your face, your eyes." The music faded into another string of commercials and gradually they stopped dancing. "You had gorgeous legs, and I wanted to put my hands around your waist where you had tied that sexy apron."

She smiled. "I thought you'd come on business."

"Josh Temple sent me here on business, but destiny walked with me. You see, milady, I've never been tempted to compromise my journalistic principles before, but one touch of your hand and I was on the verge of forgetting why I'd come."

Her heart began to thud against her ribs. "So Max the reporter met his match?"

"You made me feel sexy," he said, his voice soft and low in the shadows of the lilac leaves. "You make me feel sexy each time I see you."

"Oh, Max, don't flatter me, please."

"It's the truth," he said, his hands settling on her waist.

"But you thought I was a married woman."

"Yes, and that put me through hell until the next day when you told me the truth." His right hand moved to her shoulder as he traced the strap down to the point where it crossed over her breasts. His hand returned to her shoulder and his fingers eased the strap down her arm.

When his mouth touched her exposed skin below her collarbone, she whimpered. Burying her lips against his thick hair, she murmured, "Oh, Max, Max."

He straighted, clutching her face in his hands, staring at her before his mouth claimed hers fiercely, sucking her breath away. Time stopped as her arms encircled his neck. When his tongue skipped across her teeth, tiny fingers of desire raced through her body to ignite her passion.

Breathlessly she pulled away, trying to stop the reeling of her brain. Could one small half glass of wine have built this fire inside her? When his fingers brushed across her nipples and they responded, she knew she was on the verge of crossing a bridge over which there would be no turning back. "Max," she moaned, "please..."

His mouth blocked her words as his lips slanted across hers again. His hands lifted her from the ground to mold her body against his. Aware of his arousal, she found herself swept along in a torrent of desire. Her hands explored his back, feeling each flexing muscle beneath his shirt as he moved against her.

"I need you, Trena. I want you so much," he murmured. "I've never met a woman like you. You're beautiful, warm, passionate. You give love so willingly. Tell me you want me. I need to hear you say it."

"Max, I want—" Over his shoulder a glow appeared in one of the windows, and she stiffened in his arms.

He brushed a curl from her forehead and kissed the corner of her mouth. "What's wrong?" he asked, his voice hoarse with need.

Her lips felt swollen from his kisses, and she could hardly speak. "Boyd's awake," she whispered. "His light is on." Her breathing still ragged, she gazed into Max's stormy eyes. "It's for the best. This couldn't have led anywhere. I can't get involved with you. You were the celebrity star tonight, and for a few hours I was your leading lady. You may think you've fallen for me, but you haven't."

"Don't tell me what I feel," he replied. "Lucy tried to do that, and she was wrong every time, especially the last time, so give it up." His voice frightened her with its leashed anger.

"I'm sorry, but you know this is wrong," she said. "When *Wednesday's Child* is over, you'll go on to other projects. You'll forget all about us. You...you still hurt from losing your wife. I'm still bitter about Owen. If we became involved, it would be for all the wrong reasons. If you . . . if we . . ." She sighed deeply and pulled free of his arms. "When I'm alone with you, I lose my good sense. You make me feel so alive. But an affair is all we could hope for, and I couldn't handle that."

His eyes narrowed. "Is that what you think I'm after?"

She looked away. "What else is there?"

A chasm of silence divided them for several minutes. He reached for her hand. "I'm sorry. I wouldn't insult you by suggesting we have an affair. You were right weeks ago. We should stay friends." He dropped her hand and walked across the grass to get his jacket and tie.

Inside, he put the radio on the counter again and turned off the music. "Good night, Trenace." His jaw was tight.

"You're angry," she said, hurt by his change of manner.

He turned to her abruptly. "Hell, yes, I'm angry. Why shouldn't I be? But I'll get over it. We had a good time together. You're a woman, and I'm a man. We let our hormones get the best of us for a few minutes, but now wisdom prevails."

Tears burned her eyelids as she ran across the room to stop him. "Please don't be angry, Max. You mean too much to me to have you go away like this. I'm sorry, so sorry. Is . . . the picnic off?"

His fingers brushed a tear from her cheek. They gazed at each other through the dimly lit living room, then he smiled. "The picnic is on. I'll be here at eleven." His fingers caressed her cheek again. "Good night, Mrs. McKay. Sweet dreams."

BOYD AND GEORGE JUMPED out of the minivan with shrieks that made Trenace flinch. "Boys, not so loud. You'll bother other people."

"No, we won't, Aunt Trenace," George shouted. "Look, we've got the place to ourselves."

Max grinned. "Give up, Aunt Trena. Boys will be boys, and he's right. Seems everyone but us has gone out of town or else stayed home. Enjoy it. I'll get Mickie if you can get her chair." He swept the little girl up in his arms and scanned the area. Play equipment stood idle several yards away, and he carried her there, Trenace following along behind him.

"How's this?" he asked Mickie. "Ready for your chair?"

She looked longingly at the merry-go-round. "Could I ride on it, just once?"

"Can you sit by yourself?" he asked, glancing at Trenace.

"She does better if someone is with her," Trenace said. "I could push it if you'll hold her."

"I have a better idea," Max said. "You get on with her and I'll do the pushing." Laughing, he sat Mickie on the equipment and stepped aside for Trenace to join her. "Ready, ladies?" he asked, then gave it a running push and let go.

As Trenace steadied Mickie, she glanced at the flash of red and white as they passed Max. He'd arrived at ten-thirty wearing white sports shorts and a bright red-and-white knit shirt, along with jogging shoes that looked as if they might have actually been used for running. Dark sunglasses shielded his gaze, and a red baseball cap covered his head.

With hardly a glance toward Trenace he'd loaded blankets, a thermos of lemonade and a bowl of potato salad, then returned for Mickie's wheelchair. "Everyone been to the bathroom?" he'd asked. When they all nodded, he'd smiled. "That's one thing I remember about going places with children. Then my girls learned that McDonald's had rest rooms, and we had to change the rules." Before Trenace could say a word he'd picked up Mickie from the chair she'd been sitting on and run with her to the van, Mickie laughing all the way. By eleven they'd been on the road.

Now Max stepped to the merry-go-round and gave it another push. Mickie squealed in delight. "Faster, make it go faster. You're not afraid to go faster, are you, Aunt Trenace?" Mickie's small hand clutched at Trenace's, her other hand clinging to the rail next to her.

"Well, are you?" Max shouted as they whirled by.

"No!"

He ran alongside them for a full revolution, then gave it one hard push, spinning them away, but on the next pass he jumped onto the spinning platform. Steadying himself, he stepped over the handrails between them and sat down beside her. Trenace felt as if she were losing her balance and reached out, but when her hand touched his bare thigh, she jerked it away as if the heat of his skin had burned her. Gradually the spinning machine slowed and stopped.

Max helped them off, carrying Mickie to her chair again. "Am I the only one dizzy?" he asked.

"Not me," Mickie insisted. "That's the most fun I've ever had. Aunt Trenace can't make it go that fast."

He glanced at his watch. "Isn't it past time to eat? I've been smelling this food for hours. I'll go get the boys, and you two can help spread out the grub."

After they had made a shambles of the food, the boys asked to take Mickie down to the water. "Be careful," Trenace cautioned.

"We always are," Boyd said, pushing the chair along the narrow concrete walkway and down to the river's edge where someone had diverted the water into a shallow pool.

After the food was packed away, Max picked up one of the blankets. Snapping it several times to shake the crumbs away, he spread it on the grass again and stretched out.

"Come sit beside me," he said, patting the blanket. He folded his hands behind his head. "About last night. I acted like a horny teenage boy on a Saturday night. Chalk it up to delayed adolescence."

She couldn't tell if his eyes were open or closed with the sunglasses shielding them. "I . . . enjoyed it."

His mouth widened into a boyish grin.

"You must have had the girls fluttering all around you in high school," she teased. "You beckoned and they came running."

He took his sunglasses off and looked at her. "If I was so irresistible, where were you? Most of the girls I knew wanted to become movie stars, and they couldn't wait to leave town. None of them succeeded, but one went to New York and got a job building sets for an off-Broadway theater. I came back for our tenth high school reunion and visited with her and her husband. I don't remember seeing you there. Did I miss you?"

She shook her head. "I couldn't get a sitter, and Owen refused to go with me."

He stared up at the clouds floating high overhead. "You probably won't believe this, but I was never a horny teenager. Lucy was my first sexual partner, and it happened on our wedding night. Isn't that the craziest thing you ever heard?"

She gazed down at him, speechless. When he remained silent, she said, "Tell me about her. It's important that I know."

"We were planning for our fifteenth anniversary," he said. "We'd decided we couldn't wait until silver or golden. We were still young and impatient and very much in love. The twins had jumped two grades and were in high school already. Our lives were in order, and everything we'd ever wanted, we'd accomplished ahead of schedule. We used to laugh about our twins and tease each other, saying they couldn't have gotten their brains from either of us. I'd say maybe they'd been switched in the hospital, and she'd remind me that I'd seen them born. Life was perfect, Trenace, too perfect."

He stopped talking and she waited, afraid if she spoke she'd break this spell.

"Our birthdays were only twenty days apart," he said. "We set aside one special day so we could have our midlife crises together, and what better place than on a luxury liner in the middle of the Pacific Ocean? I'd scheduled a month off. We were going to cruise the South Pacific and explore every island we came to. Then she got sick..." His voice trailed off as he closed his eyes again.

"What was it?" she asked.

"Cancer," he said, rolling his head toward her and slowly opening his eyes again. "Bone cancer."

She gasped. "That's so painful, and so fast. Oh, Max, I'm sorry. You must have gone through hell together."

"We did, for a while. But she didn't die of cancer. She cheated me."

She laid her hand on his chest. "No, Max, she couldn't have, not knowingly. She must have been in great pain."

He dropped his hand on hers, holding it against him until she could feel the warmth of his body through his shirt. When he gazed into her eyes, her heart ached for him.

"I took her to her treatments," he explained. "She would be so sick afterward. They wanted to hospitalize her, but she refused. She felt that if she started spending time away from the house, the hospital would become her home and the end would be near. She said she'd never die in a hospital, but she was wrong."

"Maybe she wanted to spare you," Trenace said.

"She cheated me instead," Max replied. "One day about six weeks into her treatment program I couldn't get home to take her. I called a neighbor to go with her, but the neighbor said she'd gone by herself." He squeezed his eyes shut. "They found her car on the Santa Ana Freeway miles from our home or the hospital. She had run through a construction barricade and crashed into a concrete wall."

She clutched his hand. "Then she didn't cheat you at all. It was an unfortunate accident that spared her weeks of pain."

"She was still alive. She died an hour after reaching the hospital. I was able to be with her, but she didn't know me. The police and the insurance companies called it an accident, but they were wrong."

She leaned over him, caressing his cheek. "How can you say such a thing? You must be wrong, Max."

"I found a note a month later when I was going through our safe-deposit box," he explained. "She'd hidden it away where she knew I wouldn't find it until after the funeral."

"Try to focus on the good memories."

He shook his head, knocking the red baseball cap off. "There are no good memories anymore. She said she couldn't cope with the pain. She said that each time I touched her it hurt beyond description. And she didn't want to die without being able to stand my touch, so she planned to drive away until she found someplace where she could kill herself. She did, but damn it all, I needed those last few weeks to say goodbye. Didn't she know that?"

He sat up, folding his arms across his knees and resting his head against them. "I'm sorry, Trenace. I don't know why I got so loose-tongued. Other than Jocko I've never told anyone about that note, not even my daughters. I had no right to burden you with it."

She scooted close to him and put her arm around his broad shoulders. Then she brushed his hair smooth and kissed it. "I knew something had happened that had hurt you deeply. Is that why you came back to Spokane—to get away from all the memories?"

"I sold the house and the furniture," he said. "I put some of her personal belongings into storage. People wonder why I gave up a six-figure salary in Los Angeles, but what the hell was I supposed to do with that money? It couldn't make my wife healthy. It couldn't bring her back or take away the pain she'd suffered through. I thought maybe if I came back here I could start over again. I'm a fraud, Trenace. I get these letters saying what a great person I am, but it's all a facade. Each time I get one I feel as if I should return it."

"You've been hurt, Max," Trenace whispered, stroking his bowed head. "I know how that feels. When Owen told me he'd met another woman who could give him what I couldn't, I was devastated, partly because he wouldn't tell me what that something was. I'd tried hard to be a good wife, yet I'd failed. I felt betrayed, and then I got angry. My anger helped me survive."

He straightened. "You're a brave woman."

"And you're a brave man," she said, touching his cheek. "Maybe you need to vent your anger. Then you'll start to heal. Don't pretend anymore. Go out to the country and scream."

A gleam returned to his eyes.

She smiled. "That's what I did one day. The children were all in school, and I drove to the wheat fields south of here. I walked into the middle of one of the largest fields I could find and I screamed and shouted and cursed that man for every foul deed I could think of, and then I cried. Oh, how I cried. But when I stopped I promised myself I'd never let another man hurt me the way Owen had hurt me. I came home and I've felt better ever since."

He put his hand on her shoulder. "What a sight you must have made. It's a wonder some farmer didn't call the sheriff and report a crazy woman."

"Want to borrow my wheat field?" Tenderly she leaned closer and kissed his cheek.

He gazed at her, then sighed. "You're an amazing person. I reckon that right now I need your friendship more than a release for my hormones. But don't get complacent. Our time will come. Thank you, Mrs. McKay." He cupped her chin and leaned close enough to barely touch her mouth with his.

"You're welcome, Mr. Tulley," she murmured against his lips as her hand slid around his neck. "I'll be your therapist anytime. You needn't call for an appointment. Drop in anytime."

He nuzzled her ear. "Do you make house calls?"

She giggled as his tongue traced the sensitive creases of her ear. When his lips moved to her throat, she couldn't suppress the tremor that raced through her body. "Not normally, but if you keep this up, I might change my policy. Oh, my darling, that feels so wonderful."

His mouth found hers, and they clung to each other. He pulled her onto his lap, cradling her in his arms as he continued the kiss. "Let's get a sitter," he murmured.

"That's impossible on such short notice," she whispered, kissing his throat.

"Then let's find someone and make an appointment. We'll go away somewhere...and be alone. Would you go away with me? Spend a weekend together?"

"If only we could," she said, sighing. "For now, all I can do for you is tell you where my wheat field is."

He grinned. "We could bring a blanket. Have you ever made love in a wheat field?"

She chuckled. "We'd probably be invaded by ants. Now be serious. Don't you want to know where my wheat field is?"

His head tilted back and he laughed. "My folks still own their farm down at Spangle. It's leased out, but I can use it anytime, and if that one isn't available, my Uncle Max and Aunt Agnes still farm." He eased her from his lap and helped her to her feet. "If you're not willing to help me find some secluded spot, why don't we go see how the kids are. They've been awfully quiet." He put the food basket in the van and helped her with the blankets. Suddenly he stopped folding the blanket and let it drop to the grass at his feet. He reached for her hand and pulled her close again. "You called me 'darling' a few minutes ago. Did you mean it?"

"I...didn't mean to say it," she replied. "It slipped out, but...yes, I meant it. You're very special to me, Max."

His kiss was feathery. "That's encouraging."

ON TUESDAY Max drove Trenace and Mickie to the girl's doctor's appointment. While Mickie and Trenace followed a nurse to an examination room, Dr. Brockman suggested Max come with him to his office.

"Do you mind if I take notes?" Max asked.

"Not at all," Dr. Brockman replied, and began to explain Mickie's disability to Max. "Mickie was born with spina bifida. She had a congenital cleft in the vertebral column with a hernial protrusion of the..." He chuckled. "Excuse me. I'm talking doctorese. Let me explain in layman's terms. Children with this deformity seldom walk unaided, but they can become mobile. I've worked with Mickie since she was four. She's spunky."

Max inhaled sharply. "She told me her father hurt her."

Dr. Brockman nodded. "She's one of the casualties of domestic violence we see all too often in this clinic."

"Who assumes her medical expenses?" Max asked. "Trenace said there had been problems with responsibility that make her adoption possibilities doubtful."

"Mickie is a blend of several ethnic groups," Dr. Brockman explained, glancing at the open folder on his desk. "Her case fell into a snarl of red tape between the Bureau of Indian Affairs, the Immigration and Naturalization Service, tribal laws and public health service regulations. The father told them to go to hell and went out and got drunk. He was under a lot of pressure with mounting hospital bills and a pending lawsuit from one of the agencies that claimed he'd taken funds he wasn't entitled to receive. He took his frustrations out on the most innocent person—Mickie."

"Will she ever walk again?" Max asked, feeing every bit the concerned parent asking about his child's future.

"It's doubtful, but more amazing things have happened," Dr. Brockman said. "She's been examined by some of the best neurosurgeons in the Pacific Northwest. They all feel the damage of hitting the wall undid everything they'd accomplished. She's a realist, but I know she still has hopes. She notices boys, and she's beginning to mature. I see beauty in her face that others often miss."

"Not Trenace McKay," Max said, putting his notepad away. "She sees beauty in every child."

Dr. Brockman studied Max for several seconds. "I know about Trenace's husband. Where do you fit into all this?"

Max met his gaze directly. "I don't know, but I care about these children, and I need to know their situations better if I'm going to make the *Wednesday's Child* project work for them. I appreciate your including me today."

"Then let's get to our patient," Brockman said. "I may ask you to step outside during part of the examination. Mickie is a modest young lady. Sometimes we talk about things that might embarrass her if you're there. She's a jewel, that's for sure."

As the visit came to a close, Dr. Brockman smiled at them all. "Now that we're finished here I have a favor to ask of you folks. Do the children like horses?"

Mickie grinned. "Who doesn't like horses?"

Max frowned.

Trenace smiled. "George brags about having his own horse someday. Boyd watches every western rerun he can find. Why do you ask?"

"And I especially love Arabian horses," Mickie said. "I've read dozens of books about them. They're so beautiful."

Dr. Brockman glanced from curious face to face. "Michelle and I would like you to bring the children out for a weekend to our farm. We have about sixty acres near

Deer Park. We have extra beds and sleeping bags if you need them. You can stay over Saturday night, and Michelle can teach the children the basics of horsemanship. Frankly, I think it would do her good to be around some older boys and girls to get her mind off the loss of her baby." He explained the death of their child briefly to Mickie. "So you see, this is for us as much as you, Mickie, and the other children."

"When can we come?" Mickie asked. "This weekend?"

"We're going to her parents' ranch near Wisdom, Montana, this weekend," Dr. Brockman said. "How about the next weekend?"

"I think that's wonderful," Trenace said. "The boys will be excited. By then I may have some new children. Does it matter how many I bring?"

Dr. Brockman's eyes twinkled as he winked at Mickie. "The more the merrier." He turned to Max. "And you come, too."

Max grimaced. "I'm allergic to horses."

CHAPTER EIGHT

ON KSPO'S WEDNESDAY news program Boyd was featured as the Child of the Week. As Trenace watched the two-minute segment, a huge lump formed in her throat. Max and the ten-year-old boy strolled from the swing set in the McKay backyard to the fence and leaned against it, talking casually as if Max were a trusted uncle and Boyd the worshipful nephew who clung to every word of wisdom from the man.

Max Tulley had, indeed, become like an uncle to her foster children, she realized, almost as if he'd adopted them as his own benevolent cause. She recalled their picnic. When she and Max had gone to the river to get the children and take them home, Boyd and George had talked him into playing ball with them for another hour. She and Mickie had been content to sit on the grass and watch them.

After the picnic, he'd taken them for a drive into the wheat country toward Palouse, pointing out the farm where he'd grown up. A mile farther south Trenace had grinned at him. "And that's my therapy wheat field."

Two farms beyond he pointed out his uncle and aunt's wheat farm where he had Sunday dinner at least once a month. When they reached her home, he'd declined an invitation to go inside.

The Tuesday visit to Dr. Brockman's had ended with a similar decline. She knew this newly established casualness was for the best. Each time they were alone their friendship had a way of being forgotten as stronger passions erupted.

"You can stop it now," Boyd said, bringing her rudely from her daydreaming and reminding her that she held the remote control to the VCR in her hand.

She had been taping each child's appearance with Max and often, late at night when she couldn't sleep, she'd viewed the pieces again, knowing that as she watched them, it was the man more than the children who held her spellbound.

"How long before someone wants me?" Boyd asked, scooting across the carpet to kneel before her.

Trenace brushed his hair from his eyes. "Don't get excited yet, Boyd. It takes weeks of checking out anyone who is interested, sometimes months or years. Annabelle was lucky. She found her new family very quickly, but most children don't, so be patient. You have another skin graft scheduled the first of October. They might want to wait until that's over. Be patient, young man. Someone is just dying to have you."

Later that evening the phone rang unexpectedly.

"Thank goodness you're up," Mrs. Sewell gasped. "I need to place a little girl. We're at the hospital now, but they won't be keeping her. The sergeant will bring us in about an hour."

"I'll be waiting," Trenace replied. "Can you tell me about her?"

"When we get there," Mrs. Sewell said, and bid her goodbye.

Trenace went to the empty bedroom where Denise and Libby had stayed. The room seemed empty and unfriendly. Maybe the new child would feel more secure with Mickie, she thought.

When the patrol car pulled to a stop at the McKay house, the time was well past midnight. The officer opened the door to the back seat and assisted Mrs. Sewell from the vehicle. She turned immediately and motioned to another occupant, but no one appeared.

Trenace watched, anxious. She had lived through enough of these moments. Sometimes the children cried hysterically. Some refused to cooperate. But more often they obeyed like little zombies, their spirits stolen by the trauma of whatever had brought them to her house.

Mrs. Sewell shook her head and turned to Trenace. "Her name is Akeylah Johnson and she's five years old. Her mother worked late at a restaurant and her boyfriend was watching Akeylah, but he finished off two six-packs of beer in the process. When a co-worker brought the mother home, the boyfriend accused her of fooling around with the guy and promptly beat the hell out of both of them. Akeylah got caught in the middle of it and was knocked around but no bones broken. It wasn't the first time the police had been called. She needs a safe home for a few weeks."

Trenace nodded. She'd heard variations of this story many times and remembered them all.

Mrs. Sewell's shoulders rose and fell in resignation. "Her mother is in the hospital for a week at least. So Akeylah will be with you for two or three weeks. She'll probably go back with her mother on condition the boyfriend goes, but the woman can't seem to live without a man in her life, so mark my words—it'll happen again."

Trenace stepped around the robust woman and stooped to see inside the back seat of the patrol car. A small black child sat in one corner, clutching a stuffed lavender bear tightly in her arms. Her large dark eyes followed Trenace's every move.

"Hello," Trenace said, sliding onto the seat. "That's a very pretty bear. Does he have a name?"

The little girl clutched the bear tightly.

"The bear is yours to keep forever," the officer said, smiling at the frightened child. "His name is Lilac, and he needs you to take care of him." The officer nodded at Trenace. He had brought many children to her home over the years.

"Why don't you bring Lilac Bear inside, and I'll make you both some hot cocoa to drink?" Trenace suggested.

The little girl leaned forward and peeked out the open door of the patrol car toward the house with its front door standing open. "Is my mommy in there?"

"No, dear," Trenace said, glancing at the officer. "She has to stay in the hospital until she gets well."

"Bubba hit my mommy," the little girl said, her eyes glistening with tears. Her frail body trembled, and tears left twin streaks down her cheeks as she looked at the open door again. "Is Bubba in there?"

"I'd never let Bubba inside my house," Trenace assured her. "Would you come with me if Sergeant Freeman went in first and made sure Bubba isn't there?"

The girl clutched the lavender bear tighter and nodded.

Sergeant Freeman walked slowly to the open door, stepped inside out of sight for several seconds, then returned to the entrance. "It's all clear, Mrs. McKay. You and Akeylah can have your hot cocoa now." He returned to the open door of the back seat of the patrol car and squatted down on one knee. "Say, I saw a chocolate cake on the table. Do you think Akeylah likes chocolate cake?"

The frightened little girl almost smiled. "Yes," she said, her voice barely above a whisper.

Trenace held out her hand and waited. Two minutes passed before Akeylah's brown hand slid into hers, and the child left the security of the patrol car. Letting the child set the pace, Trenace held her hand and walked her into the house, Mrs. Sewell following them. The officer waited in his patrol car.

In the kitchen Trenace put a cup of milk into the microwave to heat. Mrs. Sewell handed her a small crumpled brown sack, and Trenace looked inside. "This is all she has?"

Mrs. Sewell shrugged. "Money for beer and cigarettes and drugs but nothing for shoes and clothing. Can you manage for a few days until I get an emergency allocation?"

"I have a hall closet filled with used children's clothing," Trenace replied. "God bless the thrift stores in this city."

"She had some apple sauce at the hospital, but that may be all she's had today," Mrs. Sewell said. "The child was so frightened that we couldn't get her to talk more than a word or two. Well, I really must go. It's one in the morning, and I have a meeting at eight. I've been in this business for thirty-five years and nothing's changed except to get worse."

"Why don't you retire?" Trenace asked.

Mrs. Sewell grimaced. "They'll have to fire me to get rid of this old bird." She sat down next to Akeylah. "Now you be a good little girl for Mrs. McKay, and she'll take good care of you." She patted the girl's hand that clutched the bear and hurried from the house.

After hot cocoa and two pieces of cake, Trenace washed the child's face and hands. The washcloth turned brown. Trenace looked down at the child's T-shirt and shorts. Her clothes looked as if they'd been worn for weeks. "Sweetheart, let's take a warm bath. Then I'll tuck you into bed."

In the bathroom Trenace drew the water and sprinkled a few crystals of bubble bath under the faucet, then began to undress the child. Akeylah refused to let go of the bear.

Trenace scanned the bathroom. "Lilac can sit up here," she said, patting the top of the toilet tank. "He can watch us, and you can see him." Reluctantly Akeylah put the bear on his new perch.

Trenace finished undressing her and started to lift the child into the tub.

Akeylah shrieked, clutching Trenace's blouse. "It's hot!"

Trenace put her back on the bath mat. "No, dear, it's just warm. Touch the bubbles." She raked her own hand through the bubbles and blew them away. Akeylah stared but refused to let go of Trenace's blouse. "Touch them," Trenace coaxed, and finally Akeylah's finger touched a billowing cloud.

"They won't burn me?" Akeylah asked, confused.

Silently cursing the adult who had put such fear into a child's life in so short a time, Trenace smiled and trailed her hand through the tepid water underneath the bubbles.

Akeylah's pinched features relaxed, and she scooted onto the edge of the tub and tested the water with her toe. "It's not hot." She smiled at Trenace and climbed over the tub and sat down, touching the bubbles. When Trenace blew them toward the little girl, Akeylah grinned. She looked up at the bear still perched on the toilet tank. "My bear is watching me," she said. "He won't let Bubba hurt me."

Akeylah's gaze never left the bear as Trenace took the washcloth and began to soap it. In a record five minutes Trenace had the little girl bathed and shampooed, her hair dried and combed, and had dressed her in a fresh pair of cotton piqué pajamas. Akeylah held out her hands, and Trenace put the bear back into her arms. "You can sleep in Mickie's room," she said, swinging the little girl up in her arms. In the bedroom they looked down at Mickie's sleeping form.

"This is Mickie," Trenace whispered. "She's everyone's friend. Tomorrow she'll be your friend, too."

Akeylah gazed down at Mickie's dark head in the glow of the night light between the two beds. "Whatzat?" she asked, pointing at the empty wheelchair alongside Mickie's bed.

"Mickie can't walk like you can, so she sits in the chair and rolls herself along," Trenace whispered. "She'll show you tomorrow." Trenace carried the child to the other bed and put her down. Looking down at her large dark eyes and round cheeks, Trenace wondered how anyone could abuse a child as sweet as this one. But then they were all sweet. Leaning down, she kissed Akeylah's cheek and tucked the sheet and light blanket up around her shoulders, being careful to keep the bear's face free, as well. "Good night, Akeylah, and welcome to our home," she whispered.

She waited until the little girl fell asleep, then left the room. In her own room Trenace changed into her nightgown and crawled into bed, but she couldn't sleep. She tried to read, but the story failed to hold her interest. She turned and stared at the phone. Would Max be upset if she called him? He was probably sound asleep after a long day at the station. Covering two news broadcasts must be emotionally and physically draining, she thought. She turned away from the phone, but her thoughts lingered on Max. She smiled. It had only been a day and a half since he'd accompanied them to the clinic, yet she felt as if it had been an eternity.

She missed him, plain and simple. He'd become part of their lives, part of her life. She wanted to tell him about Akeylah, to let him know they had been excited about Boyd's appearance on television. Wasn't that within the realm of friendship? She turned to the phone again. She'd let it ring twice, then hang up.

WHEN MAX'S PHONE rang, he grabbed it on the first ring. "Hello?"

Trenace's voice came across the wires, warming his heart with her greeting. "You weren't asleep?"

"I was lying here thinking about you," he confessed.

"Were you really? I'm so glad because I have so much to tell you," she said, her voice filled with excitement. She launched into a description of Boyd's reaction to seeing himself on TV, then told him all about her new child. He listened to her voice more than her words, wishing he could see her animated features as she talked. Knowing she cared enough to share her experiences with him gave him unexpected pleasure. His day had been hectic and long, and after such days he had trouble sleeping.

"Sounds like she won't be there long," he said. "Are you attached to her already?"

"You know me too well, Max," she admitted. "Will you be able to go with us to Dr. Brockman's horse farm?" she asked.

"I haven't decided," he hedged.

"Are you really allergic to horses?"

He chuckled. "I was as a child. Being around horses always ended with an asthma attack. I decided early on I could never be a successor to Roy Rogers."

"You'd make a gorgeous singing cowboy," she teased.

"I can see me sitting on an old nag, pretending to play a flashy guitar, singing my heart out to some beautiful woman like you, and wheezing through the chorus."

"Can't you get an allergy shot or something? The children will be disappointed if you can't go with us."

"And you?"

She hesitated. "I'd be disappointed, too."

He thought about the trip, knowing he'd be a fool to miss a chance to spend a weekend with her, even if it included a van full of children and probably being chaperon to the boys, who would want to sleep in the stable with the horses. "I'll call an allergist and plead my case. Maybe there's a miracle drug to save the weekend. Trena?"

"Yes?"

"I've had a lift installed in the minivan," he said. "It was previously installed in a vehicle they repossessed. The salesman remembered my interest. It's used but in good condition and I got a great price. Mickie will be getting heavier as she gets older, and having the lift will make it easier for both of you."

"But it's your van," she replied.

"Maybe I'll give the van to you when I don't need it anymore. Anyway, it seemed like the right thing to do." He glanced at the clock on his nightstand. "It's three in the morning. You'd better get some rest."

"You, too."

He thought of all the things he wanted to say to her but shoved them aside. "Thanks for calling. Night, hon." He hung up before he had a chance to make a complete fool of himself.

SUNDAY AFTERNOON Mrs. Sewell called. "I have a boy who needs a home. He's nine years old and he's a handful. This one may be a long-term placement. I'll explain when we get there."

Late in the afternoon Mrs. Sewell arrived in her own vehicle. Trenace walked outside to meet them. A sullen boy left the passenger side of the front seat only after Mrs. Sewell insisted he do as he was told. When she reached for his arm, he jerked away.

He stood on the sidewalk and stared at the house. When his gaze shifted to Trenace, he seemed to look right through her. *What a handsome boy,* she thought, studying his sandy brown wavy hair and his blue eyes, but there was some quality she couldn't put her finger on that troubled her. She thought of the children who had passed through her house over the years, but no specific child's problem stood out from the rest. They all had problems. This child was large for a nine-year-old, almost as tall as Boyd, who would be turning eleven in a few months.

"This is Terence Webb," Mrs. Sewell said. "Terry, mind your manners and say hello to Mrs. McKay."

The boy ignored both women and walked into the house without a backward glance, as if he'd played this script before.

Mrs. Sewell shook her head. "I had to remove him from the last foster home. That makes three in a row. He refuses to play with the other children. He'd rather sit in a corner and rock and hum to himself. Or else he swings by the hour. He can't read, and he's been put back twice in school. The last school finally said they couldn't put up with his unruliness. He's a strange one."

"Where are his parents?"

"His biological father has never been in the picture," Mrs. Sewell explained, glancing at the folder repeatedly.

"His birth mother married when he was about four, and now she has a new family. He caused so many problems that the new husband told her she would have to choose between his children or this one. They had a physician examine the boy, who said he was borderline retarded. But I don't think he's retarded at all. I think he's lazy. No one has ever made him mind. He's been with us since he was five or six. I can't say for sure because I inherited him from another caseworker. Maybe you can pull another miracle out of your bag. Or maybe Mr. Tulley can feature him on his show. His mother gave up legal custody years ago, so there would be no obstacle to his adoption."

"I'll talk to Max," Trenace said, her thoughts on the boy who had made her feel invisible.

Mrs. Sewell looked curiously at Trenace. "Speaking of Mr. Tulley, I saw your photo in the paper this morning. If I didn't know better, I could easily get the wrong impression."

"Photo? In the paper?"

"There's a feature on the *Wednesday's Child* dinner," Mrs. Sewell explained. "A bit late on covering it, but they used several photos taken that evening, and one is of you and Mr. Tulley." She scowled. "If I were you, I'd see that it was tossed away before Mr. McKay sees it."

"I haven't looked at the newspaper yet," Trenace said absently. She accepted a small bag of Terry's belongings and waited until Mrs. Sewell drove away. Inside, she heard the children playing in the backyard and looked out the kitchen window. Terry had made his way to the glider and was pushing it to its maximum height.

The thick Sunday paper lay untouched on the kitchen table. She poured herself a fresh cup of coffee and reached for the paper, flipping through it. On the front page of the

"People and Places" section a photo of Max and herself jumped out at her. Theirs was the central photograph, surrounded by several others, including Dr. Brockman and his wife talking with the mayor. Her attention swung back to the picture of herself and Max. They gazed at each other, smiling as if they had eyes only for each other. Mrs. Sewell was right, she decided, feeling the heat of a blush sweep up her cheek. She recalled smiling at Max, but only for a few seconds. No recollection of a photo flash, no memories of the crowd beyond the podium, only Max's encouraging smile. In the photograph they looked as if they were completely enthralled with each other.

Had the camera revealed something even they hadn't recognized? A scream came from the backyard, and she ran outside in time to see Boyd yank the new boy from the glider and slug him with his fist, knocking him to the ground.

"Boyd, don't hit him," Trenace called, racing across the yard in time to grab Boyd's arm before he could deliver another punch. "This is Terry. He'll be staying with us."

"Well, what's wrong with him?" Boyd asked, breathing hard. "He wouldn't answer me when I talked to him and he called Mickie a dirty name and he knocked George down. Akeylah tried to get on the glider, and he aimed it right for her and wouldn't stop."

"Oh, God, where is she?" Trenace asked. "Is she hurt?"

Boyd hiccuped and shook his head. "I pulled her away, but he tried to hurt her on purpose. I saw him! All he does is hum and talk gibberish like he's crazy or something." Boyd wiped a tear from the corner of his eye with a clenched fist. "He kept staring at my face, but he wouldn't answer me when I asked him why. He's weird, so I hit him." Boyd pointed at the other boy. "Look at him. I made his nose bleed and he ain't even crying."

"Boyd, you and Mickie stay with the younger ones," she said, giving the older boy an encouraging hug. "Everyone is safe now. I'll take Terry inside and we'll talk about this." She reached down to take the boy's arm.

He whimpered and pulled away. Without a word he ran into the house, Trenace running after him. "The rest of you can come inside and watch television if you want. Terry and I will be in the bathroom having a conference."

Boyd and Mickie exchanged knowing glances.

"That means she's gonna lay down the law to him," Mickie said as Trenace reached the concrete slab.

Trenace glanced over her shoulder. "That's right. We have rules to follow, but first I want to get to know Terry a little better." She found the sullen boy pressed against the refrigerator, humming in time with the motor. "Let's go into the bathroom and get your face washed off so I can see the damage," she said. "I'll put a bandage on your eyebrow. He laid a good one on you, Terry. You may have a shiner when you go to school."

"I don't go to school," the boy said. "They threw me out and told me I couldn't go back. I hate their dirty old school. Why would anyone want to go to school?"

Surprised at his outburst, she pointed down the hallway. "March, young man. The bathroom is the second door on the left." She patted the wall in case he didn't know his left from his right. She half expected him to defy her, but his rage had been vented through his verbal outburst.

He had spoken more words in anger than he had said since Mrs. Sewell had dropped him off. Trenace watched the boy's stiff walk. The welfare worker had done just that, dropped him off like a piece of unwanted baggage, and the boy seemed to be reconciled to the harsh reality that no one wanted him for long.

In the bathroom she touched his shoulder. He jerked violently away. Closing the door, she leaned against it and gazed at him. He stared at his bloody nose and swollen brow in the mirror and ignored her.

"The washcloths are in the drawer and the soap is in the dish," she said. "Do you want to do it, or shall I?"

"Don't touch me," he warned.

"Why?"

He turned to her, as if he was surprised she had asked. Reaching for the bar of soap, he turned on the faucet and let the water trickle over his soiled hands.

"Why don't you want me to touch you, Terry?" she asked, watching as he let the water flow over his wrists and forearms and collect in the bottom of the basin.

He kept his hands submerged in the warm water and glanced at her over his shoulder. His blue eyes filled with tears and his chin began to tremble. "It hurts."

"Hurts? When I touch you?"

"It hurts . . . when anyone touches me," he said. "But this feels good." He moved his hands around in the water, making swirling motions with his fingers.

Something clicked in the back of Trenace's mind as she watched him. Hadn't another child said those same words to her once? A boy older than this one, about a year after she had become a foster parent? She would look up the child's name and circumstances in the notebook she kept.

"Would you like me to fill the tub so you can sit in the warm water?" she asked.

"I won't get into trouble?" he asked, his tough facade crumbling.

"Of course not," she said smiling. She was about to touch his shoulder, then remembered his remark. "I'll start the tub." When she adjusted the controls, she turned to him again. "Try it out. Is it too hot or cold?"

He ran his fingers through the water that was collecting in the bottom of the tub. "Can you make it cooler?"

She adjusted the knobs. He felt the water again and gave his approval. "Good," she said. "Let it fill up as deep as you want, but don't let it run over. Can you work the handles?"

He nodded. She handed him a clean towel and two washcloths. "The shampoo won't burn your eyes. Can you wash your own hair?"

He nodded again, then turned to her, his young body stiff and defiant once more. "If I get water on the floor, are you gonna beat me?"

Trenace sighed. "No, Terry." She grabbed several more towels and stacked them on the floor. "If you splash, spread these around. I have a washer and dryer than can handle any mess you can make." She looked away, hoping she hadn't presented a challenge her laundry equipment couldn't live up to. "You can stay in the water as long as you want, but we eat supper at six." She glanced at the clock on the wall. "Can you tell time?"

He scowled at her. "Of course I can tell time."

She smiled. "Good. We eat at six sharp. That's when the hands are straight up and down."

He narrowed his eyes. "I know that."

She wondered who had managed to teach him that skill during his angry young life. "I'll put out a change of clothes for you in the bedroom across the hall."

"Do I have to be with someone?" he asked.

"Would you rather be alone?" she asked.

He nodded. "They don't like me 'cuz I make noises."

She thought of the only empty bedroom left. "Then you'll have a room to yourself," she assured him. "We'll be in the kitchen when you want to join us."

He pulled his T-shirt over his head, and she gasped when she spotted the bruises across his shoulders. Already turning green and yellow, they followed the lines of a belt or a switch from one shoulder blade downward to his side.

"Who hit you?" she asked.

"I fell," he said, untying his shoe.

She wondered if he'd received a beating at a foster home. Surely not, she thought.

"What do we get to eat?" Terry asked, starting to pull off his shoes and socks.

With the arrival of this child she had given supper no thought. "Consider it a surprise," she said, closing the bathroom door softly behind her.

After laying out his clean clothes, she returned to the bathroom. Knocking lightly on the closed door, she called, "How does it feel?"

"Good," his muted reply sounded.

"Need anything?"

No answer came. "Enjoy yourself," she called, and hurried down the hallway and into the living room. Drained emotionally, she leaned against the wall. Poor Terry, she thought. If his problem was the same as the other child so long ago, he'd been misunderstood most of his life, but she couldn't bring herself to find her notebook and confirm her suspicions. Not now.

The afternoon had left her feeling as if she were solely responsible for holding numerous collapsing walls from falling down on both her and the children. The air seemed to leave the room, bringing her an overwhelming sense of suffocation. Her heart thudded, and for a moment she wondered if she was about to have a panic attack. *Not now,* she scolded herself. She had no time. She opened the front door, went outside and dropped to the steps leading down from the covered porch.

Hugging her knees, she buried her face against them and took deep breaths. Her self-control continued to crumble as tears burned the back of her throat. She didn't have time to cry, and what good would tears do? Her heart pounded as her breathing became erratic. The trembling of her chin grew worse, and she bit her lip until she tasted blood.

The silence that followed an engine being turned off ebbed past the pounding in her temples and she looked up. Max's minivan was parked at her curb, and Max stood at the passenger door, reaching for something.

"Max?" she called, her voice reflecting her turmoil.

He turned, took one look at her and loped across the grass. "My God, what's wrong with you?"

"Oh, Max," she sobbed. "Of all the people I know, you're the one I need most right now. How did you know?" Her breasts heaved as she tried to stop the tearful outburst.

He took her in his arms and held her, letting her sob against his chest. Then he massaged her shoulders and the taut muscles at the base of her neck. Gradually she regained her composure and looked up at him. "I'm sorry. I had no right to greet you like this," she said, her voice hoarse.

He wiped her cheeks dry with his thumbs and pushed the damp tendrils from her face. "I've been thinking about you all afternoon," he murmured. Then his mouth settled on hers. She forgot where they stood until he released her mouth and gazed at her. His smile shimmered through another wave of tears, but she refused to let them flow.

"I had dinner with my aunt and uncle, but I wanted to be here," he said, his gaze drifting over her features. "I needed to know you were all right. You're not."

She managed a weak smile. "I am now."

CHAPTER NINE

MAX FROWNED down at Trenace's flushed face. "I was about to ask you if you've had a good day," he said, draping his arm around her shoulders. "Want to tell Uncle Max all about it?"

She slid her arm around his waist. "Maybe it would be easier to show you than to tell you. Come inside."

He stopped. "I brought dinner."

She beamed. "You are truly an angel of mercy, Max."

"Come help me," he said, returning to the van. "You can carry this one," he said, handing her a large white pizza box. "I have two more." A strange expression skipped across Trenace's features and was gone before it could fully register with Max. "I suppose you think I feed your kids too much junk food."

"The thought had crossed my mind," she said, smiling, "but as long as I balance your treats with my home-cooked meals, they'll survive."

He retrieved the second and third boxes and followed her into the house. "My Aunt Agnes sent me packing when I forgot to answer four questions in a row about how I liked being back in Spokane." Sliding the boxes onto the kitchen table, he turned to her. "Are we alone?"

She smiled. "For a moment."

"Then come here," he said, holding out his hand. His body sent unruly messages to his brain as she stepped into his arms and leaned against him. "You spoiled Aunt

Agnes's day. Did you know that? You're one hell of a friend to distract me this way." He gave her a brief description of the afternoon.

"Poor Max," she teased, sliding her hand up his shirt.

"I'm rich enough to buy pizzas." His hand found the soft skin on the side of her neck and began to stroke it.

"We agreed...to keep our feelings under control," she murmured, but brushed his mouth with hers.

"But we can modify the agreement occasionally," he hinted as his hand worked its way down her back to settle on the side of her flaring hip. A subtle movement of red and white caught his attention, and he looked over her shoulder. A sandy-haired boy with eyes as blue as his own stared back at him. In his arms were several damp towels. The boy's gaze never wavered until Max kissed Trenace lightly on her cheek and stepped away. "We have company. Want to introduce us?"

Trenace turned, smiled and held out her hand to the boy. "This is Terry," she said. "He's nine years old and he came this afternoon to stay for a while. The laundry room is through there," she said to the boy, pointing to the opposite end of the kitchen.

Max arched an eyebrow and studied Trenace's stiff demeanor. "Is he the cause of your tears?"

Before she could respond Terry returned to stare again at Max. Max extended his hand. "I'm Max Tulley. I brought dinner. Do you like pizza?"

Terry's gaze shifted from Max to the boxes on the table and back to Max. Cautiously he took Max's hand.

"Don't squeeze," Trenace warned, and something in her tone told Max to abide by her directive. "Terry, can you go tell the other children that Max brought pizza?"

Without a word the boy went outside.

"Regular chatterbox, isn't he?" Max asked.

"He needs time and space, Max," she warned. "He's a very unhappy child, but I think I can help him, or at least get him the help he needs." The children trooped in, each stopping at the sink to grab a wet washcloth to wipe their hands before surrounding Max.

He greeted each child as if they were favorite nieces and nephews. When his gaze settled on the black child clutching a pastel bear, he knelt and smiled. "I'm Max. The other children all know me. Who are you?"

She ducked her head and sidled up against Trenace's leg. The sight of Trenace's bare leg within touching distance conflicted with his effort to greet the new child. He gave up and got to his feet as Trenace picked the child up in her arms.

"This is Akeylah and she's five," Trenace said as the little girl stuck a finger into her mouth and stared curiously at Max. Trenace kissed her cheek and looked at Max. "She's had some bad experiences with men, especially boyfriends who have lived with her mom, so she's staying here for a few weeks." She sat Akeylah on a chair and waved a hand toward the boxes. "Do we want hot or cold pizza?"

AN HOUR LATER Mickie rolled her wheelchair around the table to Max's chair. "Did you see your picture in the paper? I did and so did Boyd. Wanna see it?"

Max looked across the table at Trenace, who seemed to be avoiding him. "Sure." When Mickie retrieved the paper stacked on a nearby buffet and placed the section in front of Max, a lump formed in his throat. He looked at Trenace again, but she busied herself with Akeylah. He studied the photograph and checked the name of the photographer. He knew the man. He'd give him a call and see if he couldn't get a couple of prints.

Mickie leaned against her chair arm and gazed longingly at the photograph. "Isn't it wonderful?"

"Aunt Trenace looks... beautiful," he agreed.

"And you're wearing glasses, just like my teacher did last year," Mickie said. "You don't wear them on TV."

"No," Max murmured, but his attention centered on Trenace as she worked her way around the table, clearing each spot and sending the children into the living room. She went to the sink and began to rinse the dishes and put them in the dishwater.

Mickie leaned closer and whispered, "Do you love each other?"

"I... Mickie, you ask too many questions," he whispered.

She smoothed a strand of black hair behind one ear. Smiling precociously at him, she said, "I just wondered. You keep coming here, and we all know that Uncle Owen is never coming back. Aunt Trenace lets us see the videotapes as often as we want, and she looks at them, too." She lowered her voice until he had to lean close to catch her words. "Sometimes she gets up and watches them in the middle of the night. I can hear you and Boyd and you and Annabelle talking, so I know."

"Maybe she misses the children when they leave," he said.

"Maybe. I'm never gonna leave here," Mickie said. "Even when I get to be on TV with you, I know I'll get to stay here, 'cuz nobody else loves me the way Aunt Trenace does. Do you think someday you might love me, too?"

The lump already lodged in his throat got bigger. "Mickie, I can't imagine anyone not falling in love with you. You're irresistible."

She pushed her chair backward, smiled knowingly at him and rolled herself into the living room.

Max went to the sink and trapped Trenace between his arms and the counter. "If you don't mind, I'd like to hang around here for a few hours. Compared to this house, my apartment seems incredibly dull and lonely."

"You're always welcome here," she murmured.

The evening passed quickly. Boyd sat at the desk, struggling with a page of math homework. When he asked Max to help, Max took one look at the problem and shrugged. "Better ask Trena."

Max returned to the sofa. Immediately George plopped down beside him. "I gotta write a long, long story about something I did last summer."

"How long?" Max asked, glancing at the pad of lined newsprint in the boy's hand.

"This long," George said, waving the pad.

"Write about our picnic," Max suggested.

"But how?"

Max glanced up at Trenace, who leaned over Boyd's shoulder.

"I'll take care of math," she called across the room. "You can handle the creative writing."

George shoved the pad of paper onto Max's lap and grinned. "You gonna write it for me?"

"Not on your life," Max said. "That would be cheating. When you're in school, you should always do your own work."

Trenace covered a snicker with her hand.

"Didn't you ever cheat?" George asked, resting his cheek against Max's arm and gazing up at him.

"Only in desperation," Max admitted. "Just ask yourself these questions." He turned the cover page over and tapped the back side of the page with his pencil.

Carefully he printed the words "Who, What, When, Where, Why and How." He returned the pad to a puzzled George, who sat staring at the words. "Think about the picnic and answer each of those questions. By the time you're finished, you'll have written your story."

"That's too easy," George argued.

"Who said it had to be hard? Try it."

Still skeptical, George slid off the sofa and sprawled on the carpet. Thirty minutes later he leaned against Max's leg. "Did I do it?" Max quickly read the story, trying to ignore the misspellings. Before he could respond George grinned. "My teacher says we don't have to worry about spelling. We're gonna work on that next week."

Max chuckled. "Then you've done a great job."

Baths were taken and each child was tucked into bed. Boyd and George managed to coax Max into reading to them. "We know how to read," Boyd explained, "but we like to listen to grown-up voices, and we don't like baby stories. Aunt Trenace gets Indian stories from the library and reads them."

George narrowed his eyes as he looked across the room at Max. "Are you a good reader?"

"Course he's a good reader," Boyd retorted. "He's good enough to read on television."

By the time Max reached the end of a chapter, both boys were sound asleep. He left the room, closing the door behind him.

He found Trenace in the living room, siting in one corner of the sofa, her shoes kicked off and her feet tucked up beneath her. She patted the cushion next to her. "Join me?"

"Where were you?" he asked.

"With Terry," she said. "We talked." She told him about the episodes earlier in the day. "Max, he's gone through most of his life rejecting any show of affection because it hurts to be touched.''

Max frowned. ''I thought everyone liked to be touched.''

She shook her head. ''He doesn't like crowds, either. Too many children pushing and shoving drives him wild. That's one of the reasons he gets expelled from school. Can you imagine never being able to enjoy a hug or being cuddled? I wanted to hold him, but I didn't dare, so I read to him. I don't think he's ever been read to before.''

''Did he let you sit next to him?'' he asked.

''Yes, but on his terms,'' she replied. Her hand touched Max's trouser leg and looked up at him. ''He touched my leg, just with his fingers, and he wanted to know if it hurt. When I said no, he wanted to touch my arm.''

Max's arm slid around her shoulders, and she rested her head against his chest. ''And all the while you were reading the story?''

''No,'' she murmured. ''We stopped the story, and I let him touch my arms until finally he asked me to touch his arm. I did, very lightly. Oh, Max, he was so tense, expecting to be hurt again, but I caressed his skin very gently for more than ten minutes. He began to relax. I could feel it, and I knew we were making progress when he asked if he could sit on my lap, but I couldn't hug him. Only when I agreed to his terms did he sit there, and then we started reading the story again. He got drowsy and leaned against me, but I had to keep my arms loose around him. He got into bed and I read him some more. When we finished, I asked him if I could kiss his cheek, and he said I could if I didn't do it hard. My reward was a smile. No child should have to reject a kiss because it might hurt. Max, what can I do to help a child like Terry?''

He tightened his arm around her. "It sounds to me like you've already accomplished quite a bit." He listened as she told about dozens of children who had stayed with her with special problems, misunderstood children rejected by society because they didn't fit the mold.

"It's almost as if some of these children invite abuse," she remarked. "They do things that irritate adults. Some of them, like Terry, can't stand being hugged or touched. Can you imagine having a baby that doesn't like to be cuddled? I've had a child like him here before. It's very disconcerting because it goes against the grain of all our maternal and paternal instincts, yet there's a reason if someone will take the time to find it."

"What about your caseworker? Can't she help?"

"She's changed in the past five years," Trenace replied. "She's become hard and unsympathetic. She does the paperwork and places the children and shifts them from place to place, but she's stopped caring about them. She pretends to operate by the rule book, but I'm not so sure, and now she seems to expect the worst from everyone. Max, she saw the photograph and actually cautioned me to get rid of it before Owen saw it. What am I going to do? I've got to tell her about the divorce before she finds out from someone else. The rules have been loosened, but she thinks all foster homes should have a man and woman, a married couple. She's wrong. I do fine alone."

"Except for this afternoon," he reminded her.

"I . . . just needed a sounding board," she replied.

"A friend," he said.

She played with the button at the opening of the golf shirt he was wearing. "I'm going to try to adopt Mickie. I'll have to admit I'm alone when I fill out the forms."

"Have you talked this over with Mickie?" he asked, staring across the room as he speculated on the Pandora's box she might be opening.

"Not yet. I didn't want her to get too excited."

"She's scheduled to be Wednesday's Child in two weeks. What if someone else asks for her?"

She looked up at him. "Do you think they will?"

He gazed down at her. "That's the purpose of the program. If these children get placed, I've succeeded and so have you."

She pulled away and rose from the sofa. "I'm going to apply, anyway," she insisted. "If better prospective parents come along, I won't stand in their way, but she's like a daughter to me. She's been here for almost three years. She's happy here."

He stood up. "Most of the children are happy here, but you know it can't last. You're their temporary parent, that's all."

"You don't understand," she replied, turning away.

He put his hands on her shoulders. "Mrs. Sewell and I agree on this one, Trena. You come into their lives when they need you most, but like all parents, you have to turn them loose." He spun her around. "The *Wednesday's Child* project won't last forever. When it's over, it's over, and we'll move on to other interests. When you love someone too much, they divorce you or they die or they go away and leave you. Regardless, you're left alone. You can't be with your loved ones forever. You should know that and protect yourself."

"Is that what you've done?" she asked.

His hands slid into his trouser pockets and he stared past her. "Maybe. It's getting late. I'd better go."

She followed him to the front door. "Have you made up your mind about next weekend? I need to have the car serviced if you're not going."

In spite of the dark cloud that had settled over him, he shook his head. "I have a prescription for a new antihistamine. The allergist swears it works against all animal dander."

She smiled. "The children will be so glad. I had a hard time explaining how a person could be allergic to horses. Will we see you during the week?"

He shook his head. "I have three stories I'm developing. Jocko and I will be out of town Tuesday and Wednesday."

He sensed her withdrawal. "You won't be on the six o'clock news?" she asked.

He shook his head. "The new anchor at ten got over her influenza, and she's covering for me as a return favor. I'll be here at seven on Saturday morning."

MONDAY AFTERNOON Trenace phoned Mrs. Sewell, explained her decision to formally adopt Mickie and asked her to mail the application forms so that she could begin to fill them out.

"I'll bring them Wednesday morning," said Mrs. Sewell. "I have to be in the area for another appointment, and I may have news about Boyd. But you know how I feel about foster parents becoming adoptive parents. It seldom works out. Haven't I warned you?"

"Yes, but I've thought about this for months now," Trenace insisted. "Please help me."

"We'll see," Mrs. Sewell replied. "Good day, *Mrs. McKay*." The woman's tone troubled Trenace. The social worker had never been a particularly warm person. Perhaps it was Trenace's imagination that Mrs. Sewell had put extreme emphasis on Trenace's marital status.

When the doorbell rang Wednesday morning, Mrs. Sewell's automobile was nowhere in sight. "How did you get here?"

"I had an appointment just down the street," the woman said, pushing past Trenace into the house. "Where are the children?"

"Boyd, Mickie and George are at school," Trenace said, following Mrs. Sewell. "Terry is on the glider and Akeylah is swinging."

Mrs. Sewell swung around. "You mean that boy is being civil toward another child? You'd better keep an eye on him. Akeylah will be going home to her mother the first of October, and I wouldn't want to have to explain an injury."

Trenace stiffened. "What about Terry's bruises? Did he receive them at another foster home?"

"What are you talking about?"

"He had bruises across his back," Trenace said.

"That's impossible," Mrs. Sewell said, snorting as she stalked into the kitchen. "That child must be lying. None of my foster parents beat the children." She turned to Trenace. "You must have imagined it." She reached into her purse and withdrew an envelope. "Here are the application forms, but don't be optimistic. We check out prospective homes thoroughly."

"You've known me for fifteen years," Trenace said.

Mrs. Sewell snapped her purse shut. "Your conduct has been less than exemplary in recent weeks, Mrs. McKay. I just came from the home of a concerned citizen down the street. She called the agency Monday morning and spoke to me about what she observed Sunday afternoon, right in your own front yard!"

"What are you getting at?" Trenace's thoughts scrambled as she tried to scan the past several days.

Mrs. Sewell arched a bushy gray eyebrow. "This woman..."

"Who?"

"I must respect the informant's confidentiality," Mrs. Sewell replied. "She observed you and *that man* from the television station embracing openly in your front yard. She said he kissed you and you didn't try to fight him off. Really, Mrs. McKay, what do you expect the neighbors to think? This is a reflection on the agency and myself, as well as you. And what will your husband say when he hears of this?" Mrs. Sewell's features flushed a deep rose. "Of all the people I've worked with over the years, you're the last one I'd expect to be guilty of this kind of conduct."

"And I suppose you're going to tell him?" Trenace asked, knowing she could be digging her own grave in the foster home program if she didn't bridle her tongue.

"I would if I could ever find him." Mrs. Sewell leaned closer. "I haven't seen him in over two years. I've listened to one excuse after another to justify his absence."

Trenace turned away from the woman's accusing gaze. "We're divorced." She turned again to meet Mrs. Sewell's eyes. "He hasn't been my husband for almost a year, so if I want to kiss Max Tulley in my own front yard, I have every right."

Mrs. Sewell's posture stiffened. "So that photograph wasn't lying. There *is* something between you and him. I'll have to file a report on this. Having a noncustodial man in the house is bad enough when these children live with their natural mothers, but in a foster home it's unthinkable. Do I dare ask where Mr. Tulley spends his nights?"

Trenace's anger flamed. "You'll have to ask him. He doesn't answer to me. You can file any report you wish, but I'll fight you if you try to make our friendship into something sordid. You have a dirty, wicked mind, Mrs. Sewell. You see these mothers with their boyfriends, and you imagine all kinds of promiscuous behavior. You may be justified at times, but just because a man and woman are attracted to each other gives you no right to judge. You're an insensitive old witch."

"Well, I never." Mrs. Sewell's face turned livid.

A warning bell snapped Trenace to attention again. "I'm sorry, Mrs. Sewell. I didn't mean that. I've been ... under a strain these past few days. Terry isn't an easy child to work with. Akeylah has nightmares about Bubba. I haven't had much sleep, and I *am* concerned about being divorced. Sometimes money runs short. You've assumed Owen helps me financially, but he quit doing that almost five years ago, even before he left. He paid the mortgage. That was all."

Trenace took several deep breaths and tried to think rationally. "You said you had news for Boyd. He's at school. Has someone responded to the piece Max did with him?"

"Yes," Mrs. Sewell said. "A couple already approved has expressed interest, but they want to spend several weekends with him before they decide. Please have him ready to be picked up at nine o'clock Saturday."

"Saturday? But we have plans. We've been invited to spend the weekend at Dr. Brockman's horse farm. Boyd is excited. You know how surly he can get when he's up-rooted. Please ask them to postpone taking him until the following weekend. I can prepare him. Max is picking us up at seven. All the children love him, but he's especially good with the boys. Mrs. Sewell, he's been a stabilizing force in Boyd's and George's lives since he's met them. Please don't deny them that contact. He's a marvelous role model for them, even Terry." She held out her hand. "Please?"

She couldn't breathe until Mrs. Sewell reluctantly agreed. "Good, now about Owen and me. Try to understand. After a few years, he didn't like my involvement in the program. He wanted me to quit, but I love it. It's my calling. Some of the children are parents themselves now, and they send me photos of their own babies. I get letters at Christmas from many of them. I think I've made a difference."

"Your point is well taken, but I must report this regardless," Mrs. Sewell said, hurrying toward the door. "Do prepare Boyd for leaving. He's a big boy now, and it's time he learned to adjust to change." At the door she paused. "If I ever learn of *that man* spending his nights here, I'll have your license. I've been in the department long enough to know how to cut through the red tape and get action."

"Good," Trenace said, holding the door open for her. "Perhaps you can help speed up my application to adopt Mickie."

Mrs. Sewell's gray eyes narrowed. "You realize you'll no longer get paid for caring for her? That her hospital bills will be your responsibility? The wheelchairs have to be replaced, and the cost will come out of your pocket."

"I know," Trenace murmured.

GEORGE WAS ECSTATIC on Wednesday when the woman anchor substituting for Max introduced the *Wednesday's Child* segment. "That's me, see?" He pointed excitedly and scooted up to the screen.

"Get back, stupid," Boyd insisted. "We can't see."

From a corner of the living room where Trenace had given him a blanket to sit on, Terry watched the screen. He'd chosen the corner the first night of his stay, as if staking out an area that could be his alone. Trenace sensed he needed the space he found there, safely away from the chattering of the other children, yet within sight and sound of them. Slowly Terry got to his feet and came to sit beside her on the sofa. "That's the man who brought us pizza," he said, his blue eyes as perplexed as she'd ever seen them.

Trenace nodded. "He interviewed Boyd and Mickie and a little girl who used to live here. Would you like to see them?"

Terry's frown grew deeper. "Why?"

"So you can see the others," she started to explain.

"No." He shook his head. "Why did he put them on TV?"

"To try to find them a new mother and father to love them," she said, fighting the urge to pull him closer. "We'll show you as soon as the news is over." In a few minutes she called to Boyd. "Would you rewind the tape?"

For Boyd, being put in charge was his moment of glory. He grabbed the remote control and set up the video player. He offered the narration before each segment showed. When the cartridge had shown George again, Terry looked from one child's face to the next. "He didn't do you," he said to Mickie.

"I'm in two weeks," she boasted.

"I get to go home to my mommy," Akeylah said, rocking back and forth and hugging her lavender bear.

Terry turned to Trenace as if he wanted to say something. She waited. He looked away and mumbled, "I don't want to be on it." Then he stood up and left the room.

"He's weird," Boyd said.

Trenace shook her head. "He's a lonely little boy." She had tried to explain to the others that he reacted to the touch of another person with pain, and the children had left him alone to drift in and out of their play as he chose. At night, Trenace had continued to stroke his arms, and a few days earlier he'd begun to let her rub some lotion on his shoulders. At times she wondered how much of his reaction was to physical pain and how much might be to the fear of that pain. She planned to talk to Dr. Brockman about Terry's condition during the upcoming weekend.

On Friday afternoon the phone rang.

"We've had two inquiries about George," Mrs. Sewell reported. "They'll be checked out and I'll let you know. Are you still seeing that man?"

Trenace ignored the question. "I mailed you the application for adoption. Did you get it?"

"Yes, Mrs. McKay, and you'll be notified when there's an opening. The court calendar is very full."

"Isn't it only a screening?" she asked, glad she'd learned the procedure over the years.

"Yes, and I'll see what I can do to get it over with," Mrs. Sewell said. She inquired about the children, and Trenace gave brief reports on them. "I'll be in touch Sunday evening."

Trenace grimaced. "We won't be back until late. Max has a van with a lift for Mickie's chair."

Mrs. Sewell cleared her throat. "He seems to have made a commitment to the children's welfare, perhaps short-sightedly, considering the uncertainty of your own situation."

CHAPTER TEN

WHEN THE VAN rolled to a stop at the curb on Saturday morning, the boys had already dragged their sports bags to the sidewalk and were waiting in a row.

Max jumped out, hitched his jeans up and grinned from beneath a battered felt hat. "Well, cowboys, ready to go to the ranch?"

"You betcha," George shouted, tackling Max around his legs and almost knocking him off balance.

"Then load 'em up," Max said, waving his thumb to the open back door of the van.

Boyd and George scuffled for position, but Terry sat on his bag motionless. Only when the other two boys moved away did he approach the van. He tried to reach over the other bags. Max gave him a hand, and when they were through, Terry looked up at the man.

"I saw you on television."

"I report the news at six o'clock on Channel Nine," Max said.

"No, I mean I saw you with Boyd and Mickie and George," Terry said. "Someday, if I don't get into trouble, will you let me be on with you, too?"

"Sure, if it's okay with Mrs. Sewell," Max said, placing his hand lightly on the boy's shoulder. He expected him to jerk away, and when Terry didn't, Max felt as if he'd been part of a rite of passage for the boy. "We'll talk to Aunt Trenace about it."

"I think she'll say yes. She doesn't scream at me, but Mrs. Sewell doesn't like me very much," Terry murmured, easing himself away from Max's hand.

"Want to help me load the girls' stuff?" Max asked when he spotted Terry watching Boyd and George wrestling on the grass.

Terry's gaze jerked back to Max. "What if I break them?"

"Canvas bags won't break," Max replied. "If you drop one, pick it up again. Okay?" He half expected the boy to go off by himself as he usually did, but when he glanced over his shoulder, he saw Terry's first tentative step to help.

In minutes they had everything loaded. "Climb in, everyone. Let's hit the road," Max called.

"Let Terry sit in front with you," Trenace suggested. "He does better alone. I'll sit with Akeylah." She gave instructions to Terry, then rolled Mickie's chair toward the van, waiting for Max to operate the lift.

When everyone was safely settled and buckled inside, Max held the power button until the lift slid along the floor of the van, then slammed the sliding door shut. In the driver's seat he glanced in the rearview mirror. Trenace looked away. Something was wrong, he thought. She'd hardly spoken to him since his arrival. She looked wonderful, dressed in a well-worn pair of jeans that accentuated her womanly curves yet gave her enough room to sit astride a horse. The sun turned her auburn hair to a cap of fire. A pair of sunglasses hid her eyes.

The children asked a steady stream of questions about the farm as the vehicle traveled north out of Spokane. "I know about wheat farming," Max said, "not Arabian horses."

"Same for me," Trenace called from the middle of the van. "Be patient and we'll all learn together."

"Are you really allergic to horses?" George asked.

"I was as a kid, but today I have medication and a giant box of tissues, so cross your fingers," Max called back to the two grinning boys. Beside him Terry seemed to be in a world apart. He didn't participate in the chatter and didn't look out the window at the scenery. His fingers touched the soft leather upholstery of the seat and began to stroke it.

"Terry, there's a sack by your feet," Max said, motioning to his right. "Would you get it and take out what's in it?"

Terry looked curiously at Max, then reached for the sack. He pulled out a white stuffed rabbit with pink ears and a yellow stuffed dog with gray tufts on his ears and tail. The boy touched the artificial fur, then picked up the dog and placed it against his cheek.

"Soft, isn't it?" Max asked.

Terry nodded and put the dog back onto the seat.

"There's a small pair of scissors in the sack," Max said. "Can you get them and cut the tags off the animals? I didn't have time." Thank goodness he hadn't, he thought, watching out of the corner of his eye as the boy carefully cut the plastic strings and pulled off the stickers. He folded the sack, put the trash items in the litter bag hanging from the cigarette knob, opened the glove compartment and slid the scissors inside, then picked up both animals and held them, rocking and humming as he rubbed his cheeks against the soft fur.

A few minutes later when he put the stuffed animals down on his lap, he continued to steady them by burying his hands in their fur.

"Do you have a stuffed toy?" Max asked.

Terry shook his head.

"Not a bear or a dog or a cat? None?"

The boy stared down at the animals. "I used to have a bear, but my dad said only babies played with stuffed toys. He threw my bear in the fireplace." He put the animals beside him on the seat. "I don't want any more bears."

WHEN THEY REACHED the sign for the Brockman Farm, Boyd and George began to shout and point toward five mares trotting along a white wooden fence running parallel to the driveway. Each mare had a leggy foal running close beside it.

Laudon and Michelle Brockman and their two daughters met them in the yard. "This is Maria," Michelle said, placing her hand on her oldest daughter. "She's six." She turned to a younger girl with amber eyes like her father. "This is Julia. She's four and a half. They're both excited about having you all visit."

George walked over to Julia. "She's not very big. Can she ride horses?"

"Only when I lead," Michelle said. "Horses can be dangerous if you don't know what to do. You're here for fun, but we're going to learn safety while we're at it. So do as I tell you, or you'll have to stay inside. Is it a deal?"

"Can I be first?" George asked as the others nodded silently in agreement to the rules.

Michelle smiled at him and ruffled his red hair. "I suppose so, but don't worry. We have enough horses for everyone. Now follow me to the barn, and I'll show you the tack."

"What's tack?" George asked, skipping to keep up with her.

"I'll show you," Michelle said, and they disappeared into the large red barn behind the house. Terry brought up the rear, keeping a safe distance between himself and the other children.

"I don't think I've ever seen your new boy," Laudon Brockman said. "Tell me about him."

Trenace described his actions and how she'd begun to stroke him and massage lotion on his back. "When I first got into the program, I had a boy who acted just like Terry. After a year of failing to reach him, I read an article about a type of brain damage that's hard to diagnose. I called the author who lived in Seattle, and she told me all about a program that involves patterning. Mrs. Sewell said I didn't know what I was talking about, but I went to her supervisor and she listened and was able to get the boy transferred to Seattle and into this program where they take children back to a fetal position and then have them relearn to roll over and creep and crawl and walk, and they massaged him and after a year and a half the boy was able to go to school and did very well. It was like a miracle when the foster mother he'd been placed with in Seattle wrote me about his progress."

Lau Brockman peered down at her. "I've read a lot about patterning. It's not as popular as it was a few years ago. It takes time and patience, but I've seen the results. Why don't you bring Terry in next week and we'll do some tests?"

"Thank you," Trenace said. "Just remember to let him set the limits on touching. Under that aloofness and aggressiveness I think we'll find a very bright boy. He's been labeled a troublemaker, even mentally retarded, because no one understood him."

"But you did," Max said.

She pulled her glasses off and looked at Max. "Yes, because I took the time. Mrs. Sewell is so busy keeping her rules and regulations that she can't see the children for what they really are. She...we had words this past week. I called her a witch, but I wanted to change it to the B word!"

Max chuckled and took her elbow. "Brockman, if you'll excuse us, I'd like to take Trenace for a walk. If she doesn't vent some of her anger, she'll have steam coming out of her ears. Can you do without us for a while?"

Lau grinned and waved them in the opposite direction from the barn. Trenace tried to pull away, but Max tightened his hold. "Simmer down, Trena, and march." They walked in silence alongside an irrigation ditch, past three grassy meadows, to a huge poplar tree. "Tell me what the hell's bothering you. You haven't given me a civil word since I picked you up. Are you mad at me? At the children? Or only at the witch Mrs. Sewell?"

Trenace's chin began to quiver. She put her hands on her hips and turned her back to him.

"Spill it, I said."

She whirled around. "That...that woman knows I'm divorced, and she threatened to pull my license because she said I'd been caught necking with you in the front yard."

"Is that all?"

"She accused me of having an affair with you."

A surge of compassion swept through Max. The woman standing before him, wild-eyed and angry, was as fragile emotionally as the boy who had sat beside him on the drive north.

"Would that be so unthinkable?" he asked.

She stared at him, and for a moment he recognized fear and uncertainty. "What else did she want to know?"

"She asked how many nights you'd slept over."

"Did you tell her only once?"

As Trenace turned away, Max reached out and caressed her cheek. Staring at the pink-and-blue plaid of her western-cut shirt, he didn't tell her how many times he'd imagined her standing naked in front of him. This woman had him on a tightrope, both physically and emotionally. When she let herself be free, she could be wildly responsive, but at other times he could almost see the invisible wall surrounding her. He leaned forward and kissed her shoulder and the satin lobe of her ear, half expecting her to shove him away.

The sun glistened off the back of her hair as she shook her head. "No," she whispered.

His hands settled on her upper arms. "No, it's not unthinkable, or no, you didn't tell her that I slept over... albeit on the sofa?"

Her head dropped forward in defeat. "No to both," she admitted.

The creamy skin exposed at the nape of her neck was irresistible, and he kissed it. She turned in his arms.

"What did you tell Mrs. Sewell?" he asked.

"I... I told her we were just friends," she said, staring at the opening at his collar.

He wished she'd take a chance and touch him there. "And that settled it?"

She shook her head. "When she accused me of messing around with you, that's when I became angry and told her about the divorce, and that I could kiss anyone I felt like, anywhere I wanted to. She talked as if we were being sexually active in front of the children. She said she was filing a report on my conduct. I told her she had a dirty mind."

He chuckled and pulled her closer. "I confess, Trena," he said, tipping her face up to his. "I've had some pretty carnal thoughts even with the children around, but I think I've done an admirable job of concealing them. Haven't I?"

A tiny smile softened her mouth. "Except when we danced."

Images of that night enveloped them as they stared at each other. He pulled her snugly against him. At the base of her throat her pulse throbbed, revealing her own reaction to him. Then, slowly, as if in a dream, he felt her hands settle on his ribs and begin to slide around his waist.

His groan sounded wild and primitive to his own ears when his mouth covered hers. At first she resisted when his tongue slipped into the corner of her mouth, but before he could change his strategy, her mouth opened wide to receive him. She came alive in his arms, clutching at his shirt and pulling the fabric tails from his belt and jeans. Her hands sought his bare skin and began to stroke the flexing muscles of his back in the same rhythm as her tongue danced with his. Her hips moved back and forth across his groin, sending messages that erased all the justifications she had given him about friendship.

He cupped her jaws and ears in his hands as he ended the kiss and gazed into her eyes. Her blue eyes were almost black, and dilated with passion.

Her head fell back, and he kissed her throat, then her mouth again, this time gentler, more lovingly. Breathing raggedly, he smiled down at her. "What would Witch Sewell think of us now?"

"She'd know all her suspicions were correct," she replied.

"All but one," he said. A wave of sadness cooled his ardor when she looked away.

"Turn around," she said. When he did, she began to stuff his shirt back into his jeans. The intimacy of her actions rekindled his desire for her, but he knew the moment of openness had passed. "There, now, you're decent."

"Decency is important to you, isn't it?" he asked.

"Indecency could cost me my license." She took a deep breath and looked at him again. "I admit when we're together something happens. But how on earth could we find time to be alone, with children streaming through our lives at all hours of the day and night. Max, we're incompatible. We were right from the beginning. Friendship is the best goal for us." Before he could stop her she was gone.

TRENACE RAN ALONG the irrigation ditch, past the meadows and to the paddock where Lau and Michelle Brockman were working with the children. She had let herself get out of control. It didn't take much, just an innocent brush of his hand against hers or his stopping by with an armload of pizzas, even the sight of him each night on the TV screen. He didn't even have to come near her in person for her to find herself lost in some shocking fantasy.

Being surrounded by the children didn't stop the longing that threatened to break the bounds of restraint she had so carefully built. Rerunning the videos of his interviews with the children reminded her constantly of what they could have had if she had a different career or if his was less demanding.

Leaning against the green metal gate leading into the paddock, she glanced over her shoulder. The poplar tree where they had embraced was in open view of the paddock. Had the Brockmans witnessed it all? The children?

In the distance Max walked in the opposite direction, away from the horses, away from her.

He was a virile man, of that she had no doubt, thinking of all the times she had been aware of his physical reaction to her. If she continued to reject his advances, would she be driving him out of her life and into the willing arms of another woman?

Leaning against the closed gate, Trenace studied Max's tall, lean figure as he stopped and kicked at some unseen object along the ditch bank. He stirred powerful emotions in her. Was it love? Or simply the reality that she hadn't experienced sexual fulfillment for years, lonely years during which no man had held her in his arms, whispered sweet words in her ear, kissed her and taken her breath away. Then Max Tulley had confronted her at the lilac bush and changed everything.

His glance alone made her body tremble, and when he held her in his arms, she wanted desperately to have him undress her and make wild, passionate love to her. She smiled to herself. She doubted that she'd ever experienced wild, passionate lovemaking, especially not during the final years of her marriage to Owen.

Owen seemed to have forgotten about foreplay and had taken to rolling away from her and going to sleep rather than holding her afterward. She'd been too hurt to talk about the changes in their lives. After Owen left, she'd been content with her celibate life for a few years, but Max made her want to explore her full potential in the arms of a man she loved.

Oh, Max, she thought, *is that what you've done to me? Do I dare love you when I know our futures are so far apart?*

In the distance he turned toward her, and she sensed his own need for love. Perhaps he was as lonely as she.

"Look, Aunt Trenace, watch me ride all alone," George called, and she turned away from Max, her heart heavy.

George sat astride a breathtakingly beautiful Arabian stallion, its golden mane bouncing in the breeze and its coat shining like a new copper penny. The horse responded to each command from the inexperienced boy, whose face shone with pride as he sat in the saddle. George's short legs barely reached the middle of the stallion's side, yet the horse seemed to sense the subtle shifts of the light body on his back. "His name is Samson, just like the man in the Bible," he called.

Michelle joined Trenace at the gate and whistled a command to the stallion. The horse and rider cantered across the paddock to where Trenace stood. Michelle stroked the slight, curving dip of the stallion's head just above his nose, then scratched the white blaze between his dark, intelligent eyes. "Isn't he a handsome fellow?" she asked, sliding her hand affectionately down past his finely sculptured nostrils and giving him a piece of apple. "Samson and I won enough money to open this stud-farm business. He's thirteen years old now, but he's still my pride and joy. His progeny keeps winning in the show ring. And he's as gentle as a kitten with children."

"But not as gentle as a pony," George boasted.

"No, George," Michelle said, smiling up at the child. She turned to Trenace. "He brings in more income than Lau's medical practice. Isn't that crazy?" She looked across the paddock at her husband as he lifted Akeylah onto the back of a gray mare. "Lau and I met because of Samson. We were returning from a horse show and the trailer had a flat. When I got out to fix it, I was hit by a car. The driver didn't stop, but Lau was behind the hit-and-run driver. He found me and saved my life." She turned back to George. "Take him to the steps and we'll let Terry ride."

"Terry's weird," George said. "He'll be afraid to ride a horse as big as Samson." He reached forward to pat the stallion's neck. Samson sidestepped, and George clutched his mane to keep his balance.

"Remember what I told you about being aware of your horse?" Michelle asked. "You must keep him under control at all times. Now do as I say, please. Terry has already asked for his turn."

George looked surprised. "He did? I didn't think he'd ask."

Michelle patted Samson's neck and grinned up at George. "Perhaps you've underestimated Terry. He's different, but aren't we all different?"

George chewed his tongue and twisted his face thoughtfully. "I'm not like Boyd, so I guess it's okay for Terry to be different from me." He glanced at Trenace, and she nodded her agreement.

Taking Samson's bridle in her hand, Michelle smiled. "Then let's go see if Terry is ready to ride."

George bounced in the saddle. "I can tell him how to do it," he offered. "I know *all* about riding horses, don't I?"

AFTER LUNCH, Michelle rose from the table. "I think you children are ready for a ride along the irrigation ditch. Max and Trenace, come with us, please, in case the children need help. Take your plates to the sink, everyone, and hit the bathrooms, then meet me at the barn door."

She helped the two youngest girls with their plates and silverware. In minutes everyone was racing across the yard to the barn again. Max lingered behind, waiting for Trenace to join him. "Feeling better?" he asked, draping his arm around her shoulders. She didn't pull away, so he took advantage of the moment. "Someone has to bring up the rear. Why don't we?"

She looked up at him. "Did you take your allergy medication?"

He grinned. "Yes, and I have an atomizer in case it fails."

She smiled and slid her arm around his waist.

In the barn Michelle gave Max a quick refresher course in horsemanship, and they all mounted and rode out. The horses seemed to know the trail in spite of the novices in their saddles, and the trek was completed with only a few hitches. When Terry found himself surrounded with other horses and riders, he sawed on the reins of his mount, and his animal began to rear and sidestep.

"I'll ride with him," Max volunteered. "We'll bring up the rear." As they reached the barn again, Max began to wheeze. He retired to the house. When his medication gave him relief again, he remembered the stuffed animals in the van and retrieved them, taking them to the girls and presenting them as a thank-you gift from all the visitors. "Terry helped me get them ready," he said, and the boy nodded from where he sat, patting a large German shepherd named Masher who had accompanied them on their ride.

They ate outside, with Lau Brockman acting as chef, grilling hamburgers for the children and tender T-bone steaks for the adults. As the sun sank behind the mountains in the west, the younger children began to yawn and Trenace and Michelle took them inside for baths. The men and older children discussed medicine and sports and television and school.

Mickie rolled her wheelchair close to Max's lawn chair. "Thank you, Uncle Max, for bringing us. Mrs. Brockman let me feed a colt an apple in the barn, and I rode a horse all by myself. I never thought I'd ever do that. Mrs. Sewell says I should give up on walking and stuff like that, but she's wrong.'' She leaned closer and bestowed a gentle kiss on his cheek.

After all the children had been coaxed into an early bedtime, Trenace returned to the patio. She handed Max a jacket he'd left in the van, then pulled on a navy-blue windbreaker. Michelle came from the kitchen with a tray of long-stemmed glasses and a bottle of white wine.

She smiled at the others. ''This is grown-up time. We started it after Maria was born when we realized we weren't taking time for each other anymore. I love my children, but I love my husband just as much. He deserves a family, and I want to give him one.''

Lau accepted his glass. ''I grew up in an orphanage, so relationships and a family are important to me,'' he explained. ''Tell me to mind my own business if you want, but I saw you two down at the poplar tree. We call that our 'lovers' quarreling tree.' You two aren't the first ones to work out your problems there. Michelle and I have had a few bouts there ourselves.''

Michelle walked by him, and he pulled her down on his lap. She leaned against him comfortably, then twisted to kiss his cheek. ''Lau can be very stubborn at times. He left me once, and I didn't know where he went. I was miserable.''

He tightened his arms around her. ''Not half as miserable as I was.'' He chuckled. ''That's one thing we fought over—who was more miserable.'' He kissed the top of her curly head.

''I was the most miserable when you went back to med school to become a pediatrician,'' Michelle added.

''I wanted to be a doctor from the time I was nine or ten years old,'' Lau explained. ''When I got a chance to reenter medicine here in Spokane, I found a mentor in the senior partner at the clinic who encouraged me to return to medical school and get my specialty. Unfortunately that meant I left Michelle here at the farm for several months at a time.''

"I was young and insecure," Michelle said. "I had to do a lot of soul-searching before I learned to trust Lau. I knew he loved me, but I didn't trust him to be able to trust me. We almost split up, but then I got pregnant and everything changed.''

"For the better," Lau said. "Except for the death . . .'' He looked down at his wife. "Except for the loss of our son Joel, but we're adjusting to that, too.''

Michelle sighed, then leaned forward. "What about you two? Single? Divorced? Widowed? Lau tells me a little about his patients, but all I hear about Mrs. McKay is how fabulous she is with her children.''

"I'm widowed and she's divorced," Max volunteered. "We each have two children. They're all in college. And your tree's reputation has been ruined. We haven't worked out a thing.''

Lau pulled his wife back against him. "You could have fooled me, folks. When a couple is as deep in the clinches as you two were, something must be happening.''

"Lau Brockman, you voyeur," Michelle said, chuckling. "How did you get to be an expert about couples in the clinches?''

He kissed her head again. "I've been in a few with you, sweetheart." He stared at Max, then Trenace. "You'll find happiness, but not without difficulties and heartache.''

Max reached out and took Trenace's hand. "That's encouraging.''

"It's his job to make people feel better," Trenace said.

Michelle crawled off her husband's lap and refilled everyone's glass. She stopped in front of Trenace. "Don't be afraid," she said. "It's always hard to get started, but if you love each other, you'll find the rewards are worth the risk." She turned toward her husband. "On that note, why don't we say good-night?" Together they disappeared into the house.

"COME SIT WITH ME," Max suggested.

She looked skeptical. "There's no room."

"Sit on my lap and let me hold you," he said, his voice turning soft and intimate. "If not for you, then for me, Trena."

Gingerly she perched on his knees. "I've never sat on a man's lap before," she said, embarrassed with her own awkwardness. "I'm too heavy."

"You're fine." He pulled her close, and she found herself cuddling in his arms. He didn't say a word as he held her, surrounding her with warmth and affection. Gradually she relaxed, and her arm slid up his chest to rest on his shoulder.

"Don't say a word," he whispered. "Let me talk." He waited to see if she would abide by his wishes. "If I had my way, I'd take you out in the meadow and make love to you, but it's cold, and there are mosquitoes buzzing around, and I might start wheezing, and wouldn't that be romantic?" He paused, his hand stroking her arm through her jacket. "Or I'd carry you into the living room and make love to you on the sofa before the fireplace, but George would probably get up and forget where the bathroom is and find us. My sleeping bag is in with the boys and yours is with the girls, so we're destined to sit here holding each other, feeling guilty for feeling normal and waiting for Mrs. Sewell to find us and go 'tsk tsk' and shake her finger at us.''

Trenace couldn't restrain a chuckle at the picture he painted.

''Mark my words, Trena. We'll find a way to be together. Some morning you'll wake up and wonder how you got into my bed, and then you'll remember all the wonderful things we did the night before. You'll be unable to resist touching me, and I'll wake up, too, and kiss you . . . like this.'' His mouth hovered over hers until finally she slid her hand around his neck and pulled his down.

His hand slid beneath her shirt, caressing the skin over her ribs. Slowly he moved his hand upward, hesitating when he touched the lace of her bra. She shifted her position to allow him access to the front hook.

''Unfasten it,'' she whispered. ''Touch me.''

When his fingers brushed across her nipple, it hardened into a bud of throbbing desire. He cupped her breast in his hand, caressing its fullness.

His head dipped and he tasted the skin in the V of her shirt. She wanted him to unsnap it and lay the fabric open. She longed to see the desire in his eyes.

''If only we could go away together,'' she whispered.

''We'll figure something out,'' he replied. His fingers brushed across her nipple again, and he rolled it between his thumb and forefinger.

Moaning as she pulled his head down, she whispered, ''Kiss me again, make me—''

Before she could finish he swept the words away with his mouth, and his arms tightened, drawing her hard against his aroused body.

As suddenly as he had started, his arms went slack. ''We have company,'' he whispered.

She rested her head against his throat and tried to re-arrange her shirt and jacket. His hand slid from beneath her clothing, and he eased her off his lap and stood up behind her.

"Akeylah, you should be asleep," he said.

The little girl stood in the entryway, clutching her lavender bear. "I had a bad dream. Bubba came to my room, and he scared me." She ran across the patio, and Trenace swept her up in her arms.

"I'm sorry, Max," Trenace said. "I truly am."

Max tweaked Akeylah's dark cheek. "We were letting our hormones get out of control again." He stepped away, and Trenace felt a draft of loneliness. "See you ladies tomorrow," he said, leaving Trenace alone with the child as he walked through the darkness in the direction of the poplar tree.

THE NEXT MORNING after breakfast Lau Brockman suggested they divide into two groups. "Call me a sexist if you must," he said, grinning at Michelle, "but Max and I want to take the boys and go exploring. Michelle and Trenace can go to the foaling barn and show the girls all the babies we've had this year. We'll bring back lunch with us."

"Exploring where?" Michelle asked.

Lau grinned. "It's a surprise."

With a resigned shrug, Michelle agreed. "But this afternoon everyone gets to ride the horses again." The girls and women waited on the porch as the men and boys climbed into a battered Jeep that looked as if it had seen combat duty. "Buckle up," Lau insisted.

"No," Terry shouted, leaping from the vehicle and running around the corner of the house and out of sight.

"I'll get him," Max offered. He found the boy standing stiff-legged, rocking back and forth and humming softly. "Terry?" The humming stopped and gradually his rocking movements ceased.

"I don't want to go," Terry said.

Max waited patiently.

"Boyd and George...they make too much noise," Terry said.

Max knelt before the child. "And they shove?"

Terry scowled.

"And they horse around too much?"

Terry nodded slowly, as if the information was painful to divulge.

Max nodded. "And when they bump into you?"

Terry stared down at his scuffed shoes. "It hurts." He looked up at Max's face. "If I cry, they call me a baby. Why doesn't it hurt them when they play rough?"

"Terry," Max replied, taking the boy's hands loosely in his. "Does this hurt?"

Terry stared down at their joined hands. "Not if you don't squeeze." He looked up again. "You won't hurt me?"

"Son," Max said, swallowing the lump in his throat, "I'd love to give you a big, warm hug, but the last thing I want to do is to hurt you. Have you ever hugged someone?"

The boy looked puzzled.

"Do you know how?" Max asked. When Terry shook his head, Max blinked to clear his vision. "Put your hands on my shoulders, right here." He tapped the spots. When the boy's hands rested lightly on his shirt, he nodded. "Now don't worry. I'm not going to touch you, and you can stop whenever you want. I want you to slide your

arms slowly around my neck and hug me. Pretend I'm
your father and—"

Terry jerked his hands away and stepped back.

Taken aback by the boy's reaction, Max tried again.
"Okay, pretend I'm your long-lost favorite uncle, and you
haven't seen me for thirty years."

Terry frowned. "But I'm only nine."

"Ah, a good math student?"

"I'm stupid in math," Terry said. "I can't remember
how the numbers go. I'm no good in school. The teachers call me dummy and they kick me out."

"I was never kicked out, but I never did get good at
math, either," Max replied, keeping his voice low and
steady. "Let's start again. Put your hands on my shoulders and slowly slide them around my neck and hug me,
for as short or as long as you want. If you want to kiss my
cheek, you can do that, too. I shaved this morning."

The little boy grinned, took a deep breath and placed
his hands on Max's shoulders. "I'm ready." His hands
began to move tenuously across Max's western-cut shirt
to his collar.

At first Max could tell the boy was trying to follow his
instructions without actually touching Max. When a finger touched bare skin, he knew they were making progress. A small hand inched its way along the side of Max's
neck. He waited, wondering how long it might take for
this simple maneuver to be carried out.

Max shut his eyes, too choked up to be a witness to this
act of faith unfolding around his neck. He felt the boy's
hands meet and join, and gradually he was hugged. Terry's head rested heavily against Max's shoulder, but still
Max didn't move. He wanted nothing to interfere with
Terry's effort to show affection. Nothing would have
pleased him more than to hug the child in return, but he

stayed immobile, knowing any move on his part would have destroyed the foundation he'd help to lay. When Terry's lips grazed Max's cheek, Max closed his eyes.

Terry's arms slid from Max's shoulders, and he stepped away. "I'm finished now," he said shyly.

Max stood up. "Did that hurt you?"

Terry shook his head.

"Good," Max replied, holding out his hand to Terry. "Then let's go exploring. You can sit up front by yourself. I'll handle Boyd and George."

Terry's hand slid into his, and man and boy walked back to the curious group milling around the Jeep.

"We're ready to go now," Max said. "We made a deal." He grinned at Boyd and George. "I get to sit with you characters, so move apart and make room."

He looked over the heads of the girls to Trenace and nodded slightly. She wore sunglasses again, and he knew she was hiding her emotions from him once more. Damn it, he thought, she was as emotionally crippled as Terry. Last night she had responded to him, and if he could have taken her somewhere private, they could have shared an intimacy both needed and wanted.

She had accused him once of hiding behind a wall. Yet she had helped him to step out, to face his anger, confront the ghost of his deceased wife and move ahead.

Sadly he realized he'd left her behind. Now he had to go back and take her hand, just as he'd taken Terry's hand, and bring her with him into love and fulfillment. She looked away as if she might be afraid of his thoughts. She had been hurt much more deeply than she would admit when her husband had walked away from their marriage without an explanation.

She looked his way again. *You won't shut me out, Trenace,* he vowed. *I won't walk away.* She'd drawn him into the lives of these children and into her own life, as well. Indeed, he'd begun to fall in love with Trenace McKay the first moment he'd seen her.

He'd never expected to fall in love again, but he hadn't planned on meeting Trenace McKay, a woman who had given him reason to renew his faith in love and happiness. Lucy would always be part of his past, his memories, but Trenace held the future in her gentle, caring hands.

CHAPTER ELEVEN

WHEN THE MEN AND BOYS returned, they had several strings of pan-size trout. Mud clung to their shoes and pant legs.

"We went to a fishing store and uncle Max got a license and we bought big fat worms. Then we went to a great big lake up the road," Boyd said.

"Yeah," George said. "Dr. Brockman taught us how to put worms on our hooks and we caught lunch!"

"I'd forgotten how much fun fishing could be," Max conceded.

"And some of us fell in," Boyd concluded.

Trenace laughed. "It looks to me like you all fell in."

Max grinned, and Trenace's heart fluttered. "I was the only clean one, so they ganged up and shoved me in."

Trenace's eyes widened. "Even Terry?"

Max and the boys exchanged subtle grins. "I think it was his idea, but he left the dirty work to the others. Boyd and George were more than willing to be his hit men."

While the fishermen changed into clean, dry clothes, Michelle organized a cook crew. "Mickie, you hold the plates and show Julia and Akeylah how to set the table. I'll wash and salt the fish. Maria knows how to roll them in crumbs. Trenace, would you make the salad?"

Trenace began washing the vegetables at the sink, her thoughts lingering on Max. He had looked at her very strangely before he'd driven away with Lau and the boys, almost as if he were sending her a private message. But what if she misinterpreted it? If she took a risk, would she regret it? Or would she have to live with a greater regret if she decided not to take a risk?

The afternoon flew by. Trenace went with the children back to the paddock for more riding lessons. Max accompanied Lau into Spokane for an emergency with one of his young patients who wouldn't let the physician on call treat her. They returned in time for dinner and farewells.

The drive back to Spokane was noisy. Each child had to tell their favorite memory at least twice.

"Terry, what about you?" Max asked, glancing down at the quiet child.

Terry sighed, then reluctantly murmured. "What we did."

Max glanced at Trenace in the rearview mirror. "It's a secret between us."

The children became model passengers as they drove down Division Street. "Can we stop for hamburgers?" Boyd asked.

"Ask Aunt Trenace," Max suggested.

"Some of you still have homework, and you need baths, and I have tons of laundry to do," she said. "It's been a wonderful weekend, but…maybe some other time. Max, you're welcome to come inside. We could make sandwiches."

"All good things must come to an end," Max replied with a subtle bow. "I'd better swing by the station to see what's been happening."

When they reached her house, he helped carry the canvas bags into the house and turned to leave. The children refused to let him get away so easily.

"We want to say goodbye," Mickie insisted, reaching out to him. He knelt on one knee and Mickie, Boyd, George and Akeylah each gave him a hug. He looked at Terry and waited. The boy came to him and slid his arms cautiously around Max's neck, held him for a few seconds, then withdrew. In a flash he disappeared to the isolation of his bedroom.

"What about Aunt Trenace?" Mickie asked.

Max winked at Trenace. "Want to make it one hundred percent?"

"Do I have a choice?" she asked.

"Not if I have any say in the matter." When her hands settled just above his belt loops, he caught her cheeks in his hands and held her face gently, brushing her lips several times before releasing her. "Better than a hug," he murmured, then grinned at all the smiling children.

"Thank you for taking us, Max," she said.

"The pleasure was mine," he replied.

MRS. SEWELL PHONED with news about George and Boyd. Two sets of prospective parents had expressed interest in the boys. "Please have them ready Saturday morning. They'll stay the weekend at least, maybe longer. And Akeylah will be going back with her mother on Friday. Oh, yes, I've been able to set up a hearing for you about Mickie a week from Tuesday at ten o'clock."

Max didn't call or stop by, but his handsome image on the six o'clock news reminded her of her growing affection toward him. On Wednesday's news Mickie was featured as *Wednesday's Child*, and they recorded it.

On Saturday she helped Boyd and George pack small canvas totes with enough clothes to last for several days. "The couples know what school you go to, so you may be staying for a full week."

"What if they don't like us?" Boyd asked.

"I love you both," she replied, embracing them together. "Why wouldn't they love you, too? But you'll have to give them a chance to get to know you."

The doorbell rang.

"Are you ready?" she asked.

Both boys grew quiet, not their usual demeanor.

"Will I ever see Boyd again?" George asked.

"Do they know about my burns?" Boyd asked.

Tears filled Trenace's eyes as she gazed at them. They had become like brothers since coming to her home a week apart several months earlier.

She took their hands. "Boyd, you're a handsome boy, and yes, they know about the burns and the need for more surgery. That's why Max and you talked about it on camera. And, George, I'm sure you'll see each other again. Now, if we don't answer the doorbell soon, they might leave. Do you want them to go away?"

Both boys nodded, and Boyd added, "We can go outside and play like we usually do and wait for Max to bring some pizza."

"Max called last night," she replied. "He's busy this weekend. He flew to California to see his own children." She hurried from the bedroom to the front door. Standing on the porch were two couples, well dressed and in their late thirties. After introductions she called the boys and reintroduced everyone.

She watched as the two boys trudged along between the two prospective sets of parents, looking for all the world as if they were being led away to separate jail cells.

She waited until they had driven away in opposite directions, then closed the door. Now her charges were down to two.

Terry had been examined by Dr. Brockman, who had recommended an appointment with a husband-and-wife team of professionals.

"She's a registered nurse with a Ph.D. in early childhood development," Lau Brockman had said after taking Trenace to his office while a nurse had stayed with the child. "He's an M.D. who went back to school and got a Ph.D. in education. They've worked with children like Terry before. Patterning is part of their program. I think they can help him." He'd rocked his chair a few times then leaned forward. "Max told me what happened with him and Terry behind our house." He'd given her a quick rundown. "Max is a remarkably perceptive man. How is he?"

She'd looked at her hands. "I haven't seen him since our trip to your farm. He's busy. So am I."

"Find time for him, Trenace. You need each other."

That conversation seemed doubly empty now as she walked through the quiet house to the backyard. Akeylah had returned to her mother, and Mrs. Sewell had told Trenace it would be a while before more children would be assigned to her.

The days slipped by. She heard nothing about Boyd and George and reluctantly accepted the fact that they had passed out of her home for good. During the week, while Mickie was at school, she began to work with Terry doing some basic exercises she had learned during his first visit to the Spokane Redevelopment Clinic, a name that concealed its true purpose well.

She discovered that if she lay on the carpet with him and worked through some of the routines, he would follow her and cooperate. But his attention span was startlingly short. They were both glad to take the weekend off. Each session ended with Terry giving her a hug that was so light she could hardly feel the touch of his small arms. The "hug exercise," as Terry had named it, had been his input to the program.

As Trenace cleared away the breakfast dishes on Saturday morning, the phone rang, and she grabbed it on the second ring.

"I want to stop by for a few minutes later today," Max said. "I have something for Terry, but I hate to come with nothing for the other children. Can you give me some suggestions?"

She told him about Boyd and George's departure. "Terry and Mickie are the only ones left. Mickie has gone mad about sweatshirts and T-shirts with animal stuff on them. We've had a hard time squeezing the money out for one from her clothing allotment. They're expensive. But she's a budding artist, too. Perhaps a few art supplies or a sketch pad. Max, you don't have to spend money on them."

"I'll be there about seven tonight," he replied. "I have to cover a story this afternoon."

When he rang the doorbell, Mickie opened the door. "Aunt Trenace said you wouldn't be bringing pizza, so we baked chicken instead. It was pretty good, but not as good as pizza." She spotted the sack. "Whatcha got?"

Trenace watched silently as he handed Mickie a sack from one of the finer department stores in Spokane.

"The clerk insisted they were the latest rage among preteen girls," Max said. Mickie ripped the package open. Out spilled two sweatshirts. One was pink with fuzzy gray cats playing with balls of multicolored yarn scattered across the front. The other was a soft shade of turquoise with white and brown Arabian horses racing across the front panel of deeper peacock blue. Mickie squealed with delight.

"The clerk called them Animated Spumoni," he explained with a shrug. "I'm out of practice buying for girls."

Terry lingered by the kitchen entrance. "This is for you," Max said. He pulled from behind his back a stuffed gray koala bear about two feet fall. "He gets lonely at night and hates to sleep alone."

Terry edged closer. "Do I get to keep him?" he asked, reaching out cautiously to touch the soft fake fur.

"He's yours, no strings attached, not even a hug," Max said, giving him the animal.

Mickie had pulled one of the sweatshirts on over her T-shirt. "And what did you bring for Aunt Trenace?" she asked.

"He doesn't have to bring me gifts in order to come visit you children," Trenace said, anxious to shift attention back to them.

"I brought you something, anyway." Max reached into the pocket of his blue windbreaker and pulled out a thin paper sack. "I should have had it gift wrapped, but the store was closing and the clerk was a grouch and didn't even offer me a box." He shook the sack. "Hold out your hand, Mrs. McKay."

Chewing her lower lip, she held out her hand as Max tipped the sack upside down and shook it. Out tumbled a gold chain, its links glittering as it came to rest in her palm. "Max, I can't accept this. It's beautiful, but…" She looked up at him. "What can I say?"

"Try a simple thank-you." He retrieved the chain and stepped behind her. His warm fingers caressed her neck as he worked the clasp.

Will he kiss me? In front of the children?

"Wow," Mickie said. "That's almost as neat as my shirts."

Trenace touched the cool chain resting against the base of her throat. "Thank you, Max."

He stepped away and stuck his hands into the pockets of his windbreaker. "I can't stay. I'm doing the ten o'clock news. That new anchor has personal problems. It's getting a little tiresome, but Josh Temple is in a bind. Night, kids."

He turned to Trenace. "One of these days our turn will come." He brushed her cheek and closed the door softly behind him as he left.

A JUDGE PRESIDED over the adoption hearing in his chambers, with only Mrs. Sewell and another social worker, a court reporter and Trenace present. The social worker, whom Trenace had met once before, described Mickie's case history and future medical needs.

"Mrs. Sewell, you requested time," the judge said, looking at the papers in the open folder on his desk. "I believe you oppose this request. Please give your reasons."

Mrs. Sewell patted her gray hair. "It's been my experience, Judge Lusk, that foster parents make notoriously poor adoptive parents. They get emotionally involved, and that can result in favoritism with the newly adoptive child. The foster children are often neglected, or the natural children become jealous, and all kinds of harm can come to everyone. When it doesn't work out, and the foster parent decides they've made a mistake, everyone is hurt. Adoptions are difficult to undo, as you well know, and it's been my experience that foster parents should remain where they do the best job for the county. Mrs. McKay is a single woman, a recently divorced woman, actually. She's already complained about financial problems. There's also a man—"

The judge held up his hand. "I'll take note of all these. Mrs. McKay, what do you have to say? Most foster parents are couples. Won't this create a hardship on you. What about your divorce? Have you been alone long? Did Mrs. Sewell know you were having marital problems?"

Trenace tried to answer honestly but without details. "My marital status has no bearing on my ability to be a parent to Mickie. I've been a foster parent for more than fifteen years. I love all the children who come to stay with me. My own two children are in college, and they love Mickie also. I'll manage."

The judge looked dubious as he continued to stare at her.

"She's lived with me for three years," she explained. "I've seen her blossom. She's on the verge of becoming a teenager. I understand her, and I love her as my own daughter."

The judge asked several questions about her financial affairs, but she couldn't tell if he was satisfied with her answers or not. After a brief recess, the judge returned to the courtroom.

"Adoption is a noble gesture, Mrs. McKay, but if I gave my recommendation to this adoption request, you'd be in a financial bind each time the child needed hospitalization. Can you truly say that you can afford it? Be realistic. We wouldn't have need for foster homes if single parents assumed their responsibilities properly, now would we? Listen to your caseworker. Mrs. Sewell has the wisdom of her years behind her. I've been on the bench for almost thirty years, and it's been my experience that it seldom works out when foster parents get emotionally involved with their charges. You'd better serve the child's needs by remaining her foster parent."

He leaned forward and stared at Trenace. "Petition denied." With a rap of his gavel he left the chambers.

Early the next morning Trenace received a registered letter from the Health and Human Services local agency headquarters. Inside was a form letter, signed by Mrs. Sewell, that her recertification was being withheld pending an investigation. Mrs. Sewell had put a red check mark on the box that read, "Change in suitability within the foster home environment."

Trenace had the legal right to file a protest or request a hearing if she chose. The proper forms were enclosed. She had thirty days to respond.

When the phone rang that evening, Trenace's nerves were frayed. "I'm afraid Boyd's placement isn't working," a cool Mrs. Sewell said. "I have no other place for him, so I'll be bringing him back tomorrow after I pick him up at school."

"What went wrong?" Trenace asked, her heart aching for Boyd.

"You know how overbearing he can be," Mrs. Sewell said, sniffing loudly to emphasize her opinion. "Not only did he make no attempt to get along with the couple's birth child, but he kept telling the woman she did things wrong."

In spite of the seriousness of the situation, she was overjoyed to have Boyd coming home. "And George? How is he?"

Mrs. Sewell sighed loudly. "Did he ever wet the bed with you?" she barked.

"Why, no...well, once or twice when he first came," Trenace admitted. "But he's been fine since."

"He has accidents every night," Mrs. Sewell said. "They've tried everything from withholding liquids to making him do the laundry. Nothing seems to help."

"He's an insecure little boy who craves love," Trenace said. "He's with strangers. Please tell them never to spank him or hit him. He's been physically abused. Did you tell them?"

"I have his file," Mrs. Sewell said. "But parents need to establish their own set of rules. George must learn to adjust."

"Those rules must be tempered with understanding," Trenace replied. She wanted to ask for George to be brought back, too, but suppressed the impulse.

"I've found a possible home for Terry," Mrs. Sewell continued. "Dr. and Mrs. Brockman want to have him for a visit next weekend."

"The Brockmans? I had no idea. We were there two weeks ago. Dr. Brockman said nothing when I took Terry for an examination. Did you know that Mrs. Brockman lost a son several months ago?"

"Our clients don't report to you, Mrs. McKay," Mrs. Sewell said. "Tell him I'll pick him up Saturday morning."

"They aren't coming to get him?" Trenace asked.

"The doctor will be in Seattle for a medical conference," Mrs. Sewell said. "Mrs. Brockman said she'd like to be alone with Terry for the first day or two to see how everything works out. I think it's a marvelous idea, don't you?"

"What does Dr. Brockman think?"

"Why, dear, I've already told you he's in Seattle, but she assures me he gives his total support. And besides, it's not as if they're signing the final papers. She has my number, and I can always go get him if necessary. I visited their farm last night and met her and the little girls. Aren't they sweet little things? Perfect little angels. I think going to a home and having two pretty little sisters to love is just what a child like Terry needs."

THURSDAY AFTERNOON Mrs. Sewell delivered a sulky Boyd back to the McKay door, his clothes in a paper sack.

"Where's his athletic bag?" Trenace asked.

Boyd glared at Mrs. Sewell. "Chester stole it and stabbed it with his pocketknife, but he lied and said he didn't. We had a fight. That's why they kicked me out, but I don't care. I'd rather be here." He looked pleadingly at Trenace. "Is George back yet?"

Trenace hugged him warmly. "Not yet, Boyd. There are oatmeal cookies and orange juice in the kitchen. Terry is out back, and Mickie will be home any minute now."

"Even Terry would be better than that son of a bitch Chester," Boyd said angrily.

"Boyd, how dare you talk that way," Mrs. Sewell exclaimed. "Where ever did you learn words like that? Here?"

"Chester called me that all the time," he spit back.

Trenace put a cautionary hand on his shoulder. "Put your clothes away, and you can go out back and say hi to Terry."

He ran down the hallway to the familiar bedroom door and tossed the sack in toward the bed, then raced to the kitchen.

Mrs. Sewell gazed at Trenace. "In case your recertification doesn't come through we've started looking for new foster homes for Boyd and Mickie. Terry will be fine with the Brockmans."

MRS. SEWELL LOOKED down her nose at the boy clutching a large koala bear and frowned. "Isn't he a little old to be clinging to a stuffed toy?"

Trenace laid her hand gently on Terry's shoulder. "Max gave him the bear. Please let him take it."

Mrs. Sewell's scowl deepened, bringing her gray eyebrows together over the bridge of her nose. "Mrs. Brockman is expecting a normal nine-year-old boy."

"He's upset enough about leaving," Trenace warned her. "I called Michelle and told her about the bear." She met Mrs. Sewell's disapproving eyes. "She'll ask why he left it behind."

"Then bring it," the older woman said curtly.

An hour later the doorbell rang again. Maybe Terry's back, Trenace thought, but when she opened the door, her daughter Suzanne and another young woman smiled back at her. At their feet were two suitcases. Suzanne, her auburn hair darker and less curly than Trenace's, threw her arms around Trenace and squeezed, then kissed her on her cheek.

"What are you doing home from school?" Trenace asked.

"I brought my roommate home to meet you." Suzanne smiled, her blue eyes sparkling. "This is Benita Revello. She's an exchange student from Milan. I've been telling her all about the kids you take care of, and we don't have classes on Monday, so we came home. Gee, Mom, I didn't get home all summer. Don't look so surprised. We didn't decide to come until after midnight." She shrugged. "Sorry I didn't call. Maybe you don't have any spare beds...but we could sleep on the floor in the living room."

Trenace waved the two young women inside and took them to the bedroom Terry had been using. "Only Mickie and Boyd are here," she said. "We have plenty of room, and you're always welcome."

As they unpacked, Suzanne glanced up at her mother. "How's life been treating you, Mom?"

"Fine." Her recertification uncertainty, the denial of Mickie's adoption, Max's absence and her concern for George and Terry hung heavily over her, but she refused to burden her daughter with her problems. She turned away, excused herself and hurried to her own bedroom. Sitting perfectly still on the edge of the bed, she gulped deep breaths and tried to regain her composure.

Through the closed door she heard the front doorbell ring. *Grand Central Station,* she thought, hoping Suzanne would answer it. *Probably Mrs. Sewell returning one of the boys.*

MAX LEANED against the doorjamb and waited for Trenace to come greet him. He'd stayed away too long. He knew that now, but he'd needed to put distance between them in order to think rationally. Finally he'd come up with three plans to solve their problems. One he'd already implemented. That left two to sell her on if she would listen to him and not get headstrong.

The young woman who greeted him knocked him off-stride for several seconds. "Ah . . . is Trenace . . . McKay here?" He grinned. "You must be her daughter."

The young woman smiled back.

"Is . . . your mother here?"

She extended her hand. "I'm Suzanne McKay. Some people say I favor my mom. Sure, she's here, but she's a basket case. Do you know why? Say, who are you? You look familiar. Have we met?"

He accepted her confident handshake. "Your mother and I. . ." He looked away. "We're friends." Belatedly her remark registered with him. "Why is she a basket case?"

"Beats the heck out of me," Suzanne replied. "I asked how she was and she said 'fine,' then looked as if she was going to burst into tears." Suzanne grinned. "Is she upset over you?"

Noncommittally he asked, "Can I speak to her?"

"I'll ask her if she's receiving visitors." Suzanne's gaze lingered on the logo on his windbreaker, then whipped back to his face, grinning as she wagged a flame-red nail at him. "You're Max Tulley from KSPO Channel Nine. We get you on cable at the dorm. How did *my mother* ever get to know you?"

"We went to grade school together."

She continued to study him.

"I'm glad you enjoy keeping up with the news," he added.

She laughed, and the dark-haired girl standing beside her giggled. "It's not the news that makes all the girls in our dorm.gather around the television set. It's the anchor," Suzanne said. "I'll tell Mom you're here. Were you two planning to go out?"

Max's mind raced ahead. "What if I said we'd planned to go away for the weekend but couldn't get a sitter? She's been working too hard. Would you two ladies like to help me kidnap her for a day or two? I'd pay a fair price in advance for your services."

"My mother kidnapped by the best hunk on Spokane television?" Suzanne clasped her hands dramatically over her bosom. "You betcha. Bribe us with enough to bring in hamburgers or something and gas to get back to school, and it's a deal."

She extended her hand again, and he accepted it, then handed her two twenties.

She grinned. "Gourmet hamburgers?"

"If that's your pleasure," he said, liking her more all the time and wondering if his own daughters would get along with her.

"How long have you and my mother...you know?" she asked.

"We met again in July. She's a . . . fine woman."

"She's a super mom," Suzanne agreed, "but she needs excitement in her life. I've said all along that she stays cooped up here day and night with no one to spill her deepest emotions to. A woman needs a man's company once in a while, even a woman as mature as my mother."

He chuckled. "She might not want to go."

"Leave her to us," Suzanne said. "We'll present your case and help her pack a bag. The kids are out back, only there's not very many of them, so she has no argument that Benita and I can't handle the situation."

He felt indebted to this vivacious daughter of Trenace McKay. Meeting her was serendipity at its best. With her unexpected offer to help, his case might very well turn out better than he'd hoped. He went out to the yard and visited with Boyd and Mickie, who brought him up-to-date on where the other children had gone.

"She's ready, Max Tulley," Suzanne called from the sliding glass door. "She thinks we've all gone crazy, but I said every woman deserves to be impulsive once in her life." She laughed and disappeared into the house again.

Trenace stood in the middle of the living room, looking forlorn in her own home. She wore a knit sport shirt with narrow yellow-and-white stripes and a pair of yellow chino slacks. In one hand she clutched her navy windbreaker. An overnight case sat nearby with a paperback novel balanced on its handle.

He vowed to see that she would never read a single page.

She raised her chin, and he resisted the urge to kiss it. "Where are we going?" she asked. "The girls need to know."

He turned to Suzanne, who stepped closer, a notepad and pen poised to take down the information.

"Tomorrow we'll be at my uncle's farm near Spangle." He rattled off the number.

Suzanne arched a slender eyebrow at him. "And tonight?"

"That depends on this afternoon," he said. "We'll be in touch later. She'll be safe, so don't worry."

He picked up Trenace's case in one hand, grabbed her elbow in the other and nodded to the two young women. "Thanks, ladies. I owe you more than you'll ever know. When we come back, your wish is my command...within reason." He grinned and ushered Trenace out the house and toward the street.

TRENACE SANK into the corner of her seat in the minivan, seemingly content to study the passing countryside. The miles slid beneath the wheels. Max took Highway 195 to Spangle, then turned east onto a narrow paved road. He glanced over at her, but her eyes were closed. He sensed her isolation and wondered what problems could be so burdensome to make her unwilling to share them with him. His heart ached for her.

He wanted to pull over to the side of the road and haul her into his arms. That could come later, after he showed her the farmhouse and described his plans. What if he'd misjudged her completely? Was he about to become the world's biggest fool?

They drove past harvested fields of grain, the golden stubble glistening in the late-morning sunshine. He applied the brakes and turned into one of the farms. It looked like scores of others in the area, but to Max it was special because he'd been born there. They rolled to a stop in front of a white frame house, and he turned off the engine.

She looked at the house. "Isn't this where you grew up?"

"Yes." He left the van and walked around to open her door. Taking her hand, he led her up the steps and onto the porch. He pulled a key from his pocket and unlocked the front door. Inside, the house was filled with light flowing in through the windows that ran the entire front of the house. "Without furniture it seems bigger than I remembered," he said. "Come see the kitchen. My mother insisted she had to see her kids at the table when she stood at the stove, so my dad came up with this arrangement." He waved his hand to include a rectangular room that ran the width of the east side of the house.

"It's very big," she said. "I didn't know you came from a large family."

"My folks built this house to fit their dreams, but my mother got sick after the fourth child and had to have surgery. It broke her heart for a while."

She climbed the wide staircase to the upstairs and peeked into six spacious bedrooms, two bathrooms and a laundry room.

"Mom always said the dirty clothes came from up here, so why not be able to do the laundry up here, too," he said, following Trenace through the house and trying to interpret her thoughts.

She remained silent as she walked down the back set of stairs and opened another door. Sun streamed into the room.

"This is where my mother did her quilting, and my dad helped her make templates," he said. "She taught him to operate the sewing machine, and together they made many quilts during the cold winters while the fields lay fallow.

There are two more rooms down here that could be bedrooms or an office or whatever. Anyone in a wheelchair would love one of these rooms for a bedroom, and we can add a ramp leading to the porches.''

She glanced at him strangely. "We...?"

He'd slipped with that remark. Premature, to say the least. Outside, he showed her a shop and double garage. In the distance stood a red barn gradually deteriorating from neglect. "It needs a lot of work, but its support structure is sound."

She rubbed her hands nervously. "Why did we come here?"

He sat down on the first step of the back porch and patted the space beside him. When she settled next to him, he studied the wheat stubble surrounding the house. "The man who leases the farm from my folks wanted to buy the place, but he planned to tear the house down to save on paying taxes. So I bought it last week."

She stood up and stared at him. "The whole farm?"

He leaned back to admire her. At least he'd snapped her out of her lethargy. "Just the house and twenty acres. I'm having a fence installed that should keep kids and dogs from roaming. We can put in another one closer to the house for a play yard."

"We?" She turned to follow his gaze to the fields. "Why would you want to live out here so far away from your job and all alone? You must have made a bundle when you sold your home in Southern California. You can buy a lovely house in Spokane, close to a country club and so forth."

"I hate golf," he said, his temper rising. This wasn't working out at all the way he'd planned. "I thought I'd like apartment living, but I don't like people crowded next to me. I can hear their arguments through the walls, and

I certainly don't want to have golf balls crashing through my windows."

He saw a hint of a smile tugging at the corners of her mouth.

"You probably need a tax write-off," she murmured.

It was time to lay out his cards before she came to her own conclusions. He took her hand. "I want you to move here and bring your children and turn this place into a foster home. I have the money and the place and you have the expertise. Are you interested?"

She stared at his hand holding hers. "That's absolutely crazy, Max, but it's a sweet thought. Anyway, I could never afford to furnish a house this large."

"You could if you sold your house in Spokane. What you don't have, I do, and we could work it out...financially, I mean, but only if you're willing. Maybe you don't like the house or the location."

She slid her hand from his and buried it in her jacket pocket. "It's a marvelous place, but Mrs. Sewell is threatening to pull my license." She crossed her arms over her waist. "They rejected my request to start adoption proceedings for Mickie."

"Why on earth would they do that?" he asked. No wonder she had been depressed. "Why didn't you call me?" *You could have called her,* he chided himself. But he'd been too busy making plans, so she'd had to carry her burden all alone, unaware of how much he cared.

"The judge said single parents can't afford to adopt children, especially one as handicapped as Mickie," she explained, hugging herself tighter. "Mrs. Sewell took Boyd and George away, but Boyd couldn't get along with the family's other child and she brought him back home, and now she's trying to place Terry. But what he needs is long-term treatment and a safe environment. She sent

Akeylah back to her mother, and by now she's probably terrified again, if not by Bubba then by some other boyfriend who can't be bothered with her.''

He stepped closer, wanting to take her in his arms.

She looked across the few feet that separated them, and he saw the hurt in her eyes. Did she hold him responsible for her predicament? He should have used discretion in the front yard, not looked at her so hungrily at the podium, kept his distance and maintained his professionalism. He'd never become involved with a subject before. But Trenace was no abstract ''subject,'' to be reported on and then forgotten. She was a woman whom he found enchanting, beautiful, strong—a woman who made him feel masculine and complete again.

''Max, I feel so empty,'' she admitted, her eyes glistening. ''I'm drained. I've never felt like this before. I need to be filled again, but nothing seems to work. If I lose my license, the children will be taken away. I know they're only mine for a little while, but for that while I love them. I want to see them grow up healthy and strong and safe. Is that so wrong?''

He put his arm around her shoulders and walked her several yards away from the house. ''Trena, look at this house. See its potential. Come live here with me, and you'll have room for even more children. This house will accommodate ten or more easily.''

She laughed cynically. ''Now you're talking crazy. One reason Mrs. Sewell wants to take my license away is because I'm divorced. Now you want me to come live here with you and bring the children into this? She'd consider it a den of iniquity, without a doubt. We were seen kissing once in the yard, and she thinks we make love around the clock. She's a dirty old woman if I ever met one.''

"Forget her." He took her hand again and spun her around. "Listen to me, Trena. You haven't heard a word I've said, not really. While I was in California I made up my mind about certain matters that have been troubling me greatly. I had to get back here and take care of some of the loose ends before I could see you again."

"You didn't have to stay away," she said. "I missed you very much. Friends should help each other when they have problems. Just because I didn't tell you about Mickie didn't mean—"

He shook her gently. "We met in July. Do you remember?"

"Of course," she replied. Her mouth opened, but he shook his head to silence her.

"Did you feel the chemistry between us?"

Slowly she nodded. "From the first," she confessed.

"Do I have habits that are so offensive they repulse you?"

Her lips softened. "No, but then we haven't been together all that much."

"That's about to change."

"But Mrs. Sewell is threatening to—"

"Don't think about Mrs. Sewell. We can adopt Mickie and still qualify as foster parents. Will you marry me, Trena?"

"Marry you?" Her eyes looked like those of a trapped wild animal whose death sentence was about to be rescinded. "But why, Max?"

"Because... I love you!"

CHAPTER TWELVE

"MAX, HAVE YOU LOST your mind?" His declaration was the last thing she'd expected. "What would your children think?"

"I told them about you last weekend," he said. "Since their mother died, they've only thought of me as their father, an old man who's turning gray. But I sent them the clipping and photo from the newspaper, so it wasn't a complete surprise. At first they thought I had caught some kind of Rocky Mountain Fever, but when I told them more about you, they came around. Next?"

She stepped free of his hands. "I . . . I can't think when you touch me," she admitted. "Max, it just won't work. Look at yourself. You're a star, a walking success story. I've never even made any money."

"Success is measured in nobler terms than money," he countered.

"I've always stayed home."

He grabbed her hand before she could step back. "You work in a house. I work at a television station. We've both recognized our talents and made the most of them."

"But I'm just a housewife and mother."

"You're a woman who can heal abused children, who can help them face the world, a world that is often cruel and heartless. Trena, you have a heart big enough to love any child who comes your way." He took her other hand.

"Can you find room in your heart to love me? I'll return it tenfold."

She didn't know how she took the first steps to bring them together. Maybe she floated through the air. His pledge of love was all that mattered at that moment. She sank against him, and his arms tightened around her. When she gazed up into his eyes, the emotions reflected there tore her heart to shreds.

He couldn't love her any more than she loved him. Yet something held her back from telling him so.

Her gaze shifted to his mouth. She craved to know its touch, to trace the tiny grooves that time had carved down his cheek, to caress his face freely, without fear of rejection or discovery.

Blinded by his closeness, she opened her mouth slightly and reached upward, eager to taste what lay ahead if she were brave enough to risk letting her heart guide her.

When she felt the first tentative caress of his mouth on hers, a tremor raced through her. Her hands shook as she slid them around his neck and yielded to him. Surely she was floating through a new universe where only the two of them lived? Then she didn't think at all as his mouth massaged hers, stirring a fire in her body that consumed her where she stood.

When the kiss ended, he smiled. "Does this mean yes?"

Heat burned her cheeks as she kissed him lightly. "If I went home and gave it careful thought, I'd turn you down, because none of this makes any sense. It's illogical. Yet if the foster home license *is* renewed and we *could* adopt Mickie as a couple, then I…we…at least you…"

"Trena," he said, cupping her face in his hands. "I'm not asking you to say the words if you don't want to say them now. That will come with time. Maybe it's too soon for you to trust a man. Time will take care of that, too.

We're neither young, naive, nor innocent. We know life can be cruel, but it can also bring us great joy if we give it a try. I need you, and I think you need me. So here we go again. Will you marry me?''

"Yes," she said, surprised by the strength of her reply.

THEY LUNCHED at a tiny café in Palouse. The food was hearty and delicious, but they didn't linger. As they traveled, they recalled the years of their childhoods, both surprised at the many mutual memories.

"Max," she said, squeezing his hand, "you were always that cute boy who sat behind me, but I was too shy to turn around unless the teacher was in the back of the room."

"I knew every freckle on your shoulders," Max teased. "I always wondered how far down your back they went." He glanced at her, then returned his attention to the road. "I reserved a room at a motel in Hood River. I thought we'd enjoy ourselves more if we were on neutral ground. I can cancel if you'd rather."

"No, that's fine. We might as well get this over with."

He drove over the Columbia River bridge into Oregon. "Trena, this isn't judgment day."

She stared down at the water. "I'm afraid. I want to spend the night with you, but what if we're...incompatible? Owen and I made love and we satisfied each other most of the time, but there were never fireworks or sky rockets or exploding volcanoes like you read about."

He glanced toward her, his eyes narrowing. "Are you trying to say that sometimes it was boring?"

"Well...yes, over the years."

She had half expected his anger or ridicule, but instead he began to chuckle. "Are you trying to say he rolled off, fell asleep and snored."

She stared straight ahead. "Sometimes."

"I suppose all men are guilty of that from time to time," he admitted. "But do you really think it will be that way for us? I promise that I won't fall asleep before you do, and if I snore, you can kick me out of bed. Compatibility comes with getting to know each other. When two people make love... if they try, if they make adjustments, they work everything out. Damn it, Trena, there's more than one way to make love. If your ex-husband didn't know that, the hell with his ignorance."

Not long after they reached the interstate highway, the landscape changed from farms to canyon walls that caught the late-afternoon sun and formed strange pink and purple shadows across the highway.

"This is beautiful," Trenace said, anxious to make amends for her earlier tactlessness. "I'm glad you insisted we get away. I just didn't expect it so soon. I've never been to Oregon."

"Didn't you and Owen go places?"

"He liked to fish, so we went to Moses Lake again and again and again," she replied. "When my children were older, I begged off, then I started taking in foster kids and that tied me down."

He chuckled. "With the van we can load them all up and do some sight-seeing. Children should expand their horizons. So should pretty ladies who don't like boring lovemaking."

Her head jerked around, uncertain as to what she might find. He was grinning from ear to ear. "I've been contemplating what I could do to keep you interested. I wouldn't want to try to kiss you and have you yawn in my face. I don't know if my manhood could cope with that.''

She began to smile. He didn't seem to realize that even his slightest glance could make her heart race. Thoughts of being alone with him in a motel room took her breath away.

He took her hand and squeezed it. "I drove out this way for a story shortly after I returned to Spokane, but it never aired. Jocko and I found a fantastic little restaurant right on the point, where you can sit and eat and watch the wind surfers. I decided then that if I ever met a woman I could love, I would take her there for dinner and let the evening take its course.''

"And did you ever?"

His gaze lingered, making her feel as if she were being seduced. "Not until today."

AN HOUR LATER, as they pulled into the restaurant's parking lot, Trenace looked down at her slacks and sporty knit top. "I didn't bring a change of clothes, just a nightgown and toothbrush and . . . stuff."

"You're fine," he said, taking her elbow. "The sun will be setting soon. The view will be unbelievable."

Inside, they were fortunate enough to be seated at the window. As they studied the menus, he looked up. "We can come back next summer when it's warm enough to sit outside."

Their dinners of grilled salmon steaks were delicious and Max and Trenace didn't talk much as they ate. Through the window they watched several wind surfers in wet suits taking a last sail in the twilight. "They remind me of hot air balloons. I did a story on them once, too."

Max could feel her glance at him occasionally, but he concentrated on the surfers, their bright sails billowing in the breeze. He'd planned too much. The moments they'd shared had all been spontaneous. Now he felt like a lothario about to pounce on his victim.

The waitress returned to remove their plates. "I'll bring the dessert tray," she said.

He stopped her. "How about two Irish coffees instead, and then you can bring the check. Wait, here's my card," he said, and handed over his gold card.

When the coffee arrived, served in tall, stemmed glasses, Trenace took a sip. "I canceled both my credit cards," she murmured. "I didn't want to be tempted to overspend."

"Then we'll put your name on mine," he said. "I trust you."

"Not until after—we haven't talked about when."

He stroked the vein in the back of her hand. "Soon."

"Max, I don't know how we'll handle finances. Do we mix them? Keep separate accounts? Or do we have mine, yours and ours?" She told him the amount she received for each child.

"That's all?" he asked.

"I'm not responsible for medical expenses, and sometimes I get a clothing allocation. If grocery prices would just stay steady, I'd manage, but they keep going up. Over the years I've built up an emergency clothes closet, so we get by."

He shook his head. "I don't know how you keep the heat on in winter. I suppose you qualify for commodities."

She smiled. "Butter and powdered milk, sometimes honey and cheese. We never know for sure from one month to the next. Once I got cornmeal, but it had bugs in it and I threw it out. I won't take the butter. The government seems determined to load the children up with cholesterol. Is it possible there's a conspiracy to make them die young from narrowing of the arteries so they won't be a drag on society?"

"Trenace, how can you say that?" He leaned back in his chair, studying her demeanor. "Maybe I'll talk Josh Temple into doing an investigative report on that."

"The consequences of adopting Mickie will be worse," she continued. "Not only would we lose the foster care payment, but we'd have to assume all future medical expenses. We can try to petition the court for special consideration, but the court seldom authorizes such conditions. Considering what they would save, you'd think they'd shove the children through the system's pipeline and get them into adopted homes as fast as they could. They could save millions, but then people like Mrs. Sewell would be out of their jobs. It's a crazy world, isn't it?"

He waved the waitress to their table again. "Two more Irish coffees, please." He laid several bills on the tray.

As they sipped the coffees, he grinned. "You haven't scared me off yet." He told her how much he'd cleared when he sold his California home. Her face blanched. "I have two years to reinvest in a home or pay taxes on the proceeds, so I'm saving a bundle buying the house and land at Spangle. I sold all my furniture in California, and now my apartment here has rental furniture. Do you have an old worn sofa to contribute?"

She frowned. "That's all I have—old worn-out stuff."

He glanced at his watch. "It's almost ten. Shall we leave?"

She finished her coffee, and he escorted her to the van. Within minutes they were at the motel.

"It looks expensive," she said.

"I'm paying," he replied, taking her hand. "Think of this as our honeymoon. The technicality of the wedding can come later."

After he registered, he carried their two small cases to the room. He turned and found Trenace leaning against the closed door, a glazed expression on her face.

"Are you okay?" he asked, touching her pale cheek.

She closed her eyes for several seconds, then opened them again. The blue of her iris was only a narrow rim around the midnight of her pupils. "I think the Irish coffee sneaked up on me," she said, smiling as she reached out to steady herself.

"Maybe you should lie down," he suggested, sliding his arm around her waist. Her jacket slid from her shoulders and fell to the floor. She kicked her shoes off and he followed suit. Unable to resist, he kissed the corner of her mouth.

When he felt her hands slide up beneath his shirt and touch his bare skin, he swallowed a lump and tried to maintain his composure. His body was responding with all the heat and lust of a seventeen-year-old. "How do you feel now?" he asked.

"Like I'm on fire," she said. "All the way from my toes to my shoulders. My knees are jelly, and my head is spinning."

"Maybe you shouldn't have had that second coffee."

"I like the feeling," she admitted, sliding her hand farther up under his shirt. When she touched his chest and found his nipples, he closed his eyes and groaned aloud. Her fingers stroked the scattering of hair on his chest on their way to trace the muscle toward his shoulder. She had become the seducer, but they were still dressed. He wanted her nude. Then he would switch roles and show her how exciting lovemaking could be.

"Wait," he said, whipping his shirt over his head. He tossed it on top of the abandoned navy jacket and turned to her again. She'd taken her own top off and now stood before him with only a pink lace bra covering her breasts, her aroused nipples thrusting against the sheer fabric.

Cupping her breasts in each hand, he pushed them up and stooped to kiss the swell he'd created. "You have a beautiful body."

She ran her fingers down his biceps and skipped across to his chest again. "I've wanted to do this for a terribly long time," she confessed. "When we danced and when we were outside at the Brockmans, I wanted to literally paw you."

"Then paw me now." He reached behind her and unfastened her bra. Her nipples were hard buttons. When he brushed his palms across them, her body trembled. He forced himself to stand still as she ran her hands over his torso, exploring each rib. When she leaned forward and began to nibble his chest, a surge of need filled his groin, and he felt as if he might explode.

In a frenzy they finished undressing each other and lay on the bed. "Close your eyes," he murmured, waiting until she followed his suggestion. "Pretend this is the first time for us. We don't know what to expect." His voice softened. "We must learn from each other, what feels good, what brings each other pleasure."

His gaze drifted down her naked body, lingering at her breasts while he kissed each one several times, working his way around the dark areola before taking the nipple into his mouth and bathing it with his tongue. He resented having to leave her breasts, but her waist and the indentation of her navel beckoned. He ran his fingers back and forth across it and drew circles on her flat abdomen until she began to move restlessly on the bed. He leaned down and kissed the auburn curls that covered her most intimate part.

The curves of her legs were deliciously shaped, but he'd known that from the first day he'd seen her. Sliding his hand between them, he caressed the satin skin of her inner thigh. She moaned softly, then began to pant as she shifted her hips and allowed him entry to the moist place his fingers sought. She gasped and her body jerked when he touched her swollen bud of desire. Then she fell back onto the bed again, panting.

Her hand slid down his body until she found his turgid manhood and began to explore it. When he looked at her face, her hands left him and clung to the sides of his head.

"Kiss me, Max. I want to know happiness. I need your love. I need you." She showered his face with kisses. "I'm on fire."

His mouth crushed hers, twisting to bring them closer. Their tongues danced a lovers' frenzy as he shifted his body over hers. Her legs opened to receive him, and as he slid into her, it struck him how perfectly they were made for each other.

"Oh, Trena, you've become a light in my life," he whispered. He was able to keep his thrusts easy and steady until he felt her begin to respond. He jerked his mouth away from hers, gritting his teeth as he tried to control himself, but when she arched against him, gasping and moaning wildly, he knew this conquest wasn't his alone, for her passion equaled his in every way.

TRENACE OPENED her eyes. For a moment she couldn't remember where she was. She rolled over, colliding with Max's warm body.

Memories of him undressing her washed over her . . . or had she undressed him? She slid her hand across his chest and pressed her face against his shoulder. She remembered feeling the rockets, seeing the fireworks, and their brilliance had blinded her while the exploding rockets had deafened her. Confused, she lay quietly, trying to still the rioting images that flashed through her brain.

She remembered him leaving the bed and going to the bathroom. She'd stretched and rolled to his side of the bed and placed her head on his pillow, savoring its warmth and the sensual fragrance that lingered, but what had happened after that?

Now she felt his body begin to shake beneath her, and she raised herself on her elbow. He was chuckling, his face relaxed and handsome even with a morning's stubble of dark beard.

"What's so funny?" she asked, running a finger from his temple down past his ear, then tracing the strong line of his jaw to the slight cleft in his chin.

"Do you remember what you did last night?"

She ducked her head. "Some of it."

He chuckled again. "Not the rockets. You told me about the rockets right after you caught your breath. I mean after that."

Puzzled, she looked at him again.

"You rolled over and went to sleep." His chuckles changed to laughter, and he caught her chin in his hands. "I came back from the bathroom, ready to make love again. You, my beautiful wife-to-be, were sound asleep."

She sat up, and the sheet fell to her waist. "I could never have done that, not after what happened."

He grinned. "Remind me not to give you Irish coffee again."

She kissed him, her mouth covering his and rekindling desire in both of them. "Surely I didn't snore?"

"No, so I let you stay on my side," he teased.

His hand began to tease her breast. "I have this incredible urge to make love to you again. Promise me you won't yawn in my face or fall asleep beneath me?"

She laughed. "I promise." She rolled on top of him, feeling his manhood throb against her. Her breasts pressed against his chest as she kissed him again, her tongue sliding between his teeth in search of his. "Who says I have to be beneath you? Didn't you say there are other ways to make love?"

"WILL WE MAKE IT to your aunt and uncle's place in time?" Trenace asked, clutching her paperback novel in her arms as they drove over the Columbia River again and into Washington State.

"I told them we'd be there after one," he said.

"I can't concentrate." She tossed the book into the back seat. "Max, about last night...and this morning?" She turned in the bucket seat. As she tucked her leg beneath her, her gaze shifted to his thigh. Memories of kissing it brought a tiny grin of pleasure to her full lips. "It was much more wonderful than I ever imagined. I truly feel renewed. Does that sound silly?"

He shook his head. "Don't try to analyze it, Trena. Be satisfied that it happened and that it can be that way again."

She smiled. "That sounds poetic."

"Today I feel like a poet. Life is good. We have each other, and we're on our way to partake of one of Aunt Agnes's famous fried chicken dinners. What more could a person want or need?"

She grinned impishly. "To know that what we shared had nothing to do with Irish coffee."

As THEY TURNED north on Division, he reached for her hand. "We should set a date for the wedding. Have any ideas?"

"The sooner the better if I'm going to keep my license." She studied his hand. "Max, if this doesn't work out, I want you to know you're free to go... only tell me... don't disappear."

"That's not a good attitude to have," he countered. "Maybe you're the one who will want to leave."

"But if I sell my house, breaking up won't be easy."

"Then put your energy into making it work." He concentrated on the traffic. "I'll make you a deal. If we have difficulties and need space, I'll be the one to leave. My apartment lease runs through next June, and there will be times I'll be working late and I might stay in town. That way I won't disturb you or the children. If something happens, if we decide we can't stand the sight of each other, I'll have a place to go, and you and the children can remain as long as you want. But mark my words, if anyone breaks up this marriage, it will have to be you." He pointed to the glove compartment. "There's a calendar in there. Let's look at it."

They settled on the last Saturday in October. "That gives us almost two weeks to make arrangements," Max said. "We can let our kids know so they can come. My parents, too, if they can get away. Do you know a place?"

She brightened. "Why not the new house?"

He grinned, relieved that she had stopped putting obstacles in their way. "Great. We'll go shopping for furniture some morning this week while the kids are in school. Call a Realtor and get your house listed. You and the children can move as soon as the furniture is delivered. We'll hire some men to move you. Let's keep the wedding simple."

"I agree," she replied, leaning to kiss his cheek. "I still think I'm going to wake up and find this is all a dream. It's too good to be true. When I watch you on television, I have difficulty reconciling that image with this. Why you and me?"

"Because this is our destiny," he replied. "I wish we had more time alone. I'm going to miss you like hell these next two weeks, but I'll be swamped at the station. We start production on the *Wednesday's Child* special tomorrow. We've hired two extra temporary people to help with the editing. We're going over all the filming we've done because we want to come up with fresh film of the same children. And we're going to feature foster parents. You didn't want to be one the last time I asked. Have you changed your mind?"

"I'd rather not. Wouldn't it be a conflict of interest?"

"We'll see," he murmured as he turned onto La-Crosse.

When they finally reached her block, she leaned forward. "Look. Someone's at the house. Do you think the girls had trouble?" She turned to him. "At least it isn't a police car. What if Mrs. Sewell found out we were away overnight? Max, I've never left the children alone at night before. Do you think we've been irresponsible?" she asked as they rolled into her driveway.

"I'll bring in everything," he said. "You go ahead and check the place out."

TRENACE TENSED when she spotted Lau and Michelle Brockman sitting at the kitchen table, their murmuring voices tight with emotion. His seemed almost harsh. Hers held a tremor that hinted at tears recently shed.

Lau stood up when Trenace entered. "Damn, I'm glad you're home. We have to talk to you...it's about Terry."

He looked down at Michelle's bowed head. "And what my wife has done."

"Yes, yes, of course," Trenace murmured, "but first how are the children? Is everyone all right?"

He sighed deeply. "Yes, but you should know that George is back, too. Mrs. Sewell dropped him off. We told her you'd gone out, and she said she was in a hurry. She didn't come inside."

"Where are your children?" Trenace asked. "Where is Terry?"

"He's in his room," Lau said. "George is outside, happy as a lark to be back. He and Boyd jumped on each other and wrestled to the ground, and when Boyd ended up on top, George broke into a fit of giggles and they went off to the swing set as if everything was just great. Our girls are out back, playing with Mickie and the boys."

Trenace frowned, glancing up as Max joined them. She explained the return of both boys as best she could.

Max told the other couple about their upcoming marriage. "It's two weeks from yesterday. You're invited. We won't be sending out invitations. I'll go see Terry while Trenace goes out back. You two stay right here, please, and when we come back, you can tell us all about this. Frankly, I didn't think Terry was in any condition to try adjusting to a new home."

Lau ran his long fingers through his thick brown hair. "Neither did I. This scheme was cooked up by Michelle and Mrs. Sewell without my knowledge. I came home from Seattle and found Michelle in tears, Maria with a big bruise on her stomach, Julia frightened silly, and Terry totally withdrawn again."

MAX DIDN'T KNOW what he might find when he knocked softly on Terry's bedroom door, but nothing could have prepared him for the sight of the little boy rocking back and forth in the corner of the closet, clutching the koala bear in his arms and rubbing his cheek against the toy's head. The sounds that came from the closet were more like a cornered animal than a human being.

Max closed the door, praying for wisdom to make the right overtures, to say the words that would convince the boy he was safe. Terry's blue eyes were blank, almost as if he were sightless. Not a sign of a tear dampened his cheeks.

Max reached out and stroked the koala bear's fuzzy cheek. "I'm glad to see you still have the bear."

The blank expression in the boy's eyes changed to anger as his hold tightened. "He's mine. You said he was mine."

"I told you that and I meant it." Max scratched the bear's other cheek and inched closer. When he was sitting cross-legged on the carpet at the closet door, he reached out and touched Terry's hair, but the boy jerked away.

"Don't touch me!"

"Does it hurt again?" Max asked.

Terry's chin began to quiver. "Sometimes."

"Terry, what happened?"

"They hate me," the boy said.

"But they asked you to come stay with them," Max argued. "They would never have done that if they hated you."

"She said she wanted me to be her little boy, but she kept hugging me, and it hurt. She wouldn't leave me alone. I . . . kicked her. And she hit me."

Startled, Max leaned forward. "Mrs. Brockman?"

Terry buried his chin against the top of the bear's head. "I don't care."

"What happened?"

"She sent me to a room and made me stay there even when I had to go to the bathroom, but I sneaked out twice to go. I liked it there 'cuz we were alone, just Bear and me. Then *that girl* came in and poked me with a stick. She poked me again and again, and I grabbed it, but it cut my hand." He opened his palm to show the swollen red welts. "It hurt and I kicked her and made her stop. She . . . she said she hated me and . . . and I didn't care, 'cuz I hated her too. I hate 'em all!"

"Did you hurt her?" Max asked.

"*She* said I did, and then Dr. Brockman came home and he was mad at all of us."

"What did he say when he saw your hand?" Max asked. "Did he put some medicine on it."

"I didn't show him, and *that girl* would have lied about it, anyway. He said I had to come back here. I don't want him to be my dad. I don't ever want to have a dad again. They're mean, and they hit you when they get mad even if you don't do nothing!"

Max asked for divine guidance as he looked at the intense, angry boy staring back at him. "Terry, someday you'll find a new dad. Aunt Trenace is going to help you get well, and then I'll bring the television camera here again, and you and I can talk. Some man will be watching who will say, 'That is a fine boy there. I think I'd like to be his dad.'"

"You're lying," Terry snarled. "I bet even you wouldn't want to be my dad."

"I . . . oh, Terry, don't give up. I . . . son," he said, trying not to give in to the emotional strain that tore at his innards. "Remember when you put your hands around my neck and hugged me?"

A tear slid down Terry's cheek. "It didn't hurt."

"What would you say if I asked if I could give you one of those hugs that doesn't hurt?" Max asked. "Just an easy one?"

"Why?"

Max ignored the tears that trickled from the corners of his own eyes. "Because I think you're a very special boy, and I love you, and when a person loves someone he likes to give them a hug once in a while, just an easy one, one that doesn't hurt."

"You promise?" Terry asked.

Max nodded. "But I'm too big to sit in the closet with you. Can you come out here?" He edged back a few feet to put distance between himself and the child, then held out his arms. *Be patient,* he thought as an undecided Terry stared at him over the head of the koala bear.

"How do I know it won't hurt?"

Max sighed. "I would never hurt you, son. Tell you what. I'll go sit on the bed and you can come to me over there. Come sit on my lap, and I'll give you an easy hug, and I'll stop whenever you want me to. I'm only asking for one little hug." He got to his feet and ambled to the bed, fluffed one of the pillows against the headboard and rested his tense shoulders against it.

The wait began.

When the toe of the boy's canvas shoe appeared through the closet door opening, Max closed his eyes and breathed easier. It took another five minutes for Terry to work his way across the carpet to where Max sat. "Will you sit on my lap?" Max asked.

Terry nodded.

Grunting, Max lifted the boy onto his legs and eased him closer. "You're getting to be a big boy. How old are you?"

"Mrs. Sewell says I'm nine...but I don't know my birthday."

Max grinned. "I'll bet when you're all grown up, you'll be as tall as I am."

Terry's eyes filled with doubt. "Will that be a long time?"

"About ten years," Max replied. "Can I hug you now?"

Terry nodded again.

Slowly Max put his arms around the child and eased him closer. "Will you put your head right here?" he asked, patting his chest.

Terry laid his brown head against Max, accepting Max's arms around him. He could feel the child beginning to relax. "Does that hurt?"

"No."

"How does it feel?"

"Kinda warm."

Max smiled and kissed the boy's head once, then leaned back against the wall and pillows again, enjoying the peacefulness of the moment. *Kinda warm... It's a beginning,* he thought.

Terry adjusted his position, gradually snuggling in Max's embrace. Resting his cheek against Max's shirt, he sighed. "I wish someday you could be my dad."

CHAPTER THIRTEEN

IN THE BACKYARD Trenace found herself tackled by an overly enthusiastic eight-year-old.

"Hi, Aunt Trenace," George exclaimed, gasping and out of breath. "Are you surprised to see me here again?"

She laughed. "Somehow I'm not." She squeezed him and kissed his cheek. "Do I dare ask why?"

"I wanted to come home and play with Boyd."

"But you and Boyd are always fighting and quarreling."

"But he's fun to fight with."

She sat down in the nearest lawn chair, and he leaned against the arm. "Didn't you like the family?" she asked.

"They were dumb," George explained. "We had to sit around in great big chairs with our feet on the floor, only mine wouldn't reach, and whenever I tried to lie on the floor to watch TV, Mrs. Olson made me get up and sit in a chair again, and they made me do my homework and..."

"I make you do your homework," she reminded him.

"But that's different. You help me. She said I had to figure it out by myself." He looked across the yard. "If I did something wrong, sometimes she wouldn't let me eat, and then one night..." He leaned closer and whispered, "I had an accident. I didn't mean to. I made my bed the next morning, but she found out, anyway, and got mad. I got a licking, and then two nights later I did it again."

He swung around to the other side of the chair. "I didn't like it there."

She ruffled his red hair. "I'm sorry it didn't work out, but I'm glad you're back. Terry's back, too." She sighed. "Annabelle seems to be the only one to find a good home."

George gazed at her solemnly. "Is Terry hiding in his room?"

"Max is with him." She looked across the yard at Mickie, Boyd and the two Brockman girls. "Do you like playing with Maria and Julia?"

"Yeah," George said. "They know how to wrestle, but I don't hurt them. You know how girls are. They cry easy." He turned around and did a back bend over the arm of the chair, laying his head on her lap. "Aunt Trenace?"

She reached down and flipped him across to the other side, then pulled him onto her lap. "What, George?"

"Mickie told us about you and Uncle Max, that you went away and now you're gonna get married. Are you?"

She laughed. "How did Mickie know that?" She tickled his stomach and he giggled.

"She could tell 'cuz you looked at him all moony-eyed each time he came on TV, and she overheard Max telling Dr. Brockman. Is Max gonna live here now?"

"Yes, we're going to get married. Then we're going to move to the country and all live in a big house."

"Will we have horses?" he asked. "I need a horse of my own. If I do my chores and be good, will you buy me a horse?"

"It's doubtful, George. Max is allergic to horses, and taking care of them is a lot of work. Maybe we can get a dog instead."

"I guess a dog would be okay, but it's not like having a horse. I gotta go play now." He wriggled off her lap and raced to the swings.

She headed toward the house. For a day and a half she and Max had been in a different world. Now reality had come crashing down around them. She doubted he realized how constant the children's needs would be.

She found him sitting at the table with the Brockmans. He looked up as she slid onto the bench beside him. "How's our boy?" she asked. He jerked to attention as if her words had caught him off guard. "What's wrong? Does he need me?"

Max shook his head. "He's asleep. We talked and he told me his version of what happened. He's very upset, but he let me hold him. That's progress for us. He fell asleep in my arms. Then I put him to bed. He needs a lot of help and a lot of unconditional love, doesn't he? He's the most confused child of all the ones I've met. Why is he so fearful of being hurt?"

Lau Brockman put his arm around Michelle and leaned against the table. "It's a brain injury that is so slight it often goes unnoticed. His nervous system is overly sensitive to touch, and what feels to us like a casual hold can be a painful twisting and burning to him. He learned early on to avoid it. Unfortunately that makes unsuspecting care-givers think he's rejecting them. None of us handles rejection well, and when it comes from a child, sometimes we react in kind."

Michelle looked away. "That's what I did," she confessed. "I've never struck a child before. I never thought I could, but every time we made a little headway I'd get all excited, and I did what felt natural—I tried to hug him. He flinched and jerked away and...and I...I was carrying my own guilt, anyway. I'd called Mrs. Sewell and asked her if we could have him come stay with us for a while. Terry looks a little like my twin brother Mike. I guess I was trying to use Terry to replace my baby. Joel was only two weeks old when he...died. It took me months to say that word. I never expected Mrs. Sewell to agree to it without the paperwork, but she did, and then I hid what I'd done from Lau because I knew he'd get angry."

"Which I did," Lau said. "When I saw the bruise on Maria, I was outraged. For a few seconds I saw red, but when I found Terry hiding in the barn, in an empty stall where he thought no one could find him, I knew he was the true victim. Maria will be okay, and she admitted to teasing and taunting him. She's always been such a good child, but she's human, too. She accused us of liking boys better than her and her sister. We had a talk with both of them before we came here. Michelle did wrong. I did wrong. We all did. So we brought him back because he's not ready to tackle adjusting to a new family."

Max looked around the table. "He's a bright little boy, but you have to be willing to let him set the speed. Trena does that. I don't know why, but I seem to be able to do the right things with him. I think he trusts me."

Lau chuckled. "He looks enough like you to pass for your own son. Maybe he feels a kinship with you. What's your secret?"

"I let him set the rules," Max said, taking Trenace's hand beneath the table. "I never do anything without asking him first. If he gives permission, I can hug him. I've never had a son, but I'd be proud to claim this one. His natural father is missing a world of joy."

"His natural father was a seventeen-year-old who panicked and ran the minute the sixteen-year-old mother-to-be told him about her pregnancy," Trenace said. "Mrs.

Sewell filled me in on all the sordid details of how she gradually rejected him, leaving him alone for days when he was still in a crib. She complained that all he did was cry each time she fed him, so she left him to cry it out. Maybe that's why he seldom cries now. Mrs. Sewell says he spent most of his baby and toddler days either in a playpen or a walker. His development was erratic, and he was denied the chance to creep and crawl and pull himself up. His mother married when he was four years old, but by then the damage had been done."

Max frowned. "He told me once that his father took a bear away from him and threw it in the fire."

Lau cocked his head. "Really? It must have been the new stepfather or a boyfriend. When Mrs. Sewell forwarded his medical history, she said his natural father had never been in the picture."

"Poor kid," Max said, resting his chin on his fist.

"Add colic to his brain injury, his left-handedness that his stepfather insisted be 'fixed' and his fair complexion, and you have most of the prerequisites for children with this syndrome," Dr. Brockman added.

"What does his fair complexion have to do with his condition?" Max asked.

"Blue eyes and light hair are predominant in this problem," Lau Brockman replied. "We don't know why. He's not mentally retarded. He's brain-injured. There's a big difference, in treatment as well as education. I've read about kids similar to him who have gone on to college."

"He's had three sessions of patterning exercises," Trenace said. "Do you think we'll have to start all over again?"

Lau rubbed his temple. "Probably. Will you have time now that you two are planning all these changes?"

"I'm free until ten each weekday," Max said. "This kid has gotten under my skin. I couldn't turn my back on him now."

"He can't cope with public school, so we can take him with us when we look for furniture for the house," Trenace said, filling the Brockmans in on their new home. "I'm giving him home schooling for the rest of the year...assuming he stays with me. I've worked with home school materials before. I love the one-to-one concept. Last week he wrote sentences that dealt with anger and hatred. I doubt he'd ever be allowed to express those feelings in a regular classroom, but afterward he seemed more at ease. I hope this weekend didn't undo all we've accomplished." She glanced toward Max. "I'd hate to lose him just when we've begun to make progress."

"We don't want Terry to think we're bitter or have rejected him," Lau said. "We'd like to bring the girls here on Saturday afternoons, so they can play with your children, and maybe you can bring them all out again some weekend. I've been working too much lately, but I've promised Michelle I'll start keeping banker's hours as much as possible. My family is the most important thing in my life, but they were beginning to doubt my commitment."

Michelle laid her hand on his. "Samson earned us a lot of money last year on stud fees, and I'm buying Lau a state-of-the-art computer so he can work at home on some manuscripts. Lau is cutting his practice to four days a week and will be at home three days a week now. Isn't that wonderful?"

"I'll be interrupted a thousand times a day, but I won't mind," Lau said. "We'll be a family, and maybe we can think about adoption again, this time through the right channels."

Michelle kissed her husband's lean cheek. "I had a…tubal ligation when Joel was born because we thought our family was complete. I have to accept the fact that I can't have any more children myself."

Trenace smiled across the table. "There are many older children who need good homes. Don't let this experience sour you on that possibility. Terry just wasn't ready."

The Brockmans rose to leave.

"I'll go get the girls," Michelle said, and excused herself.

Lau turned to Trenace. "I may be setting off fireworks, but I plan to file a formal complaint against Mrs. Sewell. What she did to us was inexcusable, but what she did to Terry was cruel, heartless and illegal."

THE NEXT TWO WEEKS were filled with a whirlwind of activity of furniture buying, moving and settling into the spacious farmhouse. Phone calls were made to relatives and close friends to invite them to the wedding.

Max's daughters were unable to get away from school because of tests, but they expressed their pleasure at learning their father had purchased what they called the "Tulley Homestead."

Trenace's son Steven was also unable to come, but Suzanne promised to bring Benita. "I wouldn't miss it for the world, but we'll have to leave right after the reception."

Phones were installed and the electrical power turned on. A moving van came to the old house two days before the wedding. Before Trenace locked the door for the last time, she looked around. For twenty years she had lived here. More than two hundred children had spent time under this roof. She walked through the empty living room to the kitchen and peeked out the window into the backyard. The swing set had been taken down and moved to the farm. All traces of human occupancy had been removed. "Time to say goodbye," she murmured to the empty walls.

They echoed back to her, "Goodbye, goodbye."

FRIDAY MORNING Trenace called the social service office in Spokane and asked for Mrs. Sewell.

"I'm sorry, but Mrs. Sewell is no longer working here," the receptionist said. "Could someone else help you?"

"I'm a foster parent," Trenace said. "My name is Trenace McKay. What happened to Mrs. Sewell? Who am I assigned to?"

The woman hesitated, then said, "Jessie Sewell took early retirement the first of this week. Frankly, I don't know what happened. That woman had become a fixture around here and would have died on the job, but she up and resigned just like that." The woman snapped her fingers into the mouthpiece.

"Then let me talk to whoever has taken over her cases," Trenace insisted.

"That would be Barbara Mitchell," the woman said. "She's on the phone. Could I have your number? She's swamped trying to make sense out of Mrs. Sewell's files."

Trenace gave her the new phone number, told the operator her new address and that she was getting married the following day, and to please pass the message on.

"Sure thing, honey," the receptionist said.

ON SATURDAY AFTERNOON Max arrived in the minivan, leading a caravan of vehicles. Following close behind him was Jocko, driving a shiny new midsize metallic blue sedan. A young woman drove a KSPO van. Josh Temple and his wife were in the fourth vehicle.

Trenace blanched when she saw Jocko retrieving video equipment from the KSPO van. Suddenly the wedding seemed too public.

Max walked casually up to her, tipped her face up and brushed her lips with his. "Good day for a wedding, don't you think?" he murmured, casting an eye toward the vibrant blue sky. "I told our weatherman to hold off on any early snow." He looked at his watch. "Two hours to kill." His arm slid around her waist. "I know what we could do, but I suppose it's not practical."

She grinned. "Smart man." She reached up to kiss him just as he started to turn away, and she barely caught the corner of his mouth. Before either could try again, Josh Temple and his wife approached. Jocko called out a greeting to his wife, Becky, who had arrived earlier in the day to handle the catering.

"Come inside, everyone," Trenace said. "Lunch is a buffet."

Max held the door for his guests, then stepped inside. Trenace took his hand and led him into the living room. "How do you like it?" she asked.

He scanned the room, peeked into the kitchen, then glanced up the stairs. "You've turned it into a home. It was chaos when I saw it on Wednesday, but you've worked another of your miracles. It's just the way I imagined it. It's great, sweetheart. I have some clothes in the van to bring in. Are we still getting the big bedroom at the top of the stairs?"

Trenace laughed. "I changed my mind three times after the furniture company's van got here," she admitted. "I knew it was the largest, and three beds would have fitted in there, but you've been so generous to us all that you deserve the best."

"*We* deserve the best," he countered. "That's the only bedroom with a private bathroom. We deserve that, too. I don't want to wait my turn behind several little boys who forget to lift the seat. Neither do you. Admit it."

She leaned her head against his chest and sighed. "It's hard to believe it's all working out, Max. I feel like I'm in a dream, and I might wake up to find that you're gone, along with this house and the furniture."

"We're here to stay, sweetheart." He took advantage of the brief moment alone with her and pressed his mouth hungrily against hers, then released her and left the house to bring in his clothes.

Dorothy Abernathy, Trenace's best friend from high school, arrived with a good-looking middle-aged man in tow and threw her arms around Trenace. "I'm so thrilled for you. When you called and asked me to be your attendant, I was flabbergasted, and since then I've become a devoted fan of Channel Nine's six o'clock news. Where is this gorgeous new husband of yours?" She glanced at her watch. "I'd love to meet him, but you're not dressed. You've only got an hour."

"But someone has to...keep track of all this," Trenace said.

Dotty waved Becky into the room and explained the situation.

"Take her away," Becky said. "We'll tend to the guests. Suzanne and Benita are riding herd on the children, and I've already drafted Michelle to oversee the kitchen volunteers. I'll greet the guests, and when the minister and his wife get here with their cute little electronic organ, we'll let you know. If I can coordinate a dozen *professional* clowns at parties all over town, I can handle all these amateurs."

Upstairs, Trenace showered for the second time that day, applied a light foundation, then reached for the lingerie she'd purchased for the wedding. She pulled a new pair of nylons up her smooth legs. "Pinch me again," she murmured, stepping into a pair of peach-dyed leather pumps. Slipping a matching peach silk slip over her head, she smoothed it down over her bra and panties. She'd never owned a set of coordinated underwear before and felt a bit silly in them now, but later, when Max—

A knock sounded on the bathroom door. "Are you about finished?" Dottie called. "It's fifteen minutes until the wedding. Hurry!"

In the bedroom Trenace removed a delicate peach woolen sweater and matching skirt from a hanger and put them on. Tiny embroidered satin appliquéd roses followed the neckline of the knit top to a modest point between her breasts, showing just a hint of fullness. She fastened the gold chain that Max had given her and patted it against her throat, then put on two small loop earrings. The lipstick she'd chosen harmonized with the peach of her outfit and her auburn hair.

She gazed at her reflection in the floor-length mirror. Her shoulders sank. "This is all wrong. I don't look like a bride."

"Don't be foolish," Dottie scolded. "You look lovely. You're conservative, Trena. If you wore frilly white lace and had a showy veil, that would look wrong. This is you, and it's perfection. The groom won't be interested in what you wear." She laughed. "He'd probably prefer nothing at all." She glanced at her watch again. "Five minutes."

A rap sounded at the door, and Dottie opened it. "The minister is ready," Becky said. "Everyone is outside waiting. Suzanne says she can keep the children under control for about thirty more minutes. Let's get this wedding started before Max comes apart.''

''Is he nervous, too?'' Trenace called.

''He's a basket case.''

''I PRONOUNCE you husband and wife,'' the minister said, smiling and nodding. ''You may kiss the bride.''

The gray wool suit Max wore brought out the white at his temples. Trenace resisted the urge to touch it. As she lifted her hand and laid it against his chest, the sun caught the sparkle of the diamonds in her wedding band.

His hands settled around her waist, and he eased her against him. ''I love you,'' he murmured as his lips settled on hers.

When he released her, they turned to greet the well-wishers. Max's aunt and uncle were first in line, followed by his sister and parents from Seattle.

''Are you sure you don't want to change your mind?'' his mother asked. ''We could stay another day if you need us.''

''No, that's fine,'' Max replied. ''We want to spend our wedding night here. We'll all be together.''

When Suzanne reached them, she threw her arms around her mother and hugged her, then moved to Max. She winked and grinned. ''Do I call you Dad or Max or what?''

''Anything you want,'' he replied, accepting her enthusiastic embrace. ''For now, keep it Max. I don't feel much like a dad this afternoon.'' He glanced at Trenace. A somber exchange passed between them, but the steady stream of well-wishers prevented them from further exchanges beyond the casual.

As the guests settled into groups around the spacious yard, the kitchen volunteers set up a buffet of steaming casseroles, a boneless rump roast sliced wafer-thin, a huge pot of clam chowder, and at the end of the line on a separate table, they placed a small wedding cake.

The late-afternoon air turned cool as the guests worked their way down the buffet line. Trenace searched the crowd for Mickie. She found her in line, with Suzanne pushing her wheelchair. Suzanne had put a large tray on the arms of Mickie's chair and set two plates on it. Mickie would point and Suzanne would reach for the serving spoon. Trenace had discussed her plan to adopt Mickie, and her daughter had been enthusiastic. But Suzanne was enthusiastic about everything. She was a young woman in love with life.

Max found Terry, and together they filled their plates, discussing the contents in the casseroles. Trenace heard the boy laugh. From the day they'd first met, Terry had established an invisible thread of trust with Max. When others had frightened him into isolation, Max had been able to show him the joy and warmth of a gentle hug. *Lau Brockman is right,* she thought. To a stranger they could easily pass as father and son. What would happen when a caseworker came to take the child away? Trenace feared the emotional damage such a separation would inflict on both man and boy.

Terry was taller than the average nine-year-old. Max was a taller-than-average man. She'd call the new caseworker and ask her to verify Terry's birthday. Usually she received such information automatically, but the space on the form Mrs. Sewell had given her had been blank. She'd have to find out Terry's date of birth soon. She always made a cake and had a small party if a child's birthday fell during his or her stay at the McKay home.

She looked down at the gold wedding ring. *Now it's the Tulley home,* she thought. Tonight she would be able to lie in his arms again. They would make love and talk about the future. She had never told him of her love. Tonight she would. The excitement of the day's activities would exhaust the children, and she would have an excuse to send them to bed early.

As she watched Max and Terry leave the line and search the yard for a quiet place, Max glanced over at her and smiled. *He's happy,* she thought. She'd feared he might change his mind once he had a chance to think through the responsibilities he'd be assuming, but she'd been reluctant to bring up the subject.

An offer on her house had come in yesterday, and she'd called Max at KSPO and told him the amount. All he'd said was that it seemed to be a fair offer. She'd called the Realtor with a counteroffer, and by seven that evening they'd agreed on an amount that was five times what she and Owen had originally paid for the house. Escrow was scheduled to close the middle of November, and she would receive a check for a full payoff. Then she would be able to start paying her share of the new home's expenses. He'd insisted she not worry about finances, but she still did. Old habits were hard to break, and she didn't want to feel beholden to Max.

The food line thinned, and Trenace took a plate. Selecting a few samples, she left the table and looked around the yard. George and Boyd had joined Max and Terry. She didn't want to intrude on their man-to-man conversation.

She spotted an empty lawn chair next to Michelle Brockman and sat down. "Thanks for helping out in the kitchen," she said.

"I enjoyed it," Michelle replied, brushing her curly hair away from her forehead. "I was so nervous when Lau and

I got married. You must be relieved to have this almost over."

Trenace laughed. "We only had two weeks to make all the arrangements, so there wasn't much time to think about it." She glanced up to find George working his way through the lawn chairs toward them. When he reached them, he stopped between the two women, looking first at Trenace, then at Michelle.

"Can we help you, George?" Trenace asked.

"Nope," the boy said. He placed his hands firmly on the arm of each chair and balanced himself, swinging his legs several times before dropping to the grass again. He leaned against the arm of Michelle's chair. "Hi," he said, grinning up at her.

"Hi, George," Michelle said. "Are you having a good time?"

He nodded. "I'm behaving myself." He glanced at Trenace and waited for her nod of confirmation.

"You're being a very good boy," Michelle replied.

He leaned closer, resting his shoulder against hers. "I like horses," he said.

"So do I," Michelle said, smiling. "I've loved horses since I was a kid."

"Me, too," George said. He balanced himself between the chair arms again, then settled against Michelle's knee. "Are you still looking for a little boy?"

A wave of pink swept up Michelle's cheeks. "My husband and I have discussed it."

He turned around and looked at Trenace, then returned his attention to Michelle. He stared at her face, then slowly reached out and touched her cheek. "You have freckles."

Michelle swallowed and tried to smile. "Not as many as I did when I was a little girl."

George nodded. "I have freckles, too. See?"

Michelle laughed. "They're hard to miss, George," she said, ruffling his red hair.

He grinned. "Aunt Trenace says most kids with red hair have freckles. Did you used to have red hair?"

Michelle gazed at the curious child. "No, but my husband's hair was reddish blond when he was younger. Why do you ask?"

George shrugged and stepped away a few feet. "I was just checking. See you around." He raced through the crowd to where Max and the other boys sat.

Trenace stared across the yard. "What do you think that was all about?"

Michelle's blue eyes glistened with tears. "I think he was making a sales pitch . . . for himself. He's so sweet."

They chatted for several more minutes. George ran back to them and stopped in front of Michelle's chair again, trying to catch his breath.

"Yes, George, what is it now?" Michelle asked.

"I have freckles and I try to be good, and I love horses, and I'm never mean to girls, and I like to be hugged." He gulped for air. "I just wanted you to know if you're still looking for a little boy, I'm willing to try."

Michelle clutched the arms of her chair. "I . . . I'll think about it."

Trenace grabbed George's arm and pulled him onto her lap. "George, you can't go up to grown-ups and solicit adoption."

He twisted around and frowned at her. "But if I don't tell her, how is she gonna know?" He leaned against Trenace's breast and frowned at the other woman. "But there's one thing you gotta know. If you take me, you gotta take Boyd, too, 'cuz we plan to stay together. We pretend we're brothers. He's bossy sometimes, but I don't pay much attention to that. He tries to be good, too, and his face isn't so ugly when you get to know him."

He scooted off Trenace's lap and stood in front of Michelle again, solemnly staring at her. "I just wanted you to know that we talked about it last night, and I promised Boyd to talk to you. If you don't want us, we'll look somewhere else, but finding new moms and dads can be awful hard, and since we already know you and Dr. Brockman and Maria and Julia, we just wanted you to know we're both willing."

He looked over his shoulder at Max and the other boys. "I gotta go now, but will you think about it?"

When Michelle nodded, George skipped across the yard.

Trenace reached out and squeezed Michelle's hand. "He's been in foster homes since he was two, and he's built up this imaginary idea of what it would be like to have a family. He swings between times when he's shy and insecure and needing to crawl up on my lap and suck his thumb to times like this when he openly applies to be your little boy. Boyd probably put him up to this. I know you and Lau aren't ready to take two rambunctious boys into your home."

Michelle wiped her eyes. "He's so...honest about it, isn't he? After what happened with Terry, I don't know. Maybe a little baby would be safer."

"It probably would," Trenace said, patting Michelle's hand once more. "I'd better go rescue my new husband from the clutches of three children. He's been very patient, but he's not as experienced about all this as he pretends. When the house fills up with children, he'll wonder what he's gotten himself into."

CHAPTER FOURTEEN

WHEN SHE REACHED MAX, he stood up and took her hands. "I thought you'd forgotten about me," he teased.

"Let's go cut the cake," she murmured, leaning against him as he slid his arm around her waist. "Our guests will be wanting to go home pretty soon."

They took their places behind the cake table, and Max held up the silver knife decorated with a white ribbon. "Before we serve the cake I want to give my beautiful bride a wedding gift."

Trenace's mouth fell open. "Max, that's wonderful, but you didn't need—"

"Ah, but I did." Max turned to the guests. "There's a new blue sedan out front. Trena was my excuse, because she's been worried about her station wagon, but she can drive the van and I'll take the little car into work." He grinned at her. "Agreeable?"

Speechless, she could only nod her acceptance.

"Good," he said, kissing her lightly on her mouth. "Now, friends and relatives, please give us your full attention." He clapped his hands, and from the side gate two clowns and three guests appeared, carrying a huge cardboard box between them, grunting and groaning to indicate its weight.

Trenace recognized Jocko and suspected the small clown must be Becky. Jocko had videotaped the entire afternoon's activities, but after handing the camera to Suzanne and showing her the controls, he'd disappeared.

Now, as Jocko McPocko labored under his load, the children who had met him before raced forward. Mickie's wheelchair wobbled dangerously, and Lau Brockman steadied it. Terry climbed to the top of the slide and sat down, viewing the scene from a safe distance over the heads of the crowd.

The clowns untied a giant orange bow, and the box fell apart. Inside a wire cage about four by three feet hopped two young French lop-eared brown rabbits and a New Zealand white. Jocko peered down at the children's eager faces. "Their house and food bowls and the legs to this contraption are in the kitchen," he said. He looked up at Terry, perched on the slide. "Young man, is your name Terence?"

Terry's eyes widened. "How did you know?"

Jocko chuckled. "I know everything. Terry, can you take charge of feeding them each morning?"

Terry frowned. "Me?"

Jocko grinned and held out his arms. "Who else?"

"I'll try," Terry replied, his features solemn.

He asked a similar question of Mickie for the evening shift.

"Yes, sir!" Mickie said with a grin.

"What about us?" Boyd asked, jerking George up close to him.

"I have something else for you two," Jocko said, reaching into the front pocket of his baggy green-and-yellow striped trousers. He felt all the way down to his knees where something began to jump about frantically. When his long arm finally reappeared, he held a three-month-old shaggy puppy of mixed heritage. He handed the wriggling puppy to Boyd. "Mad Max over there promised me he would build the house, but you and George must keep his water bowl filled and the food dish, too. Can you do that?''

"You betcha!" George shouted, dropping to his knees to pet the squirming, excited pup.

All the children in the yard followed Jocko and the three male guests as they carried the rabbit hutch to a place near the back porch.

"Now we can eat cake," Max said, and taking Trenace's hand, they did the honors.

An hour later the guests began to leave. The sun was below the horizon by the time Becky's crew had the kitchen and living room tidied and made a noisy exit.

Max leaned against the doorjamb of the kitchen, holding Trenace in the circle of his arms and watching the children playing with the puppy in the living room. "Pups piddle," he said thoughtfully. "They cry at night for their momma. I'd forgotten about that. Maybe I should have held off on the dog."

Trenace leaned against him. "Boyd and George have offered to keep him in their room for a week or two, but during the day he has to stay outside. I've already laid down some rules to them. Thank goodness rabbits don't mind being left alone."

He swung her around, putting his back between her and the children. "Speaking of being left alone, maybe we should have accepted one of those offers to stay with the children. We could have been alone by now."

"But it was your idea to stay here," she reminded him.

He made a face. "Admitted, but we all make mistakes at times. When do the kids go to bed?"

She stretched up and kissed him teasingly. "Soon."

"How soon?"

She glanced over her shoulder at the kitchen clock. "Another hour at least."

"This isn't fair," he muttered. He had changed out of his suit into a pair of jeans and a lime-green knit shirt.

"There are only four of them," she murmured, drawing her finger along the opening of his shirt to caress his skin.

He slid his hand beneath her loose cotton top and rested it on the small of her back as he buried his face against her neck.

"We're wasting our energies getting stirred up now, Max. What if the children see us?"

"They're engrossed in that television special," he replied, nipping her earlobe. "I want to make love to my wife."

She toyed with the tiny white buttons on his shirt opening. "That sounds wonderful." She gazed into his eyes, and the bridled passion reflected there ignited a fire in her own body. She looked at the clock again and sighed. "Still almost an hour."

"Damn."

She broke free and went to the sink to draw herself a glass of water. Looking over the rim of her glass, she watched him move restlessly about the kitchen, touching some of the items she'd brought with her from her old house.

This house was still new to her and she'd had trouble adjusting to the new locations of all the fixtures and crannies. Maybe with a few more weeks to settle in, she'd begin to feel it was home.

He leaned against the sink and scanned the long room. "Do you like it here?"

"It's not home yet," she confessed. She looked up at him in time to see his features go blank. "But it will be.

Max, you grew up here. I didn't, so please don't read more than I intended into what I said. I love the spaciousness, the layout. It's just that everything is in a different place."

"Sure." He folded his arms across his chest and stared broodingly down at the tips of his loafers.

"Are you having second thoughts about all this?" she asked, touching the fabric of his shirt and sighing deeply. "Maybe we should have waited until I got the proceeds from the house and could help with my share. You've put so much into all this. Sometimes I feel like . . . like I'm on welfare, too, just like the children."

He glanced down at her and tipped her chin. "Please don't feel that way. I love you and I don't mind spending some money to have you with me. This relationship is a mutual one. We contribute different gifts to make it work. Over the years it all balances out. Without you there would be no need to make good money."

"Is your job at KSPO secure?" she asked. "I mean, don't television personalities move around a lot?"

He frowned. "I'm not a personality. I'm a man who can read the news without stumbling over the words, and I can do damn good investigative reporting when I get the chance. Viewers believe what I say, but that doesn't make me anyone special. Don't start treating me differently because of what I do."

"I'm sorry," she said, turning away to stare out the window at the darkness. "I miss the streetlights," she murmured. "The darkness frightens me sometimes. Would it be expensive to install a yard light?"

He dropped his arm around her shoulders and drew her close again. "There used to be one out there. I'll check into it." They stood quietly for a few minutes. "I'm sorry if I snapped at you," he said. "Working on the special got to me. Those stories can be emotionally draining. I don't see how you do it day in and day out. I wanted to be out here with you, but I couldn't. This has been a happy day, but an exhausting one. We might both fall asleep tonight."

"I'll start the kids with their baths," she said, turning around in his arms and rubbing her cheek against his shirtfront. "Once they're asleep we can be alone." She slid her arms up and around his neck and pulled his head down until she could reach his lips, caressing them lightly.

A squeal came from the living room, and she jerked away. "That's Terry," she said, resting her forehead against him. "Someone is getting too close. He can be first to the bathroom." She smiled at him. "Will you stand guard in the living room while I get the process moving?"

Forty-five minutes later the boys were shiny clean and into flannel pajamas, their hair neatly parted and combed for the second time that day. Max took them to Terry's new room and read them a chapter out of a Thomasma Indian story, tucked Terry into bed, then followed Boyd and George to the room next door.

Snuggling down under a comforter, George looked at Max. "Where do you get to sleep?"

Max grinned. "With Aunt Trenace."

"You can sleep in here with us if you'd rather," Boyd said.

"No thanks. I want to sleep with her."

"Why?" George asked.

Max chuckled. "You're too young to understand. See you tomorrow, boys."

At the foot of the stairs he met Trenace coming from Mickie's room on the first floor. "Something's not right," he said, cocking his head and listening. "No noise, no giggling, no one asking for a drink, no one crying about the cruelties of being sent to bed. What's wrong?''

"Don't jump to conclusions, Max. Wait at least thirty minutes. Then they'll be asleep. Until then come sit on our new sofa with me. We can get used to it together. It's a shame the old one got damaged when the movers dropped it."

"Alone at last," he said, pulling her playfully down onto his lap. Before she was settled in his arms the doorbell rang.

"Who could that be?" he asked. He eased her off his lap and went to the door, flipping on the porch light. Trenace peeked around his shoulder as he jerked the door open.

On the lighted porch stood a woman in her thirties, a warm jacket pulled up around her neck to ward off the chill of the late October night air. Three children stood huddled next to her, holding hands tightly, their frightened little faces tear-stained. Their faded jackets seemed unnaturally thin for the chill in the fall air.

"I'm looking for Trenace McKay," the woman said, smoothing her short black hair.

"I'm . . . remarried," Trenace said, stepping around Max. "This is my husband, Max Tulley. May I help you?"

The other woman held out her hand. "I'm Barbara Mitchell from the Department of Health and Human Services. I've been assigned to most of Mrs. Sewell's cases. Am I glad I tracked you down at last. I went to the address in your file, but your next-door neighbor said you'd moved. The phone company gave me your new number, but when I called this afternoon, I couldn't get an answer. The phone company finally gave me your new address. Why didn't you tell someone at the office?"

Trenace stiffened. "I left a message with your secretary two days ago, but you never returned my call."

"Darn that woman," the caseworker said. "She may have to follow Mrs. Sewell out the door. The important thing is that I've tracked you down. I'm desperate, Mrs. . . .Tulley. These are the Forrester children—Courtney, Sadie and Philip. They need a safe place to stay for a few days. May we come in?"

Max's hand tightened at her elbow. *Say no, Trena, not tonight,* he seemed to be saying without speaking a word.

But she couldn't turn away these children in need. She had never refused a child. "Come in, please," she said, nudging Max aside gently.

Barbara Mitchell looked around the living room. "Is there somewhere the children can sit while we talk?" she asked.

"Sure," Trenace said, glancing at Max for understanding. She pointed to a shelf and a toy box near the sofa. "Children, there are toys and books there. Would you like to see them?"

The three children stared at her. She took the oldest child's hand and coaxed her forward. "Courtney, can you show your brother and sister the toys?"

The little girl nodded.

In the kitchen Ms. Mitchell opened her briefcase and retrieved a folder. "We've had these children before, but their previous foster home is overloaded. The children were back in their own home for three weeks, but the parents are both alcoholics, and this morning they put each other in the hospital." She glanced toward the living room. "Knives. The police called our emergency number, and I picked the children up at the station. I need you to keep them for at least a week."

Max held up his hand. "Ms. Mitchell, I understand your predicament, but surely you can appreciate our situation. We held a wedding in our backyard today. It was our own. This isn't how I expected us to spend our wedding night. Isn't there some other place they could stay?"

Barbara Mitchell stared at him for several seconds. "I'm sorry, but your wife is my last hope. If you can't take them, I don't know what I'll do." She smiled. "I'm sure the children will settle down. They've been dragged from one place to another all day. They'll drop off to sleep the minute their little heads touch the pillows. We're desperately in need of more foster homes, and with Mrs. Sewell being asked to take early retirement, our caseloads are almost unmanageable. Mrs. Tulley, please help me."

Trenace and Max exchanged glances. Max stood up, his features wooden. "It's your decision, Trena. I'm going to bed." He turned away and left the room.

Trenace closed her eyes. Settling children into a strange house could be a challenge, but the quicker she got them to bed, the sooner she could join Max. Surely he would understand.

"I'm sorry to cause problems between you two, but didn't he know how this could be when he married you?" Ms. Mitchell asked. "I'm telling you the truth. I have no other place to put them."

Trenace sighed, knowing that she had let herself be trapped by her own commitment to the program and the guilt she would feel if she turned them away. "Tell me about them," she said.

Ms. Mitchell opened the folder. "Courtney is six years old but behind in school. It says here she flunked kindergarten." She smiled sadly. "Can you imagine that?"

"I'm afraid so," Trenace replied.

"Sadie is four," Ms. Mitchell continued. "Her hearing is damaged from chronic ear infections, so when you talk to her make sure she's facing you. If she stays in the system this time, we'll try to get her some help." She studied her file again. "Philip is three years old. He knows his name but not much else. They're very protective of each other, so it might be best if they sleep in the same room. They took turns crying most of the afternoon. By now they're exhausted."

She got up. "Well, my boyfriend came to spend the weekend, so I'd better get back to my apartment before he gives up and goes back home." She extended her hand. "Thank you, Mrs. Tulley, and congratulations. May you have a long and happy marriage."

The caseworker returned to the living room and spoke in whispers to the oldest girl, Courtney, then left the house.

Before Trenace reached the sofa three-year-old Philip began to wail. His sister, Sadie, immediately joined him. Courtney looked from her crying siblings to Trenace and her chin began to tremble. Trenace swung Philip up into her arms and headed toward the stairs. "Come, children, follow me, and we'll go to the bathroom and then to bed." Halfway to the second floor she glanced over her shoulder to find the girls still at the bottom, sobbing their hearts out, unable or unwilling to climb the stairs.

She put Philip down and started down the stairs, but he began to scream and jump up and down on his spindly legs. His pants darkened as he wet himself.

"Need some help?"

Trenace jerked around. Max stood at their bedroom door, a pair of blue pajama bottoms hanging low on his hips, his eyebrows furrowed.

"Yes," she hissed. "Keep Philip from falling down the stairs, but be careful, his pants are wet. I'll get the girls."

"You go on up," he said, brushing past her. "I'll get the girls." He took the stairs two at a time, swept a sister up under each arm and carried them back up the stairs, ignoring their hysterical sobbing and kicking. "Where do you want them?"

She carried Philip to the end bedroom where she'd set up two twin beds and a set of bunk beds. Max followed her. As they passed a bedroom door, George stuck his head out.

"Get back in bed," Max ordered, "and no questions. We have some new kids, that's all. Now get."

The door closed again without a word.

Inside the crowded bedroom they surveyed the available beds. "The boy in the bunk bed?" Max asked.

"Yes, but not until he's out of his wet clothes," she said. "Put the girls down and I'll take them to the bathroom, then you can take Philip. I put rubber pads beneath the sheets already. We don't need to christen these new mattresses."

Thirty minutes later the children were in pajamas, in separate beds, and still wailing at the top of their lungs.

Max glanced at Trenace. "Time for a consolidation?"

"Anything for some peace and quiet," Trenace said, lifting a sobbing and kicking Philip and carrying him to the middle bed. Max did the same with Sadie. Only when the three children were huddled together did they stop crying, but their eyes remained wide open. "A book. Maybe if I read to them. Max, can you find an extra-easy book?"

She listened as he loped down the stairs and returned a few minutes later carrying a large picture book with colorful illustrations of objects depicting the alphabet. He sat down beside her on the spare bed and rested his head in his hands while she began to read and show the children the pictures. When she finished the letter *H* showing a shaggy pony, she looked up to find Philip's eyes closed, but the girls were still awake. Not until she showed them a picture of a striped zebra, did they fall asleep.

She leaned toward Max. "Are you asleep, too?"

Wearily he followed her out of the room. Inside their bedroom he closed the door and leaned against it. "I'd rather report from the front lines of a war than go through that again. Do all new kids cry like those did?"

She could feel his gaze follow her as she disappeared behind the bathroom door. They were alone at last, but where was the joy and exhilaration? The pent-up desire to be in his loving arms? This was to be that special night when they could come together as husband and wife and she could tell him that she loved him more than anyone else in her life.

But all she felt was utter fatigue. She dropped her clothes into a pile and pulled on a yellow knee-length cotton gown. She'd planned to wear something sheer, short and sexy, but what if one of the children woke up with nightmares? If the Forrester children awoke, they would cry, and that would wake up the other children, and then no one would get any rest. Removing her wristwatch, she looked at the time. Two in the morning. Where had the time gone? In four hours the house would be filled with seven hungry children. How could she possibly find time for her husband, too?

When she reopened the bathroom door, the bedroom was dark. She could see Max's form beneath the covers. Was he naked? Did he expect her to be suddenly filled with passion? As she walked toward the bed, her heart began to pound and her hands trembled. Moisture burned the backs of her eyes and her throat felt raw. Torn with uncertainty, she eased her body beneath the covers and waited for him to touch her.

He lay unmoving on his side of the bed.

"Max?" She turned on her side and tried to see his face through the darkness. "Oh, Max, I'm so sorry." Her voice broke as the tears began to trickle down her cheeks.

His arm slid around her and he pulled her close. "Just lie with me," he murmured. "There's been enough tears shed in this house tonight. Be still now and try to relax." He pulled her closer, coaxing her head down to his shoulder.

The more he consoled her, the harder the tears came, until finally she lay exhausted in his arms, drifting between sleep and wakefulness. His hand smoothed her gown down over her hips, but he made no move to make love to her.

"This isn't the way it was supposed to be," she said, touching his chest. "Oh, Max, you're soaking wet," she whispered.

He felt under his pillow, found his pajama top and wiped his chest and shoulder dry, then made a thin pillow out of the garment and coaxed her head down again. Smoothing her damp hair from her cheek, he kissed her once and lay back against the pillow again.

"Maybe when we wake up," he promised.

"But the children will be awake then."

"Then we'll try for tomorrow night. Want to make an appointment?"

"Don't make light of this," she murmured. "How long will you stay a happy husband if we never find time to make love?"

"Don't look for problems that don't exist." They lay quietly for several minutes. "Is this typical of what happens when you get children?"

A tremor shook her shoulders, and she sighed. "It's usually not so traumatic or so noisy and not so late at night."

"Good, then I'll cope. Now get some sleep. I need my rest in order to build a doghouse and assemble that damn rabbit cage."

WHEN MAX AWOKE, he was alone. Thoughts of the previous night came rushing back. *Trenace. How did she manage to find instant solutions to problems of children who were strangers to her?*

He rolled out of bed and headed toward the shower, then shaved and dressed. Downstairs he scanned the seven curious faces staring back at him. Trenace slid a small pancake onto Philip's plate and turned to Max.

"Good morning," she murmured. Did he hear uncertainty in her voice, or had he imagined it? She came to him, held the cast-iron griddle and quilted hot pad in her hand out of the way and tried to kiss his cheek, but he turned in time to catch her lips.

"Good morning," he replied. "If I can't beat 'em, I'll join 'em." He took the empty chair at the end of the table and grinned at everyone. "Morning, children. Did you save me a pancake?"

MAX DROVE the last nail into the doghouse roof at three in the afternoon, then made quick work of putting the food and water containers inside the rabbit cage. Finally he wired them in place. Three-year-old Philip stared at Max through the wire mesh of the cage. He clutched a ratty pink cat in one arm and held an oatmeal cookie in the other.

"Hello," Max said.

The boy stared.

Max opened the door and lifted one of the brown rabbits from the cage. "Want to pet him?"

Philip didn't answer, but when Max sat down on the grass and began to stroke the rabbit, the boy toddled to him, dropped his pink cat into Max's lap and touched the rabbit's fur.

"It's soft, isn't it?" Max asked.

Philip petted the rabbit again before retrieving his pink cat and walking away.

Trenace leaned over the porch railing and smiled. "Short attention span, huh?"

He chuckled. "Short vocabulary, too." He put the rabbit back into the cage and clipped the catch on the door, then scooted through the railing to join Trenace on the porch. "Tired?"

"If I had time to stop and think about it," she admitted. "Did the children wear you out today?"

He leaned on the railing and glanced over his shoulder, counting heads in the yard. "I seldom get to relax quite like this on Sundays. Sometimes I go to the station and work in the editing room just to keep busy, but today, well, this is great, really great." He pulled her between his legs, and she grasped his shoulders, pulling his head against her breasts.

Stroking his hair, she said, "I'm sorry about last night. I'm used to this, but I'm not sure about you. If there's a secret to this life, it's being flexible and patient. Tonight will be different."

He turned, burying his face between her breasts for a few seconds, and quickly kissed the skin at the base of her throat. "Patience is my middle name."

The phone rang and they stepped apart.

"I'll get it," she said, and he followed her into the kitchen. "It's for you." She held out the receiver.

When he hung up, his features were flushed. "That was Josh Temple. He says the weekend anchor is down with the flu. He wants me to come in and do the late news."

"What about the new woman from Montana? Can't he call her?"

"She's out of town for the weekend," Max replied. "Josh says only one other reporter is available, and he keeps stumbling over the script. We're gearing up for the November ratings period. I've got to help out."

Trenace slapped a towel against the counter. "It's not fair of him to ask you."

He arched a brow. "It's my job, Trena, just like last night was yours."

Trenace followed him to the hallway. "Will you be back tonight?"

He stopped, feeling as if he was being pulled apart by two different worlds. "There's always the late-breaking news to process, and then we have to put things away. I'm sorry, honey. Right now I'd better get cleaned up and in to town. We haven't had the TV on since Friday. I don't even know what's happened in the world."

He headed upstairs to clean up. Thirty minutes later he bounded down the stairs, freshly shaven and wearing the same gray suit he'd worn at yesterday's wedding.

Trenace's mouth tightened, and he longed to have the time to kiss her hurt away. "Don't stay up for me," he said, caressing her cheek. "I won't be home before midnight."

She turned away, avoiding his intended kiss. "Perhaps it would be more convenient if you stayed in town overnight."

He stared at her unyielding posture and frowned. "I wouldn't be disturbing you then, would I?"

"Drive carefully," she said, and the deadness in her tone gave him a message he'd never expected to hear.

CHAPTER FIFTEEN

A LIGHT TAP sounded on Max's office door. When he glanced up, he found the assistant news director standing in the open doorway, a piece of yellow paper in her hand.

"Yes, Maddie?"

"This came in from the Spokane Police Department," Maddie said. "I've already set it up as a final item on this evening's show. It's about a little girl. Do you want to read it?"

"Sure." Max took the paper and dropped it onto the stack of stories already cluttering his desk. He took a sip of coffee and choked. "Oh, God, no."

"What's wrong?" Maddie asked, running to the desk. "It's a terrible story, but not so different from others we report."

"I know the child," Max murmured, staring down at the brief story. He glanced at the clock. Thirty minutes to airtime. Would Trenace watch the news this late, or was she ticked off enough that she was already asleep? He couldn't take the chance. Reaching for the phone, he punched out the numbers of the farmhouse and waited while it rang several times.

Trenace's voice sang through the line and filled him with longing. "Tulley residence," she said, and her use of their married name sent a tremor through his hand.

"Trena, this is Max."

"Oh."

"How are the kids?" he asked.

"They're asleep. The Forrester children cried for an hour when I put them to bed, but it's quiet now. I was just thinking about going to bed myself, but I wanted to see the news first."

He hesitated, then said, "That's why I called."

"To make sure I was being loyal to KSPO?"

He scanned the story once more. "Trena, I'll be reading a late-breaking story near the end of the program. It's about Akeylah."

He heard her catch her breath.

"The Spokane police found her."

Trenace's voice broke. "She's . . . dead, isn't she?"

"How could you know?"

She sniffed. "I had this premonition that she wouldn't survive. I don't know why. Read me the story."

He read an abbreviated version, leaving out some of the graphic violence given in the police report. "Trena, I wish I could be there with you."

"I'll be fine," she insisted. "This isn't the first time tragedy has claimed one of my kids, Max. You'll find that out if you stay around long enough." She paused, then asked, "Are you coming home after the show?"

"Do you want me to?"

"It's your decision. Terry has his therapy at nine, and I need to arrange a sitter if I take him. I hadn't counted on having three young ones. I never gave enough thought to how far we are from Spokane when I agreed to this move." The words ran together as if she was anxious to end the conversation.

"If you find yourself stuck, give Aunt Agnes a call," he suggested.

"I don't know her well enough to impose. You know that." Her voice turned cool.

"I'll sleep at the apartment, but I'll be there in time to take Terry. But when I bring him back, I'll have to head in again right away. Josh has called a staff meeting at eleven tomorrow morning. He wants to move the *Wednesday's Child* special to the Thanksgiving weekend, probably Friday night when families are together. That means long hours for all of us."

"Then you'll be staying in town for the rest of the week?"

"It's for the best, but call me if you need me," he said, knowing that she wouldn't. She was as conditioned to solving her own problems and making her own decisions as he was.

CURLED UP in the corner of the new sofa, Trenace absorbed every nuance of her husband's polished delivery of the late-night regional news. His image blurred when he smiled into the camera as he read a story with a funny twist. Did he affect other women this way, or had love heightened her response? She wiped the corner of her eyes and continued to stare at the screen, fearful of missing some subtle message he might want to send to her.

Silly, she thought.

After a commercial break, Max came back on-camera, looking somber. Trenace straightened her legs and leaned forward.

"Spokane police detectives are investigating the death of a five-year-old girl. Her battered body was found this afternoon in an apartment formerly occupied by her mother, Tabina Johnson, and a male companion identified as Bubba Oliver. Neighbors reported the couple moved out yesterday, but a curious building manager called police to report the child had not left with them. Police found a bloodstained skillet on a burner of a filth-encrusted stove. The child lay in a corner of the kitchen, clutching a lavender stuffed bear. Exact cause of death has not been released. Whereabouts of the mother and her companion is unknown, but an all-points bulletin has been issued.''

A police photo of Johnson and Oliver filled the screen for several seconds before it faded to a commercial.

When the news resumed, the caption Editorial was superimposed below Max's chest. He peered into the camera, his blue eyes intense.

"KSPO will be presenting a week-long series focusing on physical child abuse starting one week from tomorrow. We never expected the Johnson child to be our lead-in story. I knew this child for a few weeks. She was sweet and innocent but terrified of a man named Bubba. The system designed to protect this child failed her because the authorities failed to heed the warnings.''

His voice tightened as he continued. "No child should be put back into a family environment that is life-threatening. All children deserve a safe home in which to grow, a place where a caring adult will provide them with healthy food and a warm, dry place free of filth, drugs, weapons and violence, a place where hugs and kisses are given unconditionally.''

He made a subtle motion with his finger and a commercial break began to run. When the program returned, the camera kept its distance from Max's face, filling half the screen with the KSPO logo. The credits began to roll, and she watched him unclip his microphone and collect the papers scattered in front of him.

Usually he chatted and smiled with the technical staff, giving the home viewer a chance to see the camaraderie between Max and the staff. Tonight he sat perfectly still, his head bowed, as if he'd found something of critical importance in his notes. The screen switched to the KSPO logo again, then a soft drink commercial blasted the airwaves with flashing neon lights and a heavy metal rock band playing the company's well-known melody.

Trenace reached for the phone. She had to talk with Max, if necessary plead for him to come home. He'd comforted her last night. Tonight she would comfort him. Violence and death in the world of foster care was an aspect many workers in the field chose not to discuss, yet anyone who worked in the field long enough was exposed to it. The only solace a worker could have was the knowledge that they'd provided a child with a brief respite from the real world.

"Max Tulley, please," she said when a man answered.

"Sorry, ma'am, he's not here."

"This is his wife. I . . . did he say where he was going?"

"Trenace, I didn't recognize your voice," Josh Temple said. "He left here like a bat out of hell. I assume he's on his way home."

"Oh, well, thank you." She hung up and waited thirty minutes, then dialed the number of his apartment. No one answered. Flipping through the channels, she settled into the corner of the sofa to wait in case he came home.

A SCHOOL VAN equipped with a wheelchair lift picked up the children at eight sharp. A few minutes later Trenace called to Terry. "Are you ready? Max will be here any minute."

Terry and the three Forrester children came out on the porch and sat down on the first step to wait. Trenace joined them. When Max had failed to come home or to answer his phone in Spokane, her concern had gradually shifted to anger. How dare he avoid her?

In the distance Max's blue car materialized. "Terry, here he comes."

"I'll go meet him," Terry called excitedly, running toward the road and reaching it before Max could turn in.

Her heart sank when Max braked, opened the door for the boy, then drove back toward the city without so much as a wave.

TRENACE KEPT an eye on the clock as the morning ticked away. When wheels crunched on the gravel driveway, she ran to the door, only to discover a green compact automobile parked next to the steps. Barbara Mitchell got out and motioned to Terry.

"How did you two meet?" Trenace asked, coming down the steps.

Terry scowled at her and trudged into the house.

Barbara Mitchell smiled. "I stopped at the treatment center to speak with the director about another child who might benefit from their programs and ran into your husband and Terry. Mr. Tulley mentioned his tight schedule, and since I was planning to come out here, anyway, I offered to bring Terry home. You have a very charming husband, Mrs. Tulley."

"Come in," Trenace said, knowing no good would come of her challenging the woman's impression.

At the kitchen table Ms. Mitchell opened her valise and removed an envelope. "There's your certification for the coming year," she said. "I'm sorry if Mrs. Sewell caused you difficulties. She gave all her foster parents a hard time for some reason. Her co-workers said she'd changed this past year."

"She did," Trenace replied. "It was as if she'd forgotten the children."

Ms. Mitchell nodded. "She returned Akeylah to her mother in spite of her supervisor's objection, and then when she took Terry to the Brockmans without proper authorization and Dr. Brockman filed a formal complaint . . . well, I'm telling you this in confidence, but my supervisor convinced her that she had two choices—early retirement or dismissal. She had only a year to go and she could have retired at full benefits."

She reached into her valise again and removed a folder. "I'm pleased to tell you that the Brockmans have filed a formal application for adoption." She looked across the table and smiled. "My supervisor has worked with Dr. Brockman and his wife for years now, as far back as when they developed a health program together for migrant workers near Chelan. She's writing a letter of recommendation."

"I'm glad," Trenace said. "Michelle has a lot of love to give . . . to the right child, and Lau Brockman has the patience of a saint with young children."

"Did you know he grew up in an orphanage?" Barbara asked.

Trenace smiled. "Yes. He's a good man, and their children are well adjusted, in spite of what happened between Terry and Maria."

"Dr. Brockman told me about that. Sometimes children provoke violence. Terry may have done that. And all children are angry at times, so Maria may have acted out her own aggressions on Terry, a child who threatened to take her place as the oldest in the family. Dr. Brockman tells me they've had some long talks with both children about their desire to adopt other children. By the time they're approved and a child found, the girls should be accepting. Now, about the Forrester children. We've located an aunt. She and her husband live in Walla Walla. I'll be meeting them here on Friday to get the children.''

Trenace looked questioningly at the other woman. "Does she know they're criers? Each night they seem to need an hour of sobbing. Sometimes they take turns, and no matter what I do—''

"Yes, she knows. The children's mother has left them there before, for months at a time. The aunt's sure they'll settle in quickly. She and her husband have two children of their own, and the children are quite excited about having their cousins back." Ms. Mitchell took a sip of coffee. "How is Terry's home schooling coming?''

Trenace smiled. "He knows more than I thought he did. We're starting to string words together into sentences. We're going to try writing a story this afternoon, just a simple, one-page story using words he's familiar with, but I think he'll do well. By next fall he might be ready to try public school, but only if they understand his condition.''

They discussed the other children for several minutes, then went out into the backyard where the Forrester children were talking about the rabbits among themselves. Terry sat perched on top of the slide, watching them.

After lunch, while the Forrester children took their naps, Terry joined Trenace at the kitchen table. "Remember all the angry words you learned to spell last week?" Trenace asked.

He picked up a pencil but looked dubious. "Sure.''

"Remember how we've practiced short words and sounded them out and then you strung them together into sentences?''

Terry nodded. "And we went through the alphabet again and I knew all those stupid letters, didn't I?''

She grinned. "Letters aren't stupid when you use them to express yourself."

He laid his head on his arm and grinned up at her. "Yeah."

"Now we're going to use what we've learned the past two weeks and write a story," she explained.

"You, too?"

"You write the story, and I'll be your helper in case we find a new word you can't sound out. Ready?"

He nodded.

"Think of something or someone who makes you feel happy."

She waited until he nodded.

"Ask yourself who this person is and write a sentence that describes him."

Terry fidgeted in his chair, twisted his mouth and began to print, "Max is a tall man."

Trenace swallowed the lump in her throat. "Now ask yourself, what? You can write anything you want as long as it answers the question, What about Max?"

Terry began to print, "Max is my..." He looked up. "How do I spell *friend?*"

She closed her eyes and slowly spelled the word.

"What next?" he asked.

Her eyes flew open, and she stared down at the two sentences. "Write about when something happened."

He looked at her. "Really?"

"Sure, but remember today it must be something good or fun."

He gripped the pencil in his hand, stuck his tongue out and printed, "I hugged my friend Max when he asked me to."

She inhaled sharply. "Now tell us where it happened."

"We were behind a farmhouse," he printed. "I like this. What's the next question?"

She smiled. "Write about why you like your friend Max."

He started to print again. "I like Max because he doesn't hurt me."

"Oh, Terry, Max would be so pleased to read your story," Trenace said. "Is there anything else you'd like to add to it?"

He nodded. "Yes, but I can't spell all the words."

"I'll help you if you get stuck," she assured him.

"I wish Max could be my—How do you spell *father?*" he asked, looking trustingly up at her.

Through her tears she spelled the word and he printed it.

"When will he be home?" Terry asked, folding the piece of paper carefully into a neat square. "I'm gonna give it to him."

"Not for a few days," she said. "He has to work late all this week at the station." How could she ever explain to this vulnerable child who had only recently learned to trust grown-ups that Max might never return?

"Can I mail it to him there?" he asked.

She mulled over his question. What would Max think? That she'd put Terry up to this? "I think that's a great idea." Terry had written his story from the heart, and it deserved to be read by the recipient of his trust and affection. She helped him address the envelope, told him how to lick the postage stamp, and together they walked to the gray mailbox at the end of the lane.

The next morning Terry stood at the gate, waiting for the mail truck. From the porch Trenace watched as he talked with the postman. Quite an accomplishment, she thought, for a child who had been so noncommunicative a few months earlier.

On Wednesday she had to remind Terry that sometimes the post office had lots of mail and it didn't always get sorted right away, so Max probably hadn't received his letter yet.

On Thursday evening they gathered around the television set to watch the six o'clock news. To Trenace's dismay the young woman whose job absence had cost Trenace and Max time together smiled at the camera. "This is Hope Randall, sitting in for Maxwell Tulley who is on special assignment. Max will return next Tuesday. Shooting broke out in downtown Spokane today when..."

The children turned to Trenace.

"Where did he go?" Mickie asked.

"I'm...not sure," Trenace hedged.

"Why didn't he stop and say goodbye?" Boyd asked.

"He's very busy, working on a television special and a new series." Trenace could taste salty blood as she bit her lip.

"He never comes home anymore. Is he mad at us?" George asked.

"No, I'm sure he's just...busy."

"Then why doesn't he say hi to us during the news like he did that first time?" Boyd asked.

Terry got up and went to his room.

THE FORRESTER CHILDREN were picked up by their aunt and uncle late Friday afternoon. Late Saturday evening Trenace called Max's apartment but got no answer. She looked up Becky Grimes's number and asked for Jocko.

"He's gone with Max and a crew to get some special film for their child abuse series. Didn't Max give you the number?"

"He's been staying in town all week," Trenace said, striving to keep her voice steady. "I've misplaced the paper he gave me with the new number. Do you have it?"

"Sure," Becky replied, quickly rattling off the phone number.

"Thanks," she murmured.

"Trenace, is something wrong?" Becky asked. "Jocko says Max seems preoccupied the past few nights, and he has dark circles under his eyes. Jocko says he's moody. You two aren't...?"

"No, of course not." She replaced the receiver and glanced at her watch. Ten o'clock and the children were in bed asleep. Would Max be at the number Becky had given her? She didn't know if it was a motel or business or where it was located.

She went up to her lonely bedroom and dialed the number.

A man answered. "Ellensburg Inn. May I help you?"

Trenace cleared her throat. "Yes, the KSPO people... are they registered there?"

"Sure are. Hold on and I'll put you through."

The phone rang twice, then a woman answered, "Hello, is that you, honey?"

Trenace's heart pounded. "I... may I speak to Maxwell Tulley?" A wave of anger burned her cheeks. "This is his wife."

"Oh, great," the woman said. "I'm Maddie Swanson. I'm the new assistant news director. Geez, I wouldn't want you to think... oh, geez, my boyfriend says I talk before I think. Max has the room next door. Some of us are going out for a late dinner, but Max said he was tired. I'll transfer the call. Let it ring in case he's asleep. He looks like heck. We've been telling him he ought to take some time off and stay home.''

"And what did he say to that?'' Trenace asked.

"He said he didn't have time.''

CHAPTER SIXTEEN

HE DOESN'T HAVE TIME. He doesn't have time. Max's excuse rang in her ears. *We'll see about that.* He had no right to cut her out of his life without so much as a "Thank you, ma'am, but I've made a mistake and I want out."

Her anger had been simmering all week. Tonight she didn't care if it boiled over. If he wanted out, he was free to go, but not before they cleared the air and she told him a few things about love and commitment.

"Hello? Is someone there?" Max's voice broke through her thoughts, and his mellow tone—as if he'd done nothing to cause this pain in her chest—pushed the lid off her control.

"Say something or I'm hanging up," he threatened.

"No...don't hang up." She took two gulps of air. "I'm me." He had probably forgotten what her voice sounded like.

"Trenace? What's wrong? Is someone sick? Injured?" *He's thinking only about the children.*

"Trenace, are you okay? Damn it, say something."

"We need to talk," she said, picking up the phone and pacing the length of the bedroom. "I won't mince words, Max. Are you ever coming home again?"

"Yes."

Planning her next attack, she missed his reply. "If you're not, then we need to talk about this property...this house...our marriage, if one can call it that.

I'll pay you as much as I can for your share of the house as soon as the proceeds for the sale of my house come in. I don't intend to move again, so you can't throw me out. I'll sign a note, but you'll have to be reasonable about the monthly payment, and I positively don't have money for a divorce. You'll have to take care of the legal costs. If...if you've found another woman—"

"Trenace, be quiet."

"No," she shouted back. "I have more to say. I like this house. At first I wasn't sure, but now I want to buy your half. I know, I know, it will take me fifty years at least to pay it off because I don't get much for the children. Of course I could ask for several more, but a woman alone can only handle so many children by herself and do justice to their problems."

"You're already so busy you can't think straight," he said.

She bristled at his insult. "That's the pot calling the kettle black. You can't find your way twenty miles down the road, so don't you dare accuse me of being too busy. I'll manage just fine."

"And burn yourself out as a woman?"

"My sex has nothing to do with our discussion." She hoped he would keep quiet. When he did, she plunged ahead. "The children are asking questions and I don't know how to answer them. Terry misses you the most. You'd be so proud of him, Max. His lessons are going very well, and last week he wrote you a letter. He goes down to the gate each morning and waits in case you've answered it. Max, he talks to the postman. Can you imagine our shy little boy doing that? I have to remind him each day that you're out of town, but he thinks you took his letter with you. Once you're back in Spokane, please find time to answer it. If you decide not to, let me know. I'll blame the postal service for losing it.''

"What did it say?"

"Every sentence was his own, Max. I helped him with the spelling, that's all. Writing that letter was a big step for him. He's grown very fond of you."

"What about you?"

She stood up again. "What?"

"What about you? Have you grown fond of me, or am I just a temporary intrusion in your orderly life?"

"I don't know what you're talking about," she said, her anger boiling again. "I didn't . . . I don't . . ."

"Love me?"

"Of course I love you!" Her head began to throb, and she couldn't think straight.

"No, you don't."

"I *do* love you! I would have never married you if I didn't love you."

"Why haven't you ever told me so?"

"What?"

"Goddamn it, Trenace, we've known each other since July," he said. "And each time we're close I want to sweep you in my arms, carry you off somewhere and make love to you, but even when we went to Hood River, you never once told me how you felt. That's a hell of a way to communicate. We've had sex . . . twice . . . but did you ever look into my eyes and whisper, 'Max, I love you'? Do you know how much I wanted to hear you say those words? I give you credit. You never lied. Well, neither did I.''

"Max, I—"

"No, you started this and we'll finish it. I opened up to you when I told you how my first wife died. I could talk to you, and you understood. Somewhere along the way I hoped you would fall in love with me, but I needed to hear the words. Didn't you know that?''

"I . . . Owen and I . . . we never—''

"Damn it, I'm not Owen. I'm Max Tulley. I need a wife who loves me just because of me. Did you marry me because people recognize my name? If I wore bib overalls and grew wheat, would you have married me? Damn it, Trena, sometimes I feel like you've emasculated me. Was that your intention? Get my name? Get my money? Then close your legs and hope I'd fade away?''

"Max, you have no right!''

"Shut up, Trenace, I have every right. I'm your husband,'' he shouted. "If the shoe pinches, maybe you chose the wrong model, but mark my word, woman, you won't get away with it, not with this husband.'' He slammed the receiver down, deafening her for several seconds with its crash.

THE CHILDREN GATHERED around the television set on Tuesday, eager to see Max again. Trenace busied herself in the kitchen, trying to resist the urge to watch him. At last she gave up her plan and stood in the doorway, gazing across the room at the television.

Tonight he wore a navy woolen pullover instead of his usual dress jacket. His customary pale blue shirt and red tie completed his outfit. She wondered if he might be wearing jeans. Thoughts of the soft denim hugging his lean hips warmed her, but after the crushing rejection she'd experienced only days before, her feelings were still raw and inflamed. His scathing accusations were unforgivable. If he ever had the nerve to show up again, she'd tell him just what she thought of his narrow view of marriage.

"And now this," he said, the corners of his mouth turning into an unexpected grin.

A commercial break began and she turned away. The children began to giggle. "Did you see that?" Boyd asked. "Uncle Max sent a commercial to Terry. That's fantastic."

Trenace walked into the living room, wiping her hands on a towel. "What are you talking about?"

Mickie grinned. "It was only on for about fifteen seconds, but on the bottom of the screen it said Paid Commercial Announcement. It really did and there were three balloons."

Trenace turned to Terry. "Could you read the words?"

"Every one of them," he replied, awed by the experience. "It said, 'Dear Terry, I got your letter. Hang in there.' It was signed Mad Max. What did he mean?"

She dropped to the sofa, clutching the damp towel. "I don't know. Let's see if there's more."

The news program resumed, and Max introduced the first installment on physical child abuse. The children watched attentively.

"He's talking about Akeylah," Mickie murmured.

Trenace watched the children's reaction to the piece, resisting the temptation to turn the segment off. This was an aspect of growing up they had all experienced in one form or another. No one spoke during the segment. When Max came on the screen again and began a new story, they remained quiet, soaking up every word he spoke.

His sensitivity shone through the entire broadcast that evening, and his manner made her misery doubly painful. If only he would once again be willing to show some of that kindness to her.

ON WEDNESDAY AFTERNOON, Barbara Mitchell dropped by with some new regulations and a welcome notice that approval had been received to authorize a five percent increase in the amount foster homes would receive for each child placed.

"What an unexpected surprise," Trenace murmured. "An early gift from Santa?"

"It's long overdue," Barbara replied. "We've managed to find homes for all the children currently in the system, but it won't last. I'm updating our records on the capacity within the county. How many more children are you willing to accept?"

Trenace thought of the promise she'd made to Max about buying his half of the place. "I have room for eight, possibly ten if you have a crisis, but I'd like to ask a favor of you. I'm exhausted. Will you hold off on bringing any new kids until Thanksgiving at least?"

Barbara smiled. "Of course, and I have good news for you concerning Dr. and Mrs. Brockman."

"They've been approved for future adoptive placement?"

"Not only that," Barbara said. "They want George and Boyd to come spend the weekend with them, and if it works out, they'd like them to stay for a longer trial period."

Trenace brightened. "George will be ecstatic." She told Barbara about his pitch the afternoon of the wedding. "But I'll miss them. They've both been with me for over a year."

"Mrs. Brockman and the girls will come for them Friday after school. This time it's being done by the book. I have a good feeling about this placement."

"So do I," Trenace replied.

They discussed all the children for several minutes before Barbara rose to leave. "Mrs. Tulley, please tell your wonderful husband that we at the agency are appreciative of his current series and look forward to the *Wednesday's Child* special."

"He'll be glad to know that," Trenace said. "Why don't you write him a letter and send it to KSPO so the others involved can read it. They've all worked hard on both projects."

After the six o'clock news had ended, Trenace took the two boys to their room and told them the exciting news.

"I knew it, I knew it!" George exclaimed, jumping around excitedly. "I wished and prayed and it worked. See, Boyd? I told you they would want us."

Boyd leaned against the post of his bed. "Are you sure they want me, too? Why not Terry?"

She pulled him playfully onto her lap. "Because they think you'll be happy with them. They like you, Boyd."

"What if I get too bossy?" he asked.

She kissed his cheek. "Mrs. Brockman has a solution for that. She wants to teach you about the feeding program. It involves lots of measuring and weighing and math. When you think you understand it, she plans to put you in charge. What do you think of that?"

He grinned. "It might work. I love math. I don't mean to be bossy. It just happens."

"You're a natural leader," Trenace said. "That will be a marvelous talent when you get older, but for now, do you think you could get used to being the oldest in a family of four children?"

He slid off her lap and sat down beside her. "I didn't think anyone would ever really want me. I'll try real hard."

"Don't worry, Boyd," George shouted from his bed across the room. "If you get too bossy, I'll let you know!" Suddenly he grew quiet and his eyes glistened. "I'm finally gonna have a mom and dad. Do you think they'll really love me?"

"Of course, they will," she assured them, hugging them both.

"Even if I have an accident?" George asked.

"Even then."

AFTER THE BROCKMAN FAMILY came for the boys, the house seemed abnormally quiet. Mickie tagged along behind Trenace wherever she went for the next few hours. Twice, as she moved from the sink to the refrigerator, she bumped into Terry.

Trenace caught herself before she snapped at them. She hurried out of the kitchen as her chin began to tremble dangerously. Outside, she walked toward the road. In the excitement of George and Boyd leaving she had forgotten about the mail. Since the message from Max, Terry had stopped waiting for the postal truck. The mailbox was filled with several unsolicited catalogs, a magazine, and on the bottom of the stack was an envelope with an official KSPO letterhead in the upper left-hand corner.

She tore it open. A single sheet of paper lay folded inside. "I love you, Trena Tulley." Around the words he had taken a red felt pen and drawn a simple heart with an arrow piercing it and signed the note, "Max." A postscript read, "Forgive me."

She checked the envelope to see if she'd missed anything. Why had he written it? Why not come home? His career, of course. He might love her, but first things first.

She trudged back up the gravel driveway to the house but couldn't bring herself to go inside. Letting herself through the side gate, she checked on the rabbits and the pup, who seemed to have doubled in size in the past three weeks. Boyd had made Terry promise to take over the feeding chores and had refused to go with the Brockman family until the other boy had put his promise in writing and signed his name.

She thought of Max's aunt and uncle. During the wedding reception, they had offered to take the children if she and Max had needed a break.

If she could have a few days alone, without anyone to worry about, to cook for, to coax into doing their homework, maybe she could get her life back in order and think rationally about the future. Refreshed, she would drive into Spokane and confront Max on his own turf.

Before she could talk herself out of her decision she hurried inside and dialed Max's aunt and uncle's number and asked the favor, keeping her explanation brief.

Agnes Tulley chuckled. "We've been wondering why you haven't asked before this. How many kids are there and how soon can you get here?"

"Just Mickie and Terry," Trenace said, explaining the whereabouts of the others.

"And what about you?" Agnes asked. "Max says you work too hard and never quit. Do you have plans for dinner?"

"Not really," she admitted.

"Then bring the children and their things and have dinner with us. We can watch Max on the news and then you can go home and enjoy the peace and quiet until he gets home."

ALTHOUGH THE MEAL was delicious, Trenace had to be constantly on guard to keep her marital difficulties private. Terry seemed to warm to the kindly older couple, and Mickie settled in once she was assured the school bus driver would be notified to pick her up at a different stop on Monday.

Feeling thoroughly unnecessary, Trenace drove back to the large empty house alone. She showered and felt around in the dresser drawer for something to slip into. Her hand touched the silky peach short gown she had purchased for the wedding night but had never worn.

Pulling it over her head, she looked at herself in the mirror. What a waste, she thought, her gaze following the shadowy outline of her body beneath the material. It didn't matter that the gown would never be admired by the man she loved. She would wear it, anyway.

She brushed her hair dry and kept brushing until it glistened in the soft glow of the lamplight. Glancing at the clock, she sighed. The late news would be coming on momentarily, but she couldn't bring herself to watch it. Stacking several pillows against the headboard, she crawled between the covers and settled back. A few hours of reading would put her to sleep. With no children to listen for, perhaps she could get a good night's rest for a change.

"I'VE GOT TO TALK to you, Josh."

"You go on the air in fifteen minutes. Can't it wait?"

"No, it's either now, or I'm going to exercise the early termination clause in my contract."

Josh shot from his chair. "You can't do that. KSPO management takes its contracts very seriously, Max. That's why we have legal counsel."

"Then listen to me," Max pleaded.

"Sit down but make it quick," Josh replied, dropping back into his chair.

Max glanced at his watch and frowned. "I have no choice. I want some time off...to be with my family...if I still have one."

"What the hell does that mean?" Josh asked, leaning forward and resting his chin on the heel of his hand.

"Trenace and I have spent less than a day together since we were married. Damn it, Josh, we haven't even had enough time together to...to...consummate our marriage."

Josh's eyes widened. "The hell you say. Why are you telling me this? You should be taking it up with her."

"Exactly. On our wedding night we had three little children who cried until three in the morning, then the next night you talked me into coming in here. I should have refused you, but I didn't, and then you sent us out of town, and well, damn it, either I go home and try to patch this up or I lose Trena. I'm warning you, if she divorces me, I'm leaving Spokane, contract or no contract."

Josh sat staring across the desk. "This is serious."

"You damn well better believe it's serious," Max retorted. "Now listen to me. I want the weekend and all of next week off. I'll come in later in the week to work on the *Wednesday's Child* special, but only for a few hours. I've covered for Hope Randall for weeks on end. She can return the favor. Is it a deal?"

"Well," Josh said, sighing dramatically, "it's short notice, but the ratings season is over. Maddie has been asking to sub once in a while. Maybe we can break her in during the ten o'clock slot with Hope. I've been wanting to try a team. Hope can cover for you at six, and maybe when you come back we can try a team approach there, too. Are you willing to share the camera?"

Max grinned. "Sure, as long as you don't cut my salary."

"I knew you were a reasonable man," Josh countered. "Anything else?"

"Glad you asked," Max replied. "I want you to think about making some changes in the news department's schedule. Don't get me wrong. I'm not giving you ultimatums, just strong suggestions. First, no more Max Tulley on the ten o'clock news. If you don't have another anchor, you can go on-camera yourself."

Josh's features twisted in a grin. "Catastrophic consequences," he warned.

"Then use some of the talent you've had around here all along," Max suggested, settling more comfortably in his chair. "Remember when you talked to me about developing a late-afternoon news show with local interviews and a talk format?"

Josh nodded.

"I want to give it a try," Max said. "We could move *Wednesday's Child* to that hour where women who stay home can watch it. They are the obvious untapped potential for adoptive parents. Why did we think career couples were the best targets? And think about it, is two minutes enough time to tell these children's stories? We can expand the segments to five minutes. I've filmed at least an hour on each child."

"I don't know, Max. I was thinking about canceling it when the agreement runs out."

"You must be joking," Max insisted. "How can you even think about dropping it? The special will generate more interest. Do you want to explain to the viewers why you've changed your mind about helping little boys and girls find new moms and dads?"

Josh shifted uncomfortably in his chair. "I said I was *thinking* about it."

Max shook his head. "If you cancel it, one of the other stations will pick it up faster than you can say KSPO. Hell, we'll have laid the groundwork for them. What will your investors think when they receive your explanation for loss of revenue?" He grinned slyly. "Besides, I met Trenace because of *Wednesday's Child.*"

"You've been giving all this a lot of thought," Josh said.

"I've had some damn lonely nights to think," Max admitted.

"Where's Max?" someone shouted from the news desk. "It's two minutes to airtime."

"Think about it?" Max asked, refusing to leave until he had Josh's pledge. "You cooperate with me and I promise you I'll never leave you during ratings weeks."

"Come back when you're finished the newscast," Josh said.

"Can't do that," Max called from the doorway. "I'm going home to seduce my wife."

TRENACE CLOSED the book and tossed it to the floor. She'd never expected to finish it, but sleep had escaped her. She glanced at the clock and sighed, then made a quick trip to the bathroom. By now the news was over and Max would be in his apartment. Should she phone him? Maybe he'd gone out for a late dinner. Alone?

She tried to block the possibility of driving him into the arms of some other woman. Closing her eyes, she willed sleep to come, but it seemed to be as elusive as peace of mind tonight.

A sound came from the hallway and she sat upright. A prowler? She'd never given thought to a prowler out here in the country, but city living habits had stayed with her, and each night she'd been careful to lock all the doors.

Her heart thudded against her chest as footsteps came closer and stopped. The knob turned and the door swung open. Max filled the entryway, his jacket abandoned somewhere, his tie loosened, with its knot hanging several inches below his neck. His cream-colored broadcloth shirt had been unbuttoned halfway down his chest. A bottle of wine dangled from one hand, two long-stemmed crystal glasses in the other. She'd never seen the glasses before. *Oh, God,* she thought, *is he drunk?* "Max, what are you doing?"

"I live here." His voice sounded tense but not intoxicated. He walked to the dresser and put the bottle and glasses down. Returning to the door, he kicked it closed with his shoe.

She flinched at the loud sound, and when he bolted the door, she grew apprehensive. With only a passing glance toward her he tossed the tie over the corner bedpost and removed his shirt, then disappeared behind the bathroom door.

She listened to the muffled sounds of his electric shaver running. The hum of his razor was replaced with the sound of the shower running.

She tore her gaze away from the closed door and stared across the room, but in her mind she watched soap slide down his chest and ride the narrow line of dark hair down his body to catch in the curls at his groin.

Silence replaced the drum of the shower, and she tensed, waiting for his next move. The bathroom opened, and in a cloud of steam Max appeared again. The light behind him silhouetted his shoulders and legs. He wore only a thick blue towel wrapped around his lean hips. *He has incredibly sexy legs,* she thought. Tiny droplets covered his shoulders and glistened where they clung to the curly scattering of hair on his chest.

Maybe if she looked away he would pull on a pair of pajamas and she could turn out the light.

He shifted the wineglasses to the nightstand, popped the cork from the bottle and poured each glass half full with the dark purple wine. If she reached out, she could caress his thigh.

"What are you doing?" she asked.

"We're celebrating," he replied, his voice low and sensual.

"What do we have to celebrate?" The reality of their failed marriage saddened her.

"I'm never spending another night in that damn apartment unless you're with me." He shoved the blankets away and sat down on the edge of the bed.

"What do you mean?" she asked, breathing irregularly. She busied herself with smoothing her gown, but when she glanced downward she could see the dark outline of her nipples. She looked up only to find him staring at her body. Her nipples turned into hard buttons in spite of her determination to appear nonchalant.

"This marriage is a sham," he said.

"We've already agreed on that." Her eyes burned.

"I'm changing that." He lifted a glass and offered it to her. "It's sweet, my favorite. Tonight calls for sweet wine."

"I . . . don't usually . . ."

"You don't usually do too damn many things, but sharing a glass of wine in the privacy of this bedroom, in the company of your husband, won't be on your list after tonight."

His tone frightened her. "Max, you can't force me." Her voice began to rise.

He laid his finger against her lips. "You wouldn't want to wake the children, would you?"

She tensed. He had no way of knowing they were alone. She shook her head slightly from side to side, only to discover her lips were brushing against his finger.

"Take a sip," he ordered.

"But..."

He took a swallow from his own glass and clinked it against hers. "To us."

She took a sip, watching him over the rim of her glass. "You've shaved." Why had she said that? But the sight of his smooth cheek with only a faint shadow to indicate his beard heightened her awareness of his masculinity.

"I didn't want to irritate you. I've done enough of that, haven't I?" He emptied his glass and motioned to hers. As she swallowed the wine, she felt his gaze linger on her throat. If he kissed her there, would his lips feel wet and cool from the wine? Would he become aware of her pounding pulse?

He set their glasses on the nightstand and put his hands on either side of the headboard, peering into her eyes. "You have beautiful eyes," he murmured, "especially right now when you're not sure what's going to happen next."

She pressed into the pile of pillows. "What do you mean?"

"Every night, regardless of where I am, I lie awake and wonder if you're asleep, if you're thinking of me. We started out making all the wrong moves, Trena."

She opened her mouth to speak, but he shook his head.

"No more," he said. "We've made our bed and we're going to lie in it. We're in this marriage together...all the way."

"All the way?"

Tiny drops of perspiration dotted his forehead, and she wiped them away without realizing what she had done.

One side of his mouth twitched. "Does a man always want most what he's denied? Maybe so, because I want to make love to you in the worst possible way."

Her hand dropped to the bed, but instead of resting on the rumpled sheet she felt the soft hair of his damp thigh. Before she would withdrew her hand he pressed it against him.

"I was here all along," she reminded him, unable to keep the wounded pride from her voice. "You chose your apartment."

"I was wrong," he said, leaning to brush his mouth across her temple. "I brought a lot of emotional baggage into this marriage, and so did you, but I want to start over." He lifted her and pulled two pillows from behind her, slowly lowering her to the bed again. "I need you in my life, Trena, and I need to hear you say in person what you said when you called me in Ellensburg."

Her hand moved from his thigh to his upper arm. "You mean all the bad stuff?" she asked, frowning.

The corners of his mouth curled into a smile. "No, forget the bad stuff. I want to hear the good stuff."

She gazed into his eyes. "The . . . good stuff?" Her fingers coiled in the mat of dark ringlets on his chest. His nipple hardened under her palm. As she inhaled the fresh soap-and-pine scents of his body and admired the strong planes of his face, her resistance evaporated. "I can't remember what I said."

"Nothing?" he asked, easing back a few inches.

When she saw his uncertainty, she couldn't deny the risk he had taken to come to her. "I do . . . remember telling you . . . how much I love you." Her eyes filled with moisture. "And I do, Max, I love you with all my heart."

"That's the good stuff," he said, pressing her into the pillows and taking her breath away with his kiss.

CHAPTER SEVENTEEN

MAX LEANED his shoulder against the porch post and pulled Trenace closer against him. The pup lay sprawled across their laps. To the west, the sun began to sink behind the horizon. "It's chilly. I guess winter's finally coming. Are you getting cold?"

"Love is keeping me warm," she replied, but he adjusted her sweater collar up around her neck just in case. "Max, if you'll be spending more time at home, I'd like you to help me build some play equipment."

"Wouldn't it be easier to simply purchase it?" he asked.

She shook her head. "No one makes what I've got in mind. I want to take the exercises that Terry does in his therapy and incorporate them into new play equipment in the backyard. They should be large blocky pieces where the children will have to crawl and creep through them and climb and learn to balance."

"I could use pipe," he suggested.

"No, pipe is either hot or cold," she explained. "These children need smoothness and warmth. We should make them out of wood, big thick pieces of sturdy wood. Max, many of these children can't even walk a simple two-by-four when it's on the ground. So I want to start with simple pieces and let the children work their way to the more complicated pieces at their own pace. What do you think?"

"It sounds fascinating," he said. "Maybe the director of the therapy clinic can give you some ideas."

She laughed. "I've already discussed the idea, and they think I should patent my designs. Can you help me with that, too?"

"Your wish is my command," he said, kissing her lightly. "Any more ideas or complaints?"

"Just one," she admitted. "The children say the only problem with living here is that we can't call for pizza delivery."

"I'll remedy that," Max promised. "I'll bring dinner home with me at least once a week." They sat quietly for several more minutes. "Sunday is almost over," he murmured, kissing her hair. "I promised to pick up Mickie and Terry tonight. When I called my uncle, he swore they were all getting along fine. Terry's come a long way since you first got him."

"He's become our miracle child," she agreed.

His kissed her temple and rested his chin against her head again. "How would you like to start a family?"

She tensed. "You mean a baby? Our own?" She pulled away and twisted to look at him. "Are you serious?"

He chuckled and eased the pup off their laps. "Well, that's not what I had in mind, but now that you bring it up, how about it? You know I haven't taken precautions. Have you?"

"No."

"Do you want to start being more careful?"

"Let's let nature take its course," she murmured. "If it happens, we'll love it, and if not, we have our foster children."

"I'd like to do something about that, too."

She pulled free again. "I won't stop taking in children."

He pulled her back again. "I'd never ask you to, but Terry's letter gave me much to think about. I'd like us to adopt Mickie and Terry formally. His letter and your angry phone call were two of the reasons I came home."

She turned in his arms. "Max, I didn't put him up to that. It was all his idea."

"Brilliant kid," Max replied. "Just like his father-to-be, and Mickie is as pretty and as intelligent as her future mother. What do you think?"

"Oh, Max, do you know what you're suggesting?"

"That we become a legitimate family? Yes, I know, and if a child of our own comes along, he or she will have a big brother and sister to teach him how to get along with a stubborn mom and a bullheaded dad who buys commercial time on television because he's too proud to say it in person. Let's go get the kids and talk this over with them. It's their future we're planning here. They deserve a say in our plans."

She held his face in her hands. "It's our future, too."

WHEN THEY EXPLAINED their plans to the children, Mickie whirled her chair around and grinned at Terry.

"See, I told you they were gonna do it." She smiled at Max. "When you told us you were gonna call this place the TMT Ranch and that it was for Trenace and Max Tulley, Terry said it could also stand for Terry and Mickie Tulley. We talked to Boyd and George about it, and George said if we wished and prayed every single night, it would come true."

"But we had to keep it a secret," Terry added.

"'Cuz George said it only works if grown-ups think it's their own idea," Mickie added.

Max grinned. "There's no doubt about it, folks. We're not Wednesday's Children anymore."

Terry, his blue eyes shining with pleasure, came to Trenace and shyly slid his arms around her neck and hugged her, then did the same to Max. "That's because we're going to be the Tulley family now. T-u-l-l-e-y."

Mickie sighed dramatically. "Now will you call Ms. Mitchell and get us some new kids? Since Boyd and George moved away, we don't have anyone to play with."

Harlequin Superromance®

Available in Superromance this month
#462—STARLIT PROMISE

STARLIT PROMISE is a deeply moving story of a
woman coming to terms with her grief and gradually
opening her heart to life and love.

Author Petra Holland sets the scene beautifully, never
allowing her heroine to become mired in self-pity. It
is a story that will touch your heart and leave you
celebrating the strength of the human spirit.

Available wherever Harlequin books
are sold.

PENNY JORDAN

Sins and infidelities . . .
Dreams and obsessions . . .
Shattering secrets
unfold in . . .

THE HIDDEN YEARS

SAGE — stunning, sensual and vibrant, she spent a lifetime distancing herself from a past too painful to confront . . . the mother who seemed to hold her at bay, the father who resented her and the heartache of unfulfilled love. To the world, Sage was independent and invulnerable— but it was a mask she cultivated to hide a desperation she herself couldn't quite understand . . . until an unforeseen turn of events drew her into the discovery of the hidden years, finally allowing Sage to open her heart to a passion denied for so long.

The Hidden Years—a compelling novel of truth and passion that will unlock the heart and soul of every woman.

AVAILABLE IN OCTOBER!
Watch for your opportunity to complete your Penny Jordan set.
POWER PLAY and SILVER will also be available in October.

HARLEQUIN
Romance

**This September, travel to England
with Harlequin Romance
FIRST CLASS title #3149,
ROSES HAVE THORNS
by Betty Neels**

It was Radolf Nauta's fault that Sarah lost her job at the hospital and was forced to look elsewhere for a living. So she wasn't particulary pleased to meet him again in a totally different environment. Not that he seemed disposed to be gracious to her: arrogant, opinionated and entirely too sure of himself, Radolf was just the sort of man Sarah disliked most. And yet, the more she saw of him, the more she found herself wondering what he really thought about her—which was stupid, because he was the last man on earth she could ever love....